Where White Horses Gallop

Beatrice MacNeil

Where White Horses Gallop

A NOVEL

KEY PORTER BOOKS

Library and Archives Canada Cataloguing in Publication

MacNeil, Beatrice,
Where white horses gallop / Beatrice MacNeil.

ISBN 978-1-55263-915-3

I. Title.

PS8575.N43W54 2007 C813'.54 C2007-902115-8

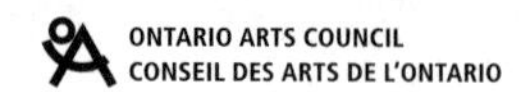

The publisher gratefully acknowledges the support of the Canada Council for the Arts and the Ontario Arts Council for its publishing program. We acknowledge the support of the Government of Ontario through the Ontario Media Development Corporation's Ontario Book Initiative.

We acknowledge the financial support of the Government of Canada through the Book Publishing Industry Development Program (BPIDP) for our publishing activities.

Key Porter Books Limited
Six Adelaide Street East, Tenth Floor
Toronto, Ontario
Canada M5C 1H6

www.keyporter.com

Text design: Martin Gould
Electronic formatting: Jean Lightfoot Peters

Printed and bound in Canada
07 08 09 10 11 5 4 3 2 1

To

Michael B. MacDonald, DCM

Cape Breton Highlanders

"Hidden amongst the heroes."

Prologue

1947

All over Beinn Barra the dandelions are dead.

Near the smelt brook, by MacGuspic's old sawmill, the dandelions died as they lived, trampled upon by the delinquent soles of children dancing their way to the brook.

In spring, when the dandelions were young and saucy, the children had plucked them by the handfuls. Fed them to the brook just to watch them drown. Adults had snapped off their golden round heads and green leaves and spoken openly of the liquid pleasures brewing in their barns. Farmers had sliced away the weeds with a vengeance, leaving their slaughtered bodies to the wind for burial.

The boy walking through the field loved the dandelions. Dead or alive. One golden smudge in his white, fisted hand sent his body into soft, rhythmic steps. His feet slid out from under him, scattering his arms and legs as if he were a come-to-life scarecrow.

The boy's father, watching from a distance, frowned on the awkward movements, the soft white skin without authority of motion, in danger of going nowhere and everywhere at once in the open field. He knew, without asking, where the boy was going to deliver his dead bouquet.

At fifty-three, he was the father of a dead son and a man-boy who had reached his peak in flower dancing. He watched as the boy's mother, his wife, dressed in black like a midnight forerunner, walked slowly towards their house. She had taken to their older son's bedroom the day the telegram arrived. Walked in quietly, as if someone were sleeping, and stripped his bed clean. Removed fresh white sheets from the old trunk and made up the bed.

"I'll be needing a weak cup of tea," she'd called out to her husband as she pulled the quilt up under her chin.

The kitchen had been dark with mourners. Old women preparing food in the pantry shook their heads.

He had stood in the doorway and looked in at his wife. She had let her hair down. Thick, black waves burdened her shoulders. Made her appear as if she were sinking into white sand.

She stared straight ahead at a picture of Babe Ruth that her son had cut out of a magazine and hung on his wall. Beside the picture, a letter from Dalhousie University lay like a white glove with frayed edges. On the dresser, in a silver frame, the faces of her two sons looked cheerfully down on her. She glanced around the room that would contain her grief. It was a sturdy room. Blue and white striped wallpaper made the ceiling look higher for the six-foot man who had left it to go to war.

On the floor, beside the bed, was a hooked rug that his grandmother had first imagined in a dream. She forced herself to look at the rug. Four white horses galloping along a beaten path. A lone figure watching from a distance. The rug was as old as her son. She must remember to pull it up and preserve its life in mothballs. Some lives can be protected.

A soft cry from his wife led to another, then three more. Men standing in the kitchen moved awkwardly towards the door and formed a large pool in the open field. He joined them. Women ushered children, date squares in their hands, out the back door. The women exchanged glances, made a pot of fresh tea. Someone began to pray, and the cries lingered on the last "Amen."

The father watched now as the boy stopped to catch his breath before walking towards his mother. His shirt had danced itself loose from his pants, and his curls leaked out from under his cap. A dark strand licked at his forehead.

Little Rachel let out a squawk. She sat royally, perched on a soft mound of hay in the red wagon the boy was pulling along behind him. The boy turned towards the hen and grinned wildly. The hen set her good eye on him and was quiet. The other eye had been lost in a battle with a rooster over feed. The boy saw his father in the field and raised one hand in a salute. His father did not respond. The boy laughed loudly and bent down to tap Little Rachel on the head.

"Him not gonna kill you no more," he assured the white hen with a smile.

The hen cocked her good suspicious eye towards the north field. The image of her would-be killer came into view.

Little Rachel had escaped the chopping block through luck and determination, but had caught the tongue of the axe when he threw it at her scrambling legs. The boy and his mother had been walking around the corner of the house. Had observed the white wings of the hen flapping like an angry choirboy's surplice.

A burnt orange sun had witnessed the scene before being drowned out where the sea and sky seal the day. The mother had soothed the terrified bird in her apron before taking it inside the house to wrap its split foot. The boy had pranced in circles around life and death. On the chopping block, the blood from another white hen had dripped slowly to the ground.

Little Rachel, so named by the boy's mother, had lamed her way around the barnyard for a week, like a young child playing hopscotch and falling out of the squares. The boy had picked up the hen and placed it in his red wagon. The hen refused to leave. Now she rode night and day along the dusty roads and through the snow-filled fields of Beinn Barra, down to the sea with the boy. She dined in the wagon from a tin bowl. Little Rachel had quit laying eggs and had neither need nor desire to limp on her foot and a half around the yard.

The boy's mother called out to him and filled her arms with the only male flesh she had held in two years. The boy did not fully understand the physical beauty of the green-eyed woman he knew as "Mama." He patted her wavy hair, parted in the middle and coiled in a bun, fastened with a shiny gold clip. The smell of rainwater came from her hair.

From deep inside her dimples wafted the fresh scent of the soap she kept in a jar. Her skin tasted like sweet dough, the kind she let him sample when she was baking.

The boy's hand moved slowly towards the gold clip as he playfully loosened the coil. They stood together under a dark rush of hair. Dancing to the song his mother sang to him in Gaelic.

The husband, still watching, could see their white hands floating in mid-air. Catching melodies. Something roamed inside his limbs. Stopped in his throat. He tried to spit it out, to kill it on the ground. But it wouldn't take direction and went down deeper. He could do nothing with this loneliness but sit on the ground and watch a lone crow fly overhead, its black wings casting double sorrow across the sun.

The boy knew that his mother was always prettier in the company of dandelions.

One

1939

THE MOON LAY WAITING, fully bloomed, behind the Barra mountain. October songs bellowed from the tall trees, and the fields below Barra chorused the twilight. Small creatures scurried for cover in the ploughed hayfields.

The wind took refuge under the cotton skirts of out-of-work scarecrows. It shivered the bones of the Barra men who awaited the coming darkness. They filled their oil lamps and set them back on shelves or braced hooks along the kitchen walls. The flames would rise at dusk. Later they would make love to their wives with the smell of kerosene and balsam in the air, a leftover white moon claiming squatter's rights on the window ledge.

A brief paralysis of golden sun rays and white mist lost its grip, tumbled down the mountain. Rising out of the mist, two boys, at the tail end of three or four sheep, hurried the animals through an open barn door. A small girl walked backwards against the wind from the barn, complaining. Weather-beaten barns rose higher than most of the white-washed houses dotting the landscape. Sturdy rhubarb stalks leaned against garden fences.

Lines of smoke rising from Beinn Barra's chimneys criss-crossed like wild geese above the heads of two men walking along the winding dirt road on their way to the parish hall. They were uneven in height, and the taller of the two pushed his hat to the back of his balding head. In the distance, they saw the curtain in the front window of the glebe house move an inch or two. The gnarled hand of the stout, elderly priest, holding back a fist of white lace, let it unravel slowly as the two men offered up a wave.

"He hasn't invited a smile to his lips in the twenty years he has been marrying the young and burying the dead of Beinn Barra," the shorter man remarked.

The priest knew this would be a busy night at the hall, with Strings Doucet on the fiddle, and God knows what to follow. *A full moon can occasion a night of eternal damnation*, he thought, making the sign of the cross painfully with one arthritic hand. Next Friday the confession line would be long and full of mortal inflictions for him to absolve.

The late October day, blending into an early evening, had turned cool, and the two caretakers pulled their collars close as they walked. They had to get the old stove fired up early to crack the chill in the hall before the Saturday night dancers arrived.

In the white shingled houses of Beinn Barra, young men were busy getting ready for the dance, shining their shoes with lard. Young women were curling their hair with rags and flushing their cheeks with red lipstick, praying it would not run in the heat.

Ona MacPherson pressed her pleated skirt with a damp cloth and hung it on a hanger over a hook fastened to her bedroom door to let the pleats settle. She polished Joachim's shoes to a brilliant shine, despite his objections that he did not want to go to the dance tonight. Her elder son, Calum, helped his younger brother, Hamish, top off his dancing shoes. Calum, nineteen, broad-shouldered, stooped his six-foot frame down to the kitchen mirror and combed back his thick, wavy hair. His laughing brown eyes caught a reflection of Hamish swirling around the kitchen with the broom.

"I don't know why you bother to take the boy to the hall," Joachim remarked to his wife. "Every day is a dance for him."

Calum turned from the mirror and patted Hamish on the back. "He's just practising," Calum said to lighten his father's mood.

Calum could see the muscles in his father's face twitch. Joachim was a slightly built man. Eyes as dark as storm puddles, set deep under heavy brows that cast a shadow over his handsome face. All the ridicule he had received when he was a child because of his lame foot had, in his mind, been passed on to Hamish. Whenever Joachim looked at the short, slightly built boy, eighteen but looking twelve, he saw his own left foot.

He was wrong, of course. People did not ridicule his son. They gave their love to the curly-haired Hamish, with eyes as green as mint, and Joachim loved the proud woman who gave their son the freedom to collect it.

Now Calum took the broom from Hamish and began to waltz around the kitchen himself. Hamish applauded loudly.

"Some people like to dance because others don't." Ona scowled at her husband, then smiled at her two playful sons. "Let Hamish dance; he's not hurting anyone," she said, as she picked out a sweater to go with her skirt. "Let the whole world dance!"

"I'll take Hamish along with me," Calum said, taking his jacket off the back of a chair. Ona watched her two sons walk through the gate, arm in arm, chatting up a storm, then turned to her husband and held his shoes under his nose.

"Here, Joachim, I'm not in the mood to waste a shine on any man this evening. Put them on!"

Joachim fastened the laces of his black shoes slowly. Stuffed a built-up arch in the left one. He watched as his wife combed out her long hair. He knew she would be the prettiest woman in the hall, with her long, slender body and skin the colour of twilight. She always reminded him of a shadow when she walked into a room. He reached out and twirled a dark curl around his finger.

"You're a sight for sore eyes, Ona MacPherson," he whispered.

"Don't get yourself in a dangerous mood this early, Joachim MacPherson, we have the whole night ahead of us!" She kissed his cheek. She felt the anxiety around her. But this was not the time to mention it, she reminded herself. Tonight they would dance and laugh and be carefree.

In the big white house a quarter of a mile up the hill, Hector MacDonald pressed his white shirt, then stood back and admired the job. Twenty years old, six-foot-three, Hector resisted wrinkles on a night that would put music in his feet and a woman in his arms. His father sat beside the stove, watching this red-haired son whose lean face squared off at the chin. He had taught his son to be a perfectionist with an iron, and in all the things he himself had had to learn since his wife's death.

"Pretty good job, don't you think?" said Hector, holding up the stiff shirt for his father to inspect. "I thought I had rinsed most of the starch out of the shirt. I poured too much in the tub."

"You were wrong. You may have to nail it to your pants to keep it in place. You'll look like a ghost."

"A ghost? How am I going to get a women to dance with a ghost?"

"Just whisper to her, that might work. You'll not have to worry about stepping on her feet."

"Why don't you come to the dance, Da? You know Benny is playing. It's going to be a great night." Hector smiled at his father, exposing the gap between his front teeth. "You're still a good-looking fellow. Women like grey-haired men with a few hard-earned sea wrinkles and strong bones."

"I just might do that, son, if I still have a pulse before the dance starts," Gunner replied, then grinned as Hector got another white shirt and began to iron it carefully.

He watched his son work on the shirt, his long arms delicately skimming the sleeves, his foot tapping under the ironing board. Then he walked up the stairs to his room, draped his thick bones in his Sunday best, and smiled at the thought that his greying hair and wrinkled forehead could entice a whirl or two on the dance floor of Beinn Barra.

Across the pond from the MacDonalds', Benny Doucet picked up his prized fiddle and checked the strings. He had the serious face that comes to men who think for a living. He whispered under his breath as his large hands moved skilfully to tune the instrument. Benny closed his eyes and played softly, then his feet picked up speed as he shifted into a set of jigs and reels.

Napoleon Doucet stood on his front step, listening to the music that floated out his son's window, then went inside and hurried Flora into her dancing shoes.

"What's the rush, Napoleon? It's not like we're teenagers again. You don't have to worry about picking up a date," said Flora as she brushed lint from her husband's suit jacket. But Napoleon's soft blue eyes already danced, his head was full of music, and his feet felt brazenly young. He pulled his petite wife into his strong arms, and she danced with him around the kitchen, a thirsty smile on her face.

Above their heads the music reeled. Benny had heard the soft shuffle of their feet and he now played to them. He felt their embrace rising up the stairs and wrapping its delight around him. A gift. A gift of blood, of honour. That's what he sent down the stairs to these two beautiful people. He played a waltz to slow the kitchen dancers. His face flushed. His grey eyes focused on a sheet of unfinished music in the corner of his room. The old cat, Jigs, poked one deep yellow eye and one white ear out from under the bed and hissed up at Benny as if he had hit a wrong note.

In the MacGregor house, a half-mile west of the Doucets', Cassie MacGregor vowed that she wouldn't be caught dead in a dance hall.

"Then let them catch you alive in one," said her daughter, Joan, her hair in rags. She had inherited her mother's striking beauty and straight hair. Her lupin eyes flashed now.

"No, siree," cried Cassie, a widow of ten years. "I'd rather go to hell in a cement hut than be seen at a dance."

Her son, Alex, listened to the conversation but did not join it. He was going to the dance with his friends, with Calum and Hector and Benny. Alex left the house and walked along the road to the shore, away from the woman he both hated and loved. His head pounded. He walked like a man scoured clean of emotional resources. One foot followed the other and pulled him in the direction of the fish hut at the edge of the shore. His six-foot-one frame trampled down hard, and a wily dust circled around him. His mouth felt dry and sour as he spit against the wind. He was in no mood to deal with his mother's wounded philosophy. He wasn't ten years old any more.

Earlier, he had heard his mother and sister in hushed conversation.

"You have to let him go sooner or later, Ma. People notice how you treat him like a child. He had to sneak away from the house when he was a boy to get a moment's peace from you."

Cassie had told her daughter to be quiet and fled to her room.

Behind her closed door, Cassie now sat rigidly beside the window. Looked out at the coming night. Indulged her fervent belief that a loving God had set upon her back His heaviest cross, as He had with His own son, and that she had carried it without the slightest complaint.

"To hell with what people say," she hissed, like a snake at the tail of its prey. She had had to be both mother and father to Alex since her husband died. She had done everything she could for him. She made sure he was well fed and his clothes were clean. She hushed him with sweets when he mentioned his father's name. She kept sorrow away from him with pies and delicate cakes smothered with boiled frosting. Even his nightmares could be settled with a date square and a glass of cold buttermilk. She had rarely touched him, except to comb his wild blond curls when she took him to church. Cassie took great pride in the fact that she had kept her son dry-eyed, despite what life had thrown in his face. She had never once seen him cry.

She looked out the window at the empty northern field. They had stood in the centre of that field, she and her husband, when they were newlyweds. He had pointed to the spot where the lupins danced their wildest premiere of summer and promised to build her a house where they could raise a family. He had kept that promise. And she'd kept hers. And now she stood up and walked across to the window facing the road. She was not sure in which direction the wind had taken her son. She had watched his brooding face earlier. His blond curls had turned darker as he got older.

A few men were out in the fields. It had been a great summer for crops. Root cellars were full of preserves. Most of the fish was salted and stored away. If the weather held up, they might catch a few mackerel this fall.

Alex MacGregor had two quarts of rum hidden in his fish hut. After a couple of swigs, he would dance with a goddamn codfish if he wanted to. Dance the night away. *Take that, Mother! Take the dancing codfish to hell with you in your cement hut!*

He waved to a neighbour coaxing her children down out of the trees with fudge in one hand and a switch in the other behind her back, the sweet and sour offerings of maternal instinct.

Alex reached the fish hut, entered, and locked the door behind him. He opened a bottle and took a long gulp of the dark liquid. He could feel something inside his chest doing a jig. He downed another. Beyond the locked door the tide was high and wide. Whose voice was that? Speaking to stones, to sand, to the coming twilight. His own. His tongue was thick and warm. His lips felt swollen, but they opened up on the rim of the bottle and suckled like a lamb. "Jesus, Jesus," slid from his throat and drowned in the bottle.

The moon was out there somewhere, sending slices under the door. It was too dark to check the time on his pocket watch. His hand felt its round face, with its dial like a bowler hat perched on the rim. He raised the bottle of rum, a salute to Winston Churchill, and took another drink.

"Here's one for you, Winnie, but I hope to Christ we never meet."

The bottle fell from his hand and rolled along the floor.

"Christ Almighty," he slurred. "You take good care of the boys. You hear me? If you can't leave them alone, then you better take goddamned good care of them."

Alex caught the bottle with his foot and slammed it against the door. Pieces of glass settled in a splintered mound. He needed a swig or two to get started. To lead him to the dance hall, where he would meet up with his friends. His feet had waited anxiously all day, stepping into and out of a shuffle. Now they lay outstretched, pointing at a mound of broken glass, moonlight striping the soles of his shoes. He couldn't find the latch on the door. Everything he touched was made of wood. The old fish barrel. The cutting table. A few broken lobster traps that needed mending. The rough walls. He stumbled back and lay on the floor. He held up a bleeding hand and wept openly for those children in the trees.

In the dance hall, the faces of the two caretakers were by now flushed from the heat of the old stove. They shuffled their feet along the hardwood floor. One of them threw Dustbane in front of the broom. The floor had to be in shape for the dancers. Too slippery was no good for the swift feet of Beinn Barra.

They had opened the windows to let in the wind off the sea. Soon the women would arrive with the food. The women would compare the heat to hell and fling open the doors to let the devil out. They laughed at the thought, threw another log into the stove, heard it crackle out what they imagined was a fiery "thank you."

A light appeared in the study of the glebe house. They could see the silhouette of the priest leaning over his desk. They knew he was preparing his sermon for Sunday morning and would be watching the clock. His rule was absolute. The music and dancing stopped at precisely one minute to midnight.

Three widows arrived at the hall armed with oatcakes and tea biscuits. They were in their mid-seventies, delicately perfumed and slightly blushed to keep gossip at bay. Cake powder exploded from the wrinkles under their chins as they complained in unison about the heat.

"You could melt the gates of hell in here. Open the doors!"

The caretakers winked at each other and raised the windows a few more inches, then opened the front and back doors.

By eight o'clock Strings Doucet was centre stage with his prized fiddle, Carmen, named after the great opera. The piano player sat with his back to the dancers. The prompter took his position on stage and called for the dancers to form the first set. Benny rosined the bow in slow glides as he looked out at the dancers whose feet he would set in motion for the next three hours and fifty-nine minutes. Eight sets of dancers took their positions on the floor, the old and the young of Beinn Barra in pairs, balsamed hands warming their wounds in the smooth, creamed hands of young women.

The MacPherson brothers and Hector MacDonald stood near the stage. Hamish heeded the prompter's call and whisked the three widows out of the kitchen, standing them opposite himself, Calum, and Hector. The widows smiled sweetly at the young men as they dabbed the sweat from their brows.

"Those men never listen," said one of the dabbers. "They always make too much of a fire."

Hector winked at Calum. They had not yet decided which widow each would choose for a partner. The women had already begun to melt before the dancing started. Hector looked over his shoulder and saw his father poised with a young woman with dark hair, waiting for the music to start. The eldest of the widows fastened her hand on Hector's shirt cuff.

"You're pretty well stiffed, Hector MacDonald," she said. "I'll have to dance that out of you before the night ends."

Hector rolled up his sleeves. He could see Benny and Calum laughing together. Hamish locked hands with the youngest of the widows and bowed to her as if he were about to dance with a queen. Ona and Joachim MacPherson arrived as the music began and joined in a set with Flora and Napoleon Doucet.

"Allemande left, allemande right..." came the command from the prompter, and the Dustbaned floor trembled under the first figure of the night. Benny had opened with a lively jig, "The Devil in the Oats."

On the third figure of the set, Benny fired the dancers up with "The Flaggon" reel. Suit coats flew in the air and landed on chairs. Joan MacGregor's rag curls unravelled down her back. The three widows grew pale and breathless. Their blush abandoned them and left their faces streaked like a paper map. They thanked their partners and bowed out gracefully to take care of their kitchen duties, blaming the heat from the damn stove for shutting them down so early in the night.

In the glebe house, the old priest had settled himself in a comfortable chair beside the window. He opened it slightly to let the music sneak in. A cool breeze ruffled a tuft of white hair and settled on the pages of the hot sermon sitting on his desktop, reminding him that he had vices like all other men, that what sneaked in under the window made him feel the proud shuffle of a man surrounded by pleasure. He watched carefully as a pool of young men gathered by the side of the parish hall. They stood in a cluster of liquid damnation. They took turns, tilting their heads back and snorting like wild bulls. He could hear their muffed voices and the sound of coarse laughter. He waited for a fight to break out. It was not uncommon to see a dozen black eyes at Mass on any given Sunday morning.

Across Beinn Barra, Cassie MacGregor opened her back door and watched as the moon came riding down over the mountain. Nights like this could cause a woman to suffer from melancholy. But she had never given in to melancholy with all the work she had to do to bring up a family. She slammed the door hard in the face of the moon, as if it were a drunken salesman, and sat at the kitchen table with a cup of tea.

She had paid her dues for being a woman. Alone. And tired. What was left of her good looks now looked away. She paid little attention to her face. It mocked her when she got up and looked in the kitchen mirror. Her children had groomed their images in this mirror and walked out the door earlier this evening. Both still handsome. Alex and Joan. And Alex the spit of his father, with his mysterious blue eyes and curly blond hair. Cassie touched what she believed was left of her own beauty. Her eyes, as mauve as a fresh lupin. She rarely sang these days, had jailed her beautiful voice as she had everything else when the kids got older. What does a tired woman sing about? Some people had predicted that she would remarry. But she had put paid to that in a hurry.

Cassie stepped away from the mirror and sat back down at the kitchen table. Her tea was cold. She closed her eyes as it slid down her throat like bad-tasting medicine.

In reflection, a comfortably distant cousin of melancholy, she sat for a long time, waiting for something that would make her smile. Nothing came but the distant hum of soft music. A great remorse welled in her chest like a stone. But her feet did not seem to belong to her body. They belonged to someone else, long ago, someone much prettier. Someone much happier as she lifted the hem of her wedding dress and began to dance in the lupin petals strewn across the floor.

By ten o'clock, Calum was watching the door for Alex. Joan insisted she hadn't seen him since he left the house before dark. Calum, Hector, and Benny sneaked out the side door during intermission and greased their throats with a swig of moonshine the caretakers had hidden for Benny behind the piano.

"Where do you think Alex went?" Calum asked.

"I say he's drunk somewhere," Hector answered. "He told me he had a quart or two riding on his hip when I saw him today. I swear he's getting worse. Drinking, and moody as a pent-up bull. By the Christ, if he shows up I'm going to sic one of those widows on him to see his reaction."

Benny passed the bottle to Hector. "You did all right for yourself with the widow—you danced the old soul off her feet."

"It was your fault, Doucet, throwing in that damn fast reel to speed things up. You did that on purpose," said Hector.

"They could have croaked in front of you," Calum added.

"Don't be so sure of yourself, Hector," said Benny. "She was keeping up to you and your stiff cuffs for a while."

"What are we going to do if Hamish brings out the widows for a waltz?" Hector asked. "Calum, will you tell him to leave them in the kitchen? Tell him they have work to do or something."

They laughed as Benny took the bottle of happy water and put it back in his jacket pocket. "That's enough for now. The dance is not over yet!"

From inside the hall, a ripple of Gaelic voices joined in song. Men and woman tore up their vocal cords to deliver the Gaelic cries of Culloden that they had learned at the patches of their ancestors' knees. The piano played softly in the background. In the kitchen, the widows hummed along as they set out the plates of oatcakes and tea biscuits with homemade jam and cups of hot tea. These Gaelic ballads could go on for miles.

Hector paused and listened to his father's voice carry over the crowd. He had often heard his father sing this ballad of Culloden out on the sea, its stormy words cast off the stern of the boat and whipped out over the waves.

"Take your history with you wherever you go," Gunner had instructed his salty son. "You will always know where you came from."

Hector lingered on the step when Benny and Calum went back in the hall. The air licked its damp tongue across his brow. He swiped at the sweat with his broad fisherman's hand. The starch was gone from his cuffs, and his collar circled his neck like a damp, limp rope. In the beauty of the night, not a breath of wind wandered. The tide had gone out. The moon rubbed its face against its smooth surface, like a child at its mother's soft breast.

Inside the hall, the battle of Culloden was coming to an end. Gunner's strong voice carried on. It was not uncommon for a Scotsman to have both music and battles under the same roof in Beinn Barra. Hector folded his arms against the railing and lowered his head. He was too young to be danced out. It wasn't tiredness that held his chest in a tight sling, it was his father's voice. And his going away from it soon, and taking his longing for it and Beinn Barra with him far across the sea. A shooting star showered above Hector's head and fizzled out along the shoreline.

In the kitchen, the three widows finished their chores and sank their elbows on the small wooden table for support. Young Barra men had held them in their arms, had rattled old, feverish memories from their heads and placed them on the tip of their tongues. They had forgotten now what they had remembered while in their arms. They were rewarding their good fortune and hard work with dark rum. They nodded at one another, ignoring the blurred faults they saw in each others' faces, faults they could no longer hide, cheeks hanging like rawhide on worn saddles. The glasses would be a clear giveaway to the rum should someone waltz in on them now. A bag of peppermints lay on the middle of the table, beside the teapot. They would leave the kitchen with fresh breath and a deluded conscience for church in the morning.

In the glebe house, the priest poured himself a small brandy to ease the ache in his bones. Then a larger one to ward off eternal damnation. He returned to the window and permitted himself a smile as the voices sang out. He was a Scotsman, a MacDonald, and the ballad of Culloden smote his chest like a blade every time he heard it sung.

No more we'll see their likes again,
Deserted is their highland glen,
Proudly the cairns lie over them,
The men who died for Charlie.

Tha tighin sodham, sodham, sodham!
Tha tighin sodham, sodham, sodham!
Tha tighin, sodham, sodham, sodham!
Rise and follow Charlie!

Alex MacGregor faced the moon at four minutes after ten. The white and happy moon illuminated his dark and brooding face and let him see the time as clearly as if he had lit a match. Somewhere behind him a lone voice sang of

Bonnie Prince Charlie, then fizzled out like water in a hot pan. He could not see anyone around when he lifted his head. In his right hand he carried the second quart of rum.

"Christ," he cried when he stumbled, then watched as the bottle floated out on a wave. His feet sank in the wet sand as he staggered his way towards the dance hall along the shoreline. He could see the outline of a building in the distance. He got down on his hands and knees to climb the steep embankment that hovered on the lip of the sea. He fell back once, then caught a good grip of seagrass and clay and wormed himself up over the edge. He continued to crawl, then stopped and wedged his back up against the building. His bones fluttered in his thin shirt like a bird that had flown inside a house. His feet were wet and cold. Again a voice cried out, but not in song.

> Mystical rose, pray for us.
> Tower of David,
> Tower of Ivory,
> House of gold,
> Ark of the Covenant,
> Gate of heaven,
> Morning star,
> Health of the sick,
> Refuge of sinners,
> Comforter of the afflicted.

Alex braced his hands against the shingles as he stood up. For one sobering moment he thought he had reached the

Pearly Gates. He steadied himself against the building and caught a glimpse of Father MacDonald's head bowed in prayer. He had mistaken the glebe for the dance hall. He knew that the priest would not retire for the night until one minute to midnight.

He could hear the music more clearly now. He walked towards the road, then down over the hill, back towards his home. He had sobered up enough to resolve that he would not make a spectacle of himself at the dance. His shine was gone. The blood in his veins felt like ice and slowed him down. The sea spit at him. The mountains shadowed him. He was somewhere between drunk and sober. And lost. He was looking for love and had landed at Culloden.

The two caretakers, teetotallers both, still enjoyed the banter that spit off the tongues of those who weren't. They ambushed the kitchen, pretending to be looking for more tea, and watched as the widows clawed at the bag of peppermints like hungry dogs at a bone.

Calum stepped out the front door of the hall and walked to the top of the hill. Everything looked white under the moon—the sea, the road, the graveyard, the fields, the mountain—as if snow had fallen while Beinn Barra danced and Culloden rallied.

He scanned down the hill and across the road. Nothing stirred but a white cat in a white field. Alex was nowhere in sight. It wasn't the first time that his friend had missed out on a good time. Calum knew Alex better than anyone else in the village did. They were the same age and had gone to school together. Calum had sat beside his friend at Alex's father's funeral. A trembling and distraught Alex had looked down into the muddy hole in the ground, a "waiting place" his mother had called it. "Here," Cassie had told her nine-year-old son, "is where your father will have to wait until the angels come and carry him home." Alex had never forgiven his mother, not for his father's death, but for failing to tell him when the angels came and lifted his father from the mud.

Calum heard the fiddle start up again inside the hall. He watched through the open window as his mother and father took their positions with the other dancers. Hamish joined in the set with Moira, the postmistress. Calum stood in a streak of white sadness. How radiant his mother looked, standing beside his father, touching him with her smile. And a grinning Hamish, already in flight, his arms rotating in small circles to warm up for the dance, his feet moving as if he were kicking up stones. His father stood with his arms at his sides like a Presbyterian corpse, his cold gaze plastered on the boy.

Watching his wife, Joachim wanted to wrap his arms around her, to kiss her as Hamish would often do, in public, at will, without rehearsal. But people frightened him, made him turn to his wife with the crack in his face he used for a smile. Ona laughed as she wiped a tea biscuit crumb from his chin, then kissed him with a smile of intent.

Calum lit up a smoke and watched them dance at the end of the yellow flame. His father seemed to be marching, rather than promenading around in a circle.

Left, right, left, right,
Hold your girl good and tight.

A flicker of yellow light in the glebe house parlour slowly crawled up the wall, like a spider, then licked its way back down. Behind Calum, in the church, the blood red sanctuary lamp danced in its perpetual soft glory. He listened to the settling sea. The sea that would take him away from Beinn Barra. The music stopped and the quiet of the night burst like a blister on Calum's tongue. He called out to his mother and father, to his brother Hamish, to his friend Alex. Nobody answered. Nobody heard him. He was alone in this white night, with its lick of red and yellow flame. He returned to the hall.

Alex sneaked in the back door of his house, up to his room, and crawled under the quilt on his bed. His body trembled. He was out of the cold, but he had taken a chill inside with him. For a split second he thought he heard a familiar voice call out his name, splitting the night air. He bolted upright in the middle of his bed. Listened. Nothing sounded but the tick of the clock beside his bed. He pulled the quilt up over his head and slid back against the pillow. He waited, in his own waiting place. At last he slept.

In the territory that was his alone, on the dance floor, Hamish waved to Benny as the fiddler disappeared through the side door for a break. Hamish still heard the music. He skimmed the floor with his shiny shoes. Tuned his head to shake up the leftover notes.

Hamish bent over to flick away a bit of Dustbane that had collected in his laces. Up again, he moved slowly like a small boy on skates having his first go on the ice. *Left foot out, right foot in. Right foot out, left foot in.* He smiled down at his feet as they carried him further out to the middle of the floor.

His mother came to his rescue. Her arms around his soft shoulders. The piano player stirred up a slow waltz, believing he was rescuing the pretty lady.

Joachim watched his beautiful wife. How the boy's feet obeyed hers. They moved in unison with the piano music, self-assured. Couples joined them on the floor. Around and around they whirled. Floating. Colourful skirt hems. Dark trouser cuffs. The clicking of heels. Stolen kisses. He watched as Calum danced up beside his mother and brother. A lovely blond girl in his arms, a stolen kiss on his cheek. Joachim watched his family dance in front of him, and something gnawed at his insides. He had to stand still, to let his mind locate the exact spot in his body that was affected. The pit of his stomach maybe. Was it moving up or down? He wasn't sure. Then he knew it was in his heart. This was the kind of pain that kept men alive, alert. It contained fear, and loss, and anger, and, yes, envy. How well she rescued the awkward strokes of the boy and refined them. With his mother in his arms, the boy danced like everyone else.

People followed them. Smiled upon them. He could never do that. Wrap his emotional strings around the boy's shoulders to rid him of his defects. Joachim felt his heart freeze. Heard the thump-thump of its rhythm as it cracked through ice. He found a chair, sat, and rested his head against the wall. He watched Calum. How smoothly he moved with a woman in his arms. Several young couples danced by. Young, strapping boys on the verge of manhood, the girls' smiles lighting up like half-moons over their shoulders.

Close by, Gunner MacDonald saw the collision of fear and loss and anger in his neighbour's eyes. He knew what the man had on his mind. The same thing he had on his own: Who would fill the arms of these dancing girls in the weeks, the months to come?

"They'll be calling for young men soon, Da," Hector had told him a few weeks earlier. "Me and the boys have decided to go when they come to Baddeck to sign up."

Gunner turned away from Joachim now and scanned the crowd. He was eager to see his son's face. To reassure himself that Hector was still here. He caught the shape of Hector's back going out the side door.

Ona pulled her husband up from the chair, into her arms, and out into the thick of the dancers.

"You're thinking too hard," she whispered into his ear. "I saw your face."

"And what was my face thinking, dear Ona?"

"It was thinking about the future."

He chose not to answer her, but to wrap everything he felt into the dance. He held her firmly, felt the heat of her body. He danced like a child in her arms. His feet were twins of mobility. He followed them wherever they went. They stepped on toes and escaped unharmed. They stumbled, asked for pardon. Pardon granted.

Joachim was new and old again when the music stopped. He searched the crowd for Calum's face. Calum was smiling down at the blond girl in his arms. But Calum's smile turned old and injured when he looked up and saw his father's face.

He left the dance and joined his friends standing outside at the side entrance of the building.

In the cool, salty breeze off the water, they finished off the bottle with a salute to Beinn Barra. "Until we meet again," they cried out with their raised fists.

"The priest is still up," said Hector, nodding towards the glebe house. They could see the flicker of light.

"He's probably asleep beside the window," said Calum. "He always retires early. Darkens the place at five o'clock every Halloween."

"I doubt he's in bed," said Benny. "He'll wait for the last note to shiver out of the fiddle before he goes to bed. To keep an eye on things."

The priest sat by the window with his head resting in his open palms. An open book of flesh. His head heavy with prayers.

"Dear Lord, in all the music you have sent into my ears, there has been none the likes of what this young man has to offer. Your gift to him is a generous one. He offers it up like a child offers his love to his mother."

The three friends watched as a slow moving light passed the parlour window and reappeared again in an upstairs window. Its flame danced on the window ledge.

"He's on his way to bed," said Hector. "Wait and see, he'll leave the lamp on in his bedroom until the music is over."

Father MacDonald changed into an old robe by a dying white flame. There were twenty-one minutes left before the dance would come to an end.

Napoleon Doucet wrapped his wife's sweater around her shoulders. They smiled at each other while they waited for the finale. Benny had kept it a secret. He said that the old cat had heard him play it and hid for three days.

The three widows stuck their heads out the kitchen windows to fill their lungs with salty air. They swayed back to the table and sat down. They knew they were waiting for something, but they couldn't remember what it was. The two caretakers waited beside the door to close up the hall.

Benny rosined the bow and turned to the piano player to give him his cue. He sat with the fiddle under his chin, his fingers searching out its pulse, the heart of the instrument. And then he walked to centre stage. A slow tune rose from the bow. The weight of its sorrow hanging in the air like branches burdened with snow. The crowd stilled. A woman stood with one coat sleeve on, the other dangling, as if moving would interfere with the fiddler. The music soared, reaching the high ceiling and trembling down the walls, filtering through the seams, the cracks in the doorways. Coaxed by the wind from the open windows, its sorrow leaked out and floated on the air. The priest knelt before the candle. The three widows blessed themselves. Hamish stood as still as a pole, his hands at his sides, staring at the musician, smiling as if he had heard it all before in another place, another time. His parents stood beside him, silent.

Benny stood in a vessel of dim light, his eyes closed, his head tilted towards his left shoulder, his mouth private, speaking only to the music. Sweat rolled down under his collar. He could feel the passion from the crowd floating back up to meet him in waves. He opened his eyes and saw his mother's face. He switched to a lively jig for her.

The widows bolted from the kitchen with peppermints locked in their jaws and grabbed the first pairs of empty arms. Hector clicked his heels and danced around the hall with a brunette. Calum held the blond girl firmly in his arms. Hamish joined in with one of the widows. At 11:59, one of the caretakers dimmed the lamp on the stage. Benny quivered the bow, bled its last shivering note to wild, thundering applause. He smiled down at the crowd as he raised the bow in the air, a formal salute to Carmen, and to them.

Two

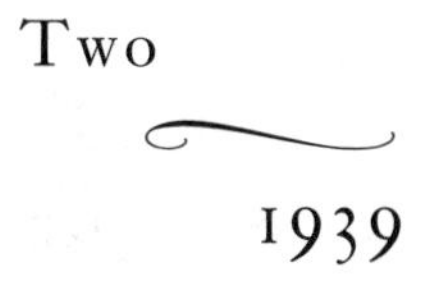

1939

MAPLE AND APPLE TREES trembled quietly as the October leaves gathered like spilled rainbows at their feet along the quiet dirt road that led to the grey building. The three clean-shaven young men standing together to enlist on that morning, in the village of Baddeck, had seen very little of the country they would take an oath to protect. Calum MacPherson had visions of England's Old World charms in his head. The Tower of London. Buckingham Palace. Big Ben. The cathedral bells of St. Paul's pealing below England's Spitfires. Daring to die, they would survive, this "breed of manly men." Calum thrilled to the official motto of the Cape Breton Highlanders, with their Black Watch tartan kilts and swirling pipes. This war would not separate their limbs or bury them in foreign soil.

"Things will never go that far," Calum said to his best friends as they waited. "It will be over before the ship's bow edges into the mouth of London's harbour. We'll get a view of historical England in the bargain." He planned on studying medicine after it was over. He had applied to Dalhousie University in Halifax after passing his grade twelve provincial exams.

He'd asked his friends not to mention that he'd be going into medicine after the war. "They'll sign me up as stretcher bearer. They like to keep men from the same area together if possible, but this would separate us if I was put on with the medics."

Hector MacDonald agreed with Calum about the timing of this war. It would not be too long before they would be back home. He was twenty and had been fishing beside his father since he got his own pair of fishing boots at nine years of age. He had fallen overboard more than once and had to be pulled back on board like a drowned rat, with his boots still on his feet, he boasted. He had given back to the sea the watery contents of his boots, with his father's two big hands coiled around his waist for safety. The Atlantic was already a battleground for him.

"History," Hector had said the evening before, tasting a mug of dark whiskey and sounding as if he were making a speech, "will repeat itself on political platforms and in the minds of old generals, and on the black-and-white movie screens of America. Nobody wants another war like the first one, where thousands upon thousands of Canadians died."

Hector's father was a returned man, having served with the 85th Battalion. Gunner MacDonald hoped that Hector would not enlist. And Hector's mother was not alive to voice her disapproval. But he could not say this to Hector. Gunner's own father had not stopped Gunner in the First World War. Gunner had enlisted without saying a word. When they were ready to leave, Gunner mentioned it.

"I've signed up for overseas," he said.

"I knew you would," his father had replied, not meeting his gaze.

A shipbuilder by trade, fiddle player Benny Doucet listened to his friends but had other thoughts. What filled his head were plans for a secret hiding place for Carmen, his prized fiddle. He would tell no one his plans. He would build a box made of cedar to preserve the wood from damage and conceal the box in a wall. To leave it visible would be too tempting for other fiddlers, who would want to keep it in tune while he was away. And his father would kindly allow them, just to hear it being played again.

The three friends had walked into this grey building on a grey morning and come face to face with young men they had arm-wrestled at picnics all across the northern highlands of Cape Breton. Now they joked, telling each other what they would do to Hitler, the European paper-hanger.

"I hope you're bringing your fiddle with you, Doucet," cried a voice from the back of the hall. "And sharpen the bow before we leave. We'll be back in Cape Breton in no time."

Benny turned to the rugged young man. "I'll bring an old fiddle along with me. My prized fiddle will be staying behind until I return."

Calum said to Hector, "With your long legs and big feet, you'll outrun the enemy in your Black Watch kilt."

Hector's voice roared above the heads of the young men in the lineup. "I'll bet you fellas don't know why there will be so many MacDonalds in the Cape Breton Highlanders, more than all the other Mac's."

"Who cares?" someone shouted.

"I care," Hector chuckled.

"Maybe because there's too many of them and they'd start their own war if they got left behind."

"It's because the MacDonalds have the best legs for the kilt. It saved many a soldier in the First World War and it will in the Second because the enemy is reluctant to take out a good pair of legs. They may be trigger-happy, but they're not stupid. Mark my word, one of these days the MacDonald tartan will rise above the Highlanders knees as the official tartan. It's not every man whose knees are bestowed such honour."

"Are you planning to fight on your knees?" a voice called from the back of the line.

A tired-looking recruiting officer appeared, sat down behind a table, and the kidding stopped as he called out in a stringent voice: "Step up."

"MacPherson, sir, Calum."

The balding officer eyed him from the boots up.
"How old are you?" he asked, staring up at the youthful face of the recruit standing straight and tall before him.

"Nineteen, sir."

"Since when?"

"Since May, sir. I was born in 1920," said Calum, holding up his baptismal certificate.

"I can add." The officer's temples quivered like dying wings.

"Yes, sir."

"Does your father know you're here?"

"Yes, sir. I told him I wanted to enlist with my friends."

"Is he a returned man?"

"No, sir. He was classified as physically disabled."

"That's not what I asked you. It's either yes or no here, MacPherson. Only idiots feel they have to elaborate."

"Yes, sir." Calum bit down hard on his tongue. He knew the officer was sizing him up. If he couldn't take an insult fired directly at him, he couldn't take what was to come in Europe. He had figured out the game plan in no time.

"Do you think you're ready for this?"

"Yes, sir."

The officer stared at him as if he had deliberately asked the wrong question to get the right answer. He passed him several sheets of white paper to fill out and called, "Next."

Hector stepped in front of the recruiting officer and looked down at him. "Hector MacDonald, sir."

"I hear your father served at Vimy Ridge," said the officer, shuffling some loose papers without looking up.

"Yes, sir," answered Hector in a proud voice. "He was a gunner, and that's what everyone still calls him, never Neil."

"I presume he knows you're here this morning."

"Yes, sir, I mentioned it to him."

"Did he mention Vimy to you?"

"Not much. He doesn't say too much about the war. But I don't think he was too happy about me enlisting."

"What have you got to say about it?" asked the officer.

"I doubt it will be anything like the first one, sir. I rather doubt it will go in that direction."

"Oh? You have some inside information that the rest of us don't? Are you planning on taking a picnic basket with you?"

"No, sir."

"This is war you're enlisting for. Are you expecting a Saturday night brawl?"

"No, sir."

"Are you planning on coming back in pieces?"

"One piece would be good, sir."

"Here, fill out these papers and let's see what happens!" The officer let out a sigh before calling, "Next!"

Some of the young men signing up for battle had come from the mines of Cape Breton, their eyes rimmed with coal, their arms hard and lean. Beside them stood sturdy balsamed lumbermen with hands as tough as bark, farmers bronzed by the sun to the colour of the soil, carpenters who had climbed down from a church belfry and blessed themselves on the way out—"In the name of the Father, the Son and the Holy Ghost." And men of the sea, ruddy-faced fishermen with the taste of salt on their knuckles.

They all knew, or had heard of, Strings Doucet, who now walked quietly up to the recruiting officer and gave his name. Benny stared down at the military man behind the table. The officer was too old for combat himself, had made it only as far as England in the First World War, but now looked for the will to go into battle in the eyes of the young men who stood before him.

He knew there were many ways a man could imagine war. In the blackest spaces where men mingle with insects and rodents for safety. Where death and grub have the same flavour, with the rat looking for his own share. Mortar tasting your skin. Death waiting to smear the dawn. And returned men with enough scars to trace their battles for life. This military man summed up the ready and able with a steely look.

He did not question Benny Doucet the way he had questioned Calum MacPherson and Hector MacDonald. He tapped along the edge of the table like a piano player searching for the right key. His breathing came in short strides, like a dog's at an empty bowl. The officer was out of shape and had to rely on his mouth to keep himself busy. He looked up at Benny and passed him his papers.

"You will be sent to different locations off the island for advanced training. Fill these out and good luck!"

Benny thanked him politely as he reached for the papers and walked away from a man who, he knew, was afraid of death.

The three friends stopped as they left the building and had a smoke with a group of boys who had signed up before them.

"Did you see the nose on that officer?" said one of the boys.

"He asked me if I could find England on the map," lamented one of the coal miners, blowing smoke rings in the air. "He said he 'rather doubted,' with me crippled English, that I was a frequent visitor to anything with words in it. I wanted to tell him, 'Yeah, I knows where to find it. It's where ya shot yourself in the arse to get out of going to the battlefield.' Me uncle told me all about him."

Everyone laughed.

"All I cares about," continued the miner, "is that that officer doesn't show his snout or his chin where we'll be training. Me uncle said they'll have us parading around the streets in skirts in a friggin' blizzard with our legs raw from going up and down the harbours looking for German submarines." He paused for another drag. "'That's what the army will do for ya, bye,' me uncle said, 'and then get ya over there in the mud ta finish ya off.'"

The three friends parted from the others and walked along the road towards their homes, bruising the foliage under their feet. They were full of whatever it takes to prime a man for infantry training.

"We'll be sent off to New Brunswick or someplace else for advanced training," said Benny. "If you are still interested after that tale."

"My father said we'd get very little training on the island. We'll be parading the lookouts on guard duty in our skirts," Hector laughed. "He doesn't believe we'll be sent overseas for a year or two. I know he doesn't want me to leave, but he won't say it out loud. I asked him about his experience overseas, but I can't get him to talk about much of it. He said it's not something vets like to talk about."

"I told my father," said Calum, "that this would be good practice for medical school. He pointed out that the sick and the dying are everywhere, then shrugged his shoulders and walked away. My mother went into the pantry without saying a word, and made a pie."

Benny gazed at the falling leaves. "I hate to leave them," he said, more to himself than to his friends. "They said they know I will return."

At their backs, a soft wind carried with it a high note from the mountains, and in the distance a church bell pealed, then went as faint as a dying lamb. Benny preserved the morning's chorus, tapping the rhythm out with his fingers in his pants pocket. *An air or a lament?* the composer wondered. Benny closed his fist on the notes until he was ready to let his fiddle taste them later in the day.

As they neared the north field, all three caught sight of Alex MacGregor. Standing in the open field, he looked older than his nineteen years, his head bowed, his arms dangling at his sides. Around him, morning dew covered the grass like an array of cracked silver plates.

Alex was not yet aware of his friends. He savoured a familiar scent on the air, the smell of hay coming through the open barn door. A pair of ragged scarecrows swung wild and dusty at each other in the potato patch, her torn skirt wrapped around his coverall legs, his straw hand reaching for her sagging breast. He was amazed at the energy two pieces of dead wood could contain. *They have more of a bloody love life than I do*, he thought. Alex pushed his hair out of his eyes with a swift stroke. Between the strands he noticed his friends in the distance.

"Say nothing to him," cautioned Calum, his eyes catching Hector. "He has witnessed more in this life than anyone should have to."

Alex watched as they threw him a friendly wave with hands that had just signed up for freedom. "For king and country" was how it went. For cowards and deserters was how it felt. Behind him, he could hear the scarecrows tearing away at each other.

Within minutes, the four of them stood shoulder to shoulder, talking about everything but war.

"You missed a great dance Saturday night," Benny said to Alex. "You should have seen the women these two had for partners."

"I almost made it. I just took a little detour."

"What kind of detour, Alex? The kind that pours?" Hector grinned. "I had a woman all lined up for you. She was drenched in enough perfume to choke a hog. Benny is jealous that he couldn't get to her as fast as I did."

"That's good. I'm sure I'll be able to pick up her scent the next time around."

"Some of the girls were asking about you," said Calum. "They said they missed seeing the good-looking one of the bunch. They mentioned something about seeing you earlier in the day."

"I told you, I almost made it."

"How far was almost?" Hector asked.

"Let's just say I made it to a tower."

"For the love of Christ, you were into those Englishmen's poems again."

"You're wrong. I told you I was sidelined. I had one gulp too many," said Alex, winking at Calum.

"Forget it!" said Hector, throwing his arm around Alex's shoulder. "We're all meeting at Benny's tonight for some music."

Alex noticed the locked fist bulging in Benny's left pocket. Opening and contracting as if to let something breathe. What Benny carried in his fist were the unfinished notes of "Farewell to Beinn Barra."

Alex watched them as they continued through the field on their way home. They gave a formal salute to the King and Queen of Straw as they passed the scarecrows. Three abreast, their sturdy shoulders cupped for the coming rain. Their faces plain with happiness. Or was it commitment to each other? Had they not signed a pact to stand together always? Alex idled awhile longer in the field until it began to rain. It was a sanctuary for the misbegotten. Dusty lovers. And dead mice carted up by screaming crow undertakers fighting for a corpse. Other scavengers arrived and dropped their calling cards over the field. He had signed up for nothing. He was going nowhere. He conceived the idea on this day, in a dusty, open field where the dead were being fought over, that pleasure is nothing more than the chemical reaction of the imagination.

The silver plates of dew had vanished from the young morning, and the noon sky signed its dark contempt above his head like a bruise he would carry for life. He walked slowly past the scarecrows, all desire now depleted from their eyes, as if they had been watched and scolded. Not unlike himself, really. People would question why he had not volunteered with his friends. Alex spat this thought out into a deep furrow of soil. The scarecrows had stood their ground since the spring planting in April, on guard until their services were no longer required this October.

He didn't know or care at this moment what he stood for.

Three

1939

Calum MacPherson left Beinn Barra for training in Sydney with a warm kiss on his smile, a black crow hovering above his head, and a broken crab shell close to his chest. He'd lingered beside the wharf that morning and watched as Hamish filled his red wagon with a treasure trove of broken shells and sandy rocks.

"Here, Lum, this for you," Hamish squealed, holding out a crab leg to his brother.

Calum tapped him on the back and thanked him for the gift, which he buried in his pocket. "I'll keep it with me," he said to Hamish, who was now paying more attention to a crow that had perched itself boldly among the seagulls. The intruder dipped its beak furiously into the wooden wharf. The seagulls bellowed a mournful gust of alarm at the crow, but it stayed on and pecked away at the wood.

Hamish noticed the young blond girl walking towards the wharf and waved her over to where he stood with Calum. He smiled as the girl approached. She wore a red sweater under her coat. Her bottom lip trembled as she spoke.

"What time are you leaving?"

"About noon. Benny and Hector will be leaving with me. We'll be home on leave now and again. The troops will be taking up defensive positions to defend Sydney Harbour and other harbour points in the vicinity."

"This sounds dangerous, Calum. How long will you be here before they send our troops overseas?"

"I couldn't tell you. I don't know what the orders will be."

Hamish pulled a small pebble from the sand and held it out to the girl.

"This is Lizza," said Calum. "You met her at the dance last Saturday, Hamish."

She hesitated for a moment before extending her hand.

"Me saw you kissing," smiled Hamish to Lizza.

"He wants to give you a present," said Calum. "A going-away present. I got a crab leg."

Lizza opened her hand slightly.

"Lum go way," said Hamish playfully. "Him doe where white horse gawup."

"What did he say?" she asked.

Calum grinned. "I told him that I'm going to where white horses gallop."

Hamish danced about the sand. "Me gonna get horse. Lum gonna get me horse. What colour him, Lum?"

"I told you, Hamish, your horse will be white."

"Him go fast, Lum?"

"Real fast, like a bird, Hamish."

"Him got feathers?"

"No, Hamish, your horse won't have feathers."

"Where him at?"

"I'm going to find him."

"How many feets him got?"

"Four, your horse will have four feet and four legs."

Calum laughed as he rustled Hamish's curls. "Enough questions, Hamish!"

Lizza turned her head and looked at the crow on the wharf. No other birds were in sight, but the crow stood brazenly pecking at something that had caught its eye. She mumbled the words to herself. *One crow sorrow.* She felt a chill bleed down her back.

Calum, noticing the fear in her eyes, kissed her cheek and walked with her towards the wharf.

Looking up from the wagon, Hamish called out, "Me come, Lum, you wait."

"No," replied Calum. "You wait there for me!"

Hamish stood beside the wagon and watched his brother and Lizza disappear under the wharf. He could hear laughter, and then nothing at all. He smiled as he thought about his mother and father kissing in the kitchen. Just like Calum and his girl.

The calm sea, wearing soft frills of unravelled lace, floated up on the sand. A slight breeze found loose hinges to rattle in the fish sheds farther along the shore. Hamish waved as Calum and Lizza returned to where he stood beside the wagon. The crow took flight and flew above Calum. A black feather spiralled to the sand. Hamish, down on his knees, picked up the feather and presented it to Lizza.

"You get col," he said with youthful authority, reaching out to fasten the three top buttons on her red sweater. He wiped the salt spray from his glasses with his handkerchief.

Calum winked at her. "He said you would be cold; that's why he buttoned up your sweater, the buttons I had undone. He'd scold me if he understood. I told you Hamish would look after you while I'm gone."

They were interrupted by the sound of greeting voices. Hector MacDonald walked towards them on the shore, his large feet scattering whirls of sand in his path. Behind him, Benny Doucet, fiddle in hand, paused and looked out towards the sea. Hamish rubbed the sand from a small stone and handed it to Hector.

"I hope this is gold, Hamish, me lad," Hector said, wrapping his arm around Hamish's shoulder.

"Yeah," Hamish chuckled, "dat is gol."

"I'll cash it in when I return from overseas and build a house up on the point."

"You house there?" Hamish inquired, pointing out towards the sea.

"I'm not going to marry a mermaid. Up there, Hamish." Hector pointed to the west. "That's where it will be. Benny is going to build it for me. I'm going to get married and live up there."

"Lum gonna get me horse," said Hamish, shaking Hector's big hand.

"Good boy yourself, Hamish," Hector laughed. "I'll borrow him to take me to my wedding. We'll decorate him in ribbons and bows and old tin cans."

"What colour my horse, Lum?"

"White, Hamish. I told you, your horse will be white."

"Him gonna be white, Tor."

Hector's deep baritone voice broke into a familiar Gaelic ballad, coaxing the others to join in, including Benny and his fiddle.

The sound of the sweet ballad, the voices melting the salt air, the fiddle mating with the wind, the sight of a young girl holding a black feather and Hamish in a fury of scattered steps were too much for the slim figure hiding behind the fish shed.

Alex MacGregor slumped down and sat against the shed. He shuddered. His cowardice was complete now. He could not bring himself to face them. The wind, tired of rattling hinges, rounded the corner of the fish shed and swooped down on him. It opened his eyes and let in the light for him to see Calum walking towards him. Calum pulled Alex up on his feet and wrapped him tightly in his embrace.

Gunner MacDonald stood in the north field and watched the scene play out below, along the shore.

Alex joined the others near the wharf at Calum's insistence. Hamish put three small stones in Alex's hand. "Them for you, Lex, them you present." Alex wrapped his arms around Hamish and thanked him for the gift.

"I'll have to get going," said Benny, placing his prized Carmen carefully into its case. "I've got something to do before we leave." He shook Alex's hand firmly and patted him on the back. Alex watched Benny walk along the sandy road until he was out of sight.

Benny descended the hill and entered the woods. A squirrel ran across his path, stopped a few feet away, and stood on its hind legs as it nibbled a fallen crabapple. Benny smiled at the animal. "I'm going to store something, just like you do." Benny swung open the back door of Rory's old shack and pulled at a few wall boards with the hammer he had previously left behind to complete this job.

Rory himself had called it the "old shack," yet it was sealed as tight as a clam. "She's all yours when I'm gone," Rory had declared to Benny years before, in the Doucets' kitchen, as he scribbled a handwritten will with a pencil and paper. "Just make sure the music doesn't die in her." Rory had taught him to play the fiddle.

Nobody came out here, this far off the beaten track, where the old shack stood on its solid timbers under a firm roof. Benny had boarded the two windows from the inside.

Benny took out the cedar box he had lined with cedar wood chips and placed Carmen inside. "*Tout fini*," he said. He secured the box inside the wall he had rebuilt with cedar boards for extra protection, then hurried back along the path, past the squirrel, still nibbling.

Down by the sea, Calum watched as Hamish continued to fill the wagon with newfound treasures.

"I'll come along with you," said Hector. "I've already said so long to Da."

Calum and Hector gave Alex a hearty farewell. "Keep an eye on Hamish!" said Calum.

Alex watched them walk away. Calum holding hands with Lizza, Hamish with his arm around Hector's waist. Alex could hear Hector singing, an old Gaelic ballad about a lost lover.

Gunner walked down to where Alex stood staring at the sea.

"They'll be leaving soon," said Alex, turning to face the elder MacDonald.

"The time is near," agreed Gunner, searching the young man's face. "Someone from the military is picking them up to take them to Sydney. I believe there will be a year of training before they are sent overseas."

"I'd like to go with them, but I know it's not what I want," said Alex, his face drawn and weary.

"It's not up to me to tell a man where he ought to go, but I can tell him where he should enter at his own free will."

"What were you thinking about, Gunner, before you left?"

"Just what they're thinking, Alex. My friends and I were as close as you boys are, but one of us stayed behind. It didn't change anything."

"Are you sorry you went?"

"In many ways, I am sorry indeed. It's not for everyone. How far would you get if the whole damn world went mad in pursuit of sanity?"

The old gunner studied the young man's face. "You are too young for home-front duties unless the army would deem you unfit for battle," he told Alex. "The home-front duties will fall into the hands of older men who are in the militia, or young men who couldn't pass their medical for overseas. And don't forget, some of us old vets will be as able as anyone else."

"I can't see myself on the battlefield, Gunner. I know I wouldn't last a day out there."

Gunner knew Alex was already at war. His war had started the day his father died. "Then you must find a place where you can maintain your sanity, Alex. As of today, the men are still volunteering. There are no conscription orders yet. But that's not to say it won't happen. Even for home-front duties. The war has not reached its full peak."

"What will these men do on the home front, Gunner?"

"Guard duty at the harbours, and the steel plant in Sydney, and the Marconi Towers in Glace Bay, and the power plants. Anything that could cause real hardship for people should these areas be tampered with."

"But what happens if they want to ship me overseas when things get worse and conscription is mandatory?"

"You will make that decision when it comes. That's what I meant when I said I cannot tell a man where to go, but where to enter on his own free will. Let's just hope it will not come to that."

The two men walked along the shore without speaking. Behind them, the tide was coming in, lacing the earth with white froth, lifting the stones with a heavy tongue. A gull dipped down low, then flew up and landed on the roof of a fish shed. Gunner looked over at Alex, whose eyes were aloof, full of dark, disturbing destinies. Going nowhere can take a man everywhere at once. His shoulders folded like a split fist around his chin, his head slanted like a man in a noose. In his pockets, Alex's big hands twitched as if to give him balance. Gunner slowed his pace as Alex trudged along beside him. Alex never once lifted his head to see in which direction they walked. His feet knew the sand and the sand knew his footsteps.

Four

1940

THE BLUEBERRIES CAME INTO SEASON plump and tempting in mid-July. Flora Doucet could not remember when the blueberry had given such a performance, luring men, women, and children to the lush purple fields of Beinn Barra with buckets and dippers in hand.

Napoleon Doucet turned down the volume of the Philco radio and glanced towards his wife, who stood in the pantry working blueberries into a pie. He hoped she had not heard all of the news report. But Flora appeared in the pantry doorway, a deep frown frosting her brow, the sweetness of the berries filling her mouth as she spoke.

"Have the Germans bombed England?"

"They've set a few fires," Napoleon replied.

"It's just the beginning."

"A beginning always has an end, Flora."

"They'll be sailing into England," she said.

"It will settle down. England is not asleep."

"I wish he had never enlisted, Napoleon. I don't think it's the place for Benny. He is not cut out for battle."

"He is not a child, Flora. He has to place himself in this world."

"I doubt any of them know what they are heading into, Napoleon. They speak about going overseas as if it were a job they had applied for. You heard them talking when they were home on leave. Then they are off to New Brunswick and Ottawa and on to Camp Borden. And God knows where, Napoleon. Didn't they mention something about coming back to Debert in Nova Scotia for their final training?"

Napoleon nodded.

"Honestly, I can't keep up with them. They are not prepared for this. They'd have to be aware of what's going on in England with the Blitz this September, or whatever they're calling it on the news. What do these young men know about fighting a war? I don't care how much training they give them. They've been away for almost a year now, training them for their own death, no doubt. All this training to shoot at people they don't even know. Benny does not have one combative bone in his body. I don't imagine many of the others do either. Look at the death toll in the First World War. We've already given our share. He is part Acadian, does this not bother you, Napoleon? What if..." She did not finish, but turned quickly and went back to her pie crust.

Napoleon could hear his wife slamming the rolling pin down hard on the thick dough, could imagine her hands disappearing behind flying white flour.

He removed his hat from behind the stove and moved quietly out the kitchen door. He felt no need to worry his wife by telling her that he felt the same way. That he had hoped Benny would never go to war so far from home soil. But Napoleon would not interfere with his son's plans. He would make no mention of the fear he and Flora had for Benny's safety. His son was a proud young man who had enlisted for duty. Who can interfere with a man's honour? He would be leaving with his two best friends. If that was his only reason for going overseas, it was still his decision to make.

Napoleon had placed himself safely in the heart of a woman he adored. He built strong-ribbed fishing boats that floated smoothly on the ocean's surface. They had been blessed with the good things in life. A son born to them in their later years was a wonderful surprise.

As a child, Benny had stood beside the boats as they were hoisted into the air. Run his small hands along the smooth juniper. Asked to be lifted up and placed among the giant ribs. Sat there for hours, like a small bird, admiring the twists and turns, the smell of the wood, the feel of the wind that bothered to fly up and rustle his hair. Beneath him, the child imagined the ripple of giant waves sailing him on a sea he couldn't name. Silver fish did the dance of death on the slippery floor of the big boat. All around him the deep purple water rushed up to swallow the setting orange sun. On smooth waters, the sky turned scarlet, melting its colours over the waves. He had to be coaxed down from his perch and taken home to supper in the fog. At the table, Benny would ramble on about the places he had sailed to.

"Will you describe them to me, Benny?"

"You should see them, Mama. The flowers were pretty like you on one island."

"Oh, you were sailing on some rough waters," she joked.

Benny turned to his father. "Papa, did you meet Mama on an island?"

Napoleon winked at his wife.

"Yes, I suppose I did. On Cape Breton Island, Benny, where we live. We lived very close to each other. We went to school together. Your mama was the smartest girl in the school."

Benny dropped his fork and listened intently while chewing on a piece of cabbage.

"Every day we threw stones at each other. In winter, we threw snowballs," Napoleon continued.

Benny's eyes opened wide. "Did you hit Mama?"

"No, Benny, never! We did it for attention. She wanted me to notice her."

Flora shook her head. "Don't you go filling the child's head with crazy stories, Napoleon!"

"Did Mama hit you?"

"I'd like to hit him now," Flora whispered under her breath.

"It's very simple, Benny," Napoleon said. "People will throw things at each other to get their attention. And when they get the attention, and each person understands what the other wants, the battle usually stops."

"How do you expect the child to understand you, Napoleon? He is barely eight years of age."

"He will someday, dear wife, he will someday."

Napoleon walked along the rim of the mountain, his hands behind his back, his hat secure on his head. He was a large-framed man with an easy sensibility to life. He greeted women with hat in hand, men with his large hand extended, children with a pat on the head.

He looked up towards the tip of the Barra mountain. An eagle folded its majestic wings and perched on a waiting branch. He stood as still as the eagle. Words would not come to him. He had never feared anyone or anything in his life. Until now. Until fear had insinuated itself into the small of his heart and ticked away like a squeaky clock, every day bringing the same minutes, hours, counting down their departure overseas.

He walked home when the fog began to roll in. Flora had set the table for supper. She looked over at her husband but didn't say a word. She knew him well enough to let him take his own solace. Her face was flushed from cooking, her eyes a deeper blue from the heat. Her greying hair was pulled into a bun, but a few wisps had escaped. He wanted to reach up and tuck them back in. Give his hands the pleasure of touching her. Let her know what he knew, without words.

Colourful bowls of vegetables blew off steam in the centre of the table. The limbs of the golden chicken on the white platter were folded sedately into their own flesh. He ate heartily in appreciation for the delicious meal his wife had prepared.

Napoleon dipped his fork into the pie crust. A rush of plump berries spilled out onto the plate in a slide of juice.

The berries had been spared her pounding, and they were succulent to the taste. The crust was hard and coarse under his fork, but he ate it with the same enjoyment he had shown for the chicken. Flora watched him carefully as he ate the crust. She was aware of the pummelling the dough had taken from the rolling pin. He looked up and gave her a blue grin.

After the meal he would turn the volume down low on the radio and listen to the news reports from overseas. Surely he would hear of things that had been spared.

Five

1941

THEY WALKED UP the gangplank of the troop carrier the SS *Orcades* on the thirteenth of November, and superstition hung over the heads of thousands of families and friends bidding the soldiers farewell along the Halifax waterfront.

Hector had studied the *Orcades* before they embarked, had stood back a few hundred feet and searched the belly of the steel whale, had joked that he was looking for torpedo bites. On deck, the three stood shoulder to shoulder, searching the crowd for familiar faces. Two of Hector's cousins made their way to the front of the line and raised a strip of the MacDonald tartan on a wooden pole high above their heads. Loud applause thundered down from the ship.

Joachim MacPherson stood among the crowd. He had caught a glimpse of his son, recognized Calum's broad shoulders, the quick tilt of the MacPherson head. He stumbled forward, manoeuvred his way to the roped-off section, and called out to his son. Cold sweat pooled on his skin as he tugged on the rope. He could feel a weight on his shoulders. Someone's hands. A stranger's voice coming in thin layers within the wind.

"It's not a good day for anyone, mister," the voice of a guard spoke kindly. "But nobody is permitted beyond this rope."

The sun, warmer than he remembered, made him squint. Joachim swore under his breath, made his way back to his truck, and locked himself in. He did not feel the heavy pain in his lame foot until he sat down. People were milling around in small and large knots. Some of the women and children were crying, their arms roped around the dark sleeves of relatives for support.

When she was fully loaded with fourteen thousand soldiers, the SS *Orcades* spread the waters of Halifax Harbour to begin her liquid journey to England.

One man held his fist in the air as he swore at someone or something. Only when the crowd thinned did Joachim notice that the man was talking to himself, atop a makeshift stand of plywood, dressed in a ragged army uniform and patched rubber boots. Ropes of black hair fell over a creased and shrunken face, giving him the appearance of a man spit out from the sea with his lungs and mouth still working. Everything else was dead. The teeth. The eyes. The clothes bleached of all colour. He approached the truck when he saw Joachim watching him. Joachim opened the window. The man was older than he had first imagined, his voice softer than he expected.

"The bastards are going to do to them what they did to the others. I tried to warn Churchill and Mackenzie King, but they wouldn't listen to me, and nobody will hear the dead man's tale. They bury them too deep."

He walked away slowly, his head held high with the satisfaction of a travelling evangelist to whom someone, at last, had listened.

Joachim rolled up the truck window as a northwest wind spiked his skin. The *Orcades* had by now made her way out of the harbour, leaving a deep grey scar to mark her passing. Joachim shifted the truck into gear. He had an urgent desire to get back to Beinn Barra and bury himself in his work. He had not planned on coming here to see them off. He had left at the last minute. He didn't even remember telling Ona that he was leaving for Halifax. If he hurried, he'd be met by a full moon halfway on his long return.

Joachim lowered the truck window again as he rode along the shore road. He was nearing home when he saw the figure on the hill.

Gunner MacDonald stood on the hill north of his house and watched as the chilling sea groaned under the cargo on her back. He locked his arms into a hammock position and rocked them slowly. Imagined a young boy asleep in his arms. He knew they were out there somewhere on the sea. On their way to England. He knew the horror Hitler had left England in after the Blitz.

He could see the shadow of a small animal leaping in the grass. It curled at his feet and licked his boots. He picked up the cat and walked down the path towards his home. Its warm breath left circles of heat on his bare hand.

A quarter of a mile east of Beinn Barra, a kitchen lamp burned well into the night, its limp white flame outlining two still figures sitting at the kitchen table drinking tea. The full moon rested on the arm patch of Benny's old woollen sweater hanging from a peg in the corner. Even the spider, following a route in the woodbox, looked whitewashed. Nothing moved but the four hands of the aging couple whispering their way along their rosary beads, she in Gaelic, he in his native French. At the stroke of midnight, he blew out the lamp. A path of moonlight escorted Flora and Napoleon to their bed.

"Tomorrow is still untouched," he said, following his wife.

"Amen," she answered, "Amen," as if someone were listening outside the light.

Joachim reached his lane, turned, noticed a lamp still burning in the kitchen. Ona was sitting in the rocking chair beside the window when he entered after midnight. She wore a white nightgown. Her curls fell against her breast; her feet were bare.

"You went to see Calum leave, didn't you?"

"Yes. I'm sorry I didn't tell you, Ona. I just got in the truck and drove."

"I'm happy you were there. I know Calum would be proud of you for making the long trip."

"I was proud of him as he walked up the gangplank. He turned and waved."

"Would you like a cup of tea, a bite to eat?"

"Nothing, thank you."

"You must be very tired, Joachim. Come to bed."

Joachim wrapped his arm around his wife as they walked up the stairs to their room. They passed Hamish's door. Ona entered, pulled the quilt up over his arms, and bent down to kiss him.

"Is he asleep?"

"Fast asleep, Joachim."

Joachim pulled his wife into his arms and rocked her tenderly, as if he had not seen her for a long time. He could hear her soft breathing as he lay awake beside her.

"Are you sleeping, Ona?" he asked.

"Not a wink. I was just wondering where they are at this moment, out there on the sea. How safe are they?"

He didn't answer, just listened to the sounds of the night. Outside their bedroom window they could hear the haunting scream of a dying lynx, caught in a snare in the back woods.

Six

1941

The Cape Breton Highlanders infantry battalion assumed responsibility for the protection of the ss *Orcades* on the second day of its eleven-day crossing to England, mounting twenty-nine separate guards at different points of the ship.

"There," joked Hector to his friends, "this means we'll get to where we're going without a torpedo bite. The Highlanders are in charge of fourteen thousand soldiers. Doesn't that tell you how tough we are? If Hitler himself were on one of those submarines he'd tell the captain, 'Hold your fire, there go the Cape Bretoners. Get out of their way!'"

"What makes you so sure?" said Calum.

"What can a Bren gun do against a torpedo?" Benny put in.

"The Bren gun is an anti-aircraft weapon, and with twenty-nine Cape Bretoners aiming at you, look out." Hector added, "If we weren't floating on water, I'd swear we were in a convent with all the drills and lectures and cleaning and re-cleaning we are ordered to do. Just like the nuns."

"This is the easiest part," said Calum.

"Look on the bright side," said Hector. "The U.S. warships will be performing escort duty for half the run to England. They're still neutral."

"Well, I'll tell you one thing," Calum cut in. "Hitler is not neutral: he's ripping up Europe by its roots. I, for one, don't know what we're sailing into here. We didn't hear about the Blitz until the following year, after we had volunteered for active duty. Hitler was too busy rooting up Poland."

"What do you think of all of this, Benny?" Hector asked. "Remember when MacPherson was planning on going overseas to listen to cathedral bells ring and Big Ben tick? Do you suppose he thought he was going to a circus? And he's the one who passed his grade twelve provincial exams with flying colours and led the pack with his high marks."

"He's right, Hector," said Benny. "Things are changing at a drastic pace. We don't know what's ahead of us."

Hector shook his head. "With that attitude, how far are you two going to get? Don't stray too far from me! In case you forgot, we're all Cape Bretoners. I thought you'd have written a duffle bag full of music, Benny, before we laid eyes on Beinn Barra again. You nailed that grade twelve yourself like a spike, even before Calum did. The teacher told me the only way I'd get out of grade ten was through the window, and she was right."

"You'll get along as well as the rest of us," said Calum, shaking his head.

"It's a war we're headed to, I know," answered a more serious Hector. "I knew Da hoped I would change my mind. I could see it in his eyes when I questioned him. The man will probably not rest until I get back to Barra."

"It's just as well that Alex didn't sign up," said Hector. "He'd never have made it past boot camp. I wonder what will become of him."

"He's too sensitive for this kind of manoeuvre," said Calum. "He never got over his father's death. We should have paid no attention to Cassie when she told us to shut up if Alex ever mentioned his father."

"It's too bad," said Benny. "He's very bright. I realize now that he needed to talk about his father. He told me once that he wanted to be a teacher. He had little trouble in high school. I always respected his knowledge, especially with literature. I'm sure the widows will keep an eye on him. They always liked him."

Calum grinned at Hector. "Remember the day at MacSween's store when you told the widows that a German submarine had been sighted near Sydney Harbour?"

"Yes indeed," laughed Hector. "They left the store in a damn hurry...to get home and nail their windows shut, they claimed. Nobody believed them. I'd say they went home and buried their rum in their root cellars."

"They'd put up a good fight, even if they were here on the ship," said Calum. "I'd love to hear their opinion on our sleeping quarters."

In the immense rabbit warren of the ship, each soldier had a canvas hammock as a bed. "What in the name of hell would you call this if you were writing home?" Hector had snarled as he jumped into his for the first time. "It's as comfortable as sleeping on the branch of a rubber tree. Be good if we were all monkeys."

Calum and Benny laughed. "It's better than the food," said Calum.

"I'll smuggle a couple of loaves of bread from the galley at night," Hector assured them. "One of the cooks told me he'd get them for me."

A dozen or more Highlanders joined in the conversation. They had come to get Strings Doucet from back home in the Barra to fire off a tune or two. Benny rosined the bow, thinking about the fiddle he had left behind. He enjoyed playing the fiddle in his hand, but it didn't have Carmen's sweet sound. Their laughter filtered through the music. It was light and daring. The kind that comes with fear, great expectations, a first date. And pounding jigs and reels. Young men drifting on a misty journey, bellies full of stale homemade cookies, freshly stolen bread, and swelling homesickness.

At the end of the day the swirling bagpipes filled the upper deck like a tempest swooning down over the Barra mountain.

As they sailed on a sea infested with German submarines, they had no idea what waited on the other side. The boys caught their first sight of land on a Friday, the twenty-first of November, as all hands on deck looked out at Scotland's

Mull of Kintyre, the ancestral home of many on board the ss *Orcades*.

Benny remembered his mother at this moment and how often she had talked about Scotland. "One of these days," she'd said, "I'll give it a whirl in my MacDonald kilt where many of my ancestors are buried." Benny smiled later as he began his letter home. He noted how much the Mull reminded him of Beinn Barra and suggested that perhaps his mother, a MacDonald, had not really left Scotland at all. She had just married a fine Frenchman who spoke bad Gaelic. Perhaps he reminded her of Bonnie Prince Charlie, who spoke French with a Gaelic soul.

Calum looked out at the great Mull and thought about Beinn Barra, miles away across the sea, the open fields running down to the sand, and his brother, Hamish. He would be dressed warmly today at his mother's insistence, in a heavy sweater under his coat and cap. He would carry with him a bag of thick molasses cookies to share with the fishermen closing things down for the winter. He would greet Alex MacGregor with a big grin and open up the bag. Alex would give him a mug of tea. They would sit together and talk about the sea, watching the gulls and the smouldering dark clouds on the blue horizon.

"Wat colour the water, Lex?" Hamish would ask.

"It's grey today, it's a misty day."

"Wat colour the sky?"

"It's blue, like my boat. Eat your cookies!"

"Wat colour you boots?"

"My boots are black, the colour of sorrow."

"Wat colour sorrow?"

"The colour of war."

"Wat colour war?

"I don't know. Drink your tea, Hamish."

Alex would look at the young man sitting beside him. He never complained, whether rain or snow fell on his shoulders. Flowers and trees welcomed his touch. Birds he couldn't name landed at his feet. The raging sea danced around them. He was the wisest soul he'd ever met, without a trace of colour in his world.

Hamish would put his arm around Alex's shoulder and pull his head down on his new sweater. He had already forgotten that its colour was blue.

"Lex, why you cry? Me you best friend," Hamish would say softly into a grey mist.

Hector had a déjà vu moment when the Mull of Kintyre appeared in the distance. He had sailed past the Mull many times in his father's stories. An image of his father came to him, alone in the big house at the edge of the cliff, the house he had shared with Hector's mother. Perhaps he would be filling the woodbox now or going through the newspaper for every detail he could find on the progress in Europe. Gunner MacDonald would know that the fire waited. That it was only the beginning of things to come. That it was the passing of innocence for his only son and his friends. That England, as black as Calvary's sky, was assumed to be losing the war.

At dusk on the twenty-fourth of November the Highlanders filled their lungs with British air and looked out from the ship at what they believed to be an air raid, but what turned out to be nothing more than faulty connections in an overhead tram. They marched off the ss *Orcades* and set foot on British soil in Liverpool.

In his first letter home, Hector wrote:

> You'd have to see this to believe it, Da. We were taken by train to Maida Barracks at Aldershot, southwest of London, in what looked to us like toy trains. I swear they were not much bigger than the go-carts I used to make from old barn boards. We're anxious to get to London to see the destruction of the Blitz and the sights. Will keep you posted. We were quickly put into training after cleaning out our quarters. But we are together, and we hear that they like to keep fellas from the same area together whenever possible. The Mull of Kintyre was a sight for sore eyes. Made us lonesome for home. But nothing can come close to Beinn Barra for its beauty.
>
> Benny, as usual, checked out everything made of wood on the ship, like a beaver, and jigged and reeled us across the Atlantic. He left his prized fiddle behind in Beinn Barra, but that man could play a tune on a clothesline. He's just that good.
>
> Do you ever see Alex these days? Give him my regards. I hope he is well. Did he enlist for home-front duties? I have a feeling he won't. I should have convinced him to come with us. Calum says he would not have made it past the

training. Too sensitive. I'm happy that he has you to talk to. I know how much he respects you. There are all kinds of personalities here. You lose your shyness or you lose your dinner, but some of the boys are far too young. Keep the home fires burning!

Regards,
Hector

Seven

1941

Alex MacGregor's decision not to enlist for overseas duty centred on an obsession. At seventeen, he had held in his callused hands the soft pages of the English poet Percy Bysshe Shelley, who had drowned at sea, and in his eye the thick white ankles of the young postmistress. At nineteen, he had fallen in love with the rest of her. He had no idea if a woman would rather be loved from her face down or her ankles up. Who could he ask? He was too shy to ask Moira. She might laugh in his face and throw him out of the post office. But he had noticed the way she smiled at him, and measured his shoulders with her eyes. She had never asked him why he had not signed up for active service. This, he believed, indicated that she was happy to have him close to home.

Moira's face was soft and pink. She wore her black hair rolled under. Once, from under her bangs, she had caught him staring. Caught him mapping the shape of her mouth, her eyes, the plump ankles oozing slightly over her loafers. Alex wondered as he mapped if he could print his name in dimples on her ankles. How long he could live in her flesh before popping out. He watched her swift hands scallop around an envelope. But it was her voice that lingered in his head.

"There is something for you today."

"There is nothing for you today, Alex."

He argued with her in his mind. *There is nothing for you any day, Alex. Nothing at all.*

She blushed as she licked a stamp with her pink tongue down over her bottom lip, her eyes on him. He nodded politely to her and left empty-handed. Her tongue strangled his dreams for weeks.

Over the top of *Farmer's Almanac*, he would watch as her large breasts swam under her blouse. *Spring... early thaw. Large ice floes.* In small waves, they rose to her chin when she reached for something on a high shelf. *Winter... high drifts. Deep frost.* Down they slid when she bent on one knee. *Snowed under.*

She was not beautiful, but she was tempting, like an apple pie left on a window ledge to cool.

Alex placed her in the poetry of Shelley, his favourite poet, which he recited to himself at night, between dreams. The more he went to the post office the lonelier he became. His heart was choked by this woman he carried around like a poem day and night. Yet he could not get up the courage to ask her out. Whenever someone mentioned her name, he blushed. He was linked to her by the tide of his blood. There was no way, he convinced himself, that he could risk spilling one ounce of her on the battlefield.

Alex did not believe he was stealing when he took her picture from the envelope. One of her relatives in the United States had sent her photographs taken when they had visited Beinn Barra. She left the photographs on the counter when she went to a back room. Alex took the one of her sitting on a fence. She is wearing a straw hat pushed to the back of her head. One hand rests on the fence pole, the other anchors her hat from the wind. Her legs are crossed, displaying her thick ankles in a bold X. Her bare feet dangle in a summer moment. Alex placed her under his pillow at night in a thick envelope to keep her from wrinkling. By day, when he went fishing, he tucked her into his wallet.

"How are your friends getting along overseas?" she asked him one afternoon, as he stood with a letter in his hand.

"This letter is from Calum," he stammered, before thanking her and walking out. She watched him as he passed the window and walked along the road. Watched his broad shoulders brace against the wind. Watched him hold the letter like a child holding a delicate flower. What was inside the envelope could not be crushed, could not be wrinkled. He read the letter as he walked home.

Dear Alex,

Benny and Hector send their regards as the year comes to a close. Here's hoping you're keeping the home fires burning for us. We will miss not being in Beinn Barra for Christmas.

We are eagerly waiting for a batch of fudge and fruit-cake to arrive. We will enjoy them even though they likely will not arrive in time for Christmas. Hector plans on learning to cook when we return so he can get the taste of real food back in his mouth. This is something to look forward to, Hector making fruitcakes. And Benny is still checking out wood. Hector calls him Private Pinocchio every time he sees him checking out another piece.

I know you must see Hamish on his journeys. Tell him for me that I miss him every day. Keep an eye on him for me! I know you and Hamish are great friends, and that he is safe with you at his side.

Things are rather bleak here in England. The destruction of London is an eyesore. But it is the death toll from the Blitz that is staggering. When we landed, we were taken by train to Maida Barracks at Aldershot, in the southwest of England. We are kept busy, preparing for a war we haven't met eye to eye. There are route marches and wiring parties, fieldcraft and map reading exercises.

Benny is eager to play the fiddle at the mention of Beinn Barra, and Hector provides us with the humour that is needed here. Nobody can describe the beds we have to sleep in like Hector can. He calls them "beaver traps" because they are made of iron and fold in two. The mattress comes in two parts, called "biscuits." More often than not, the bottom biscuit slips to the floor during the night and we wake up to the fact that we've slept on iron. It is quite a sight to see Hector's big feet dangling over the iron. Someday we'll gather again at the shore and tell all our stories. For now, remember us well.

Your friend,
Calum

Alex folded the letter as neatly as a handkerchief and placed it in his shirt pocket. He could smell the rain before it began to fall lightly on his back. He stood for a while and watched the drops fill a small pothole in the middle of the road. His thoughts were in Europe. He had heard stories of Vimy Ridge from men who had returned from the First World War. Everyone had an opinion on this war. They would not stay in England forever. It was just a holding tank before the boys were sent into the fire. Everyone knew that. How calmly Calum spoke about the future. And then there was Hector, who could find comedy in everything.

A strange anger stirred in Alex's chest, crawled around and pushed itself up into his throat and dripped like sour milk on the tip of his tongue. "Why in the hell did you go, Benny?" he heard himself shouting into the light rain. "You are a creator, not a destroyer."

The rain fell faster, like a stranger roaring back a response. Alex stirred the deep puddle with his foot. He watched as the falling rain turned into mud.

He was angry at himself for not saying anything to Benny before he left to go overseas. He remembered that day down by the wharf, a month or so before they went off to training camp in New Brunswick. They were on leave from their Sydney posting. Calum had sneaked a bottle of rum under his shirt. And a snort of dandelion wine for Hamish. They drank to the future under a white haze, the yellow of the sun paled by the swirling sand. They moved like ghosts between jigs and reels. Intoxicated by heat, liquor, and anticipation. Hamish offered up gifts cast off by the sea. A beer cap, a piece of netting from a lobster trap, two clam shells.

From his vantage point by the fish shed, Alex watched a car stop and a stranger emerge with camera in hand to capture the moment. Two weeks later, the picture of the three Cape Breton Highlanders appeared in the Halifax *Mail-Star*.

When they left the shore, Alex followed behind Benny. He wanted to tell Benny that he had made a big mistake by signing up. He caught up to Benny on the road, and walked side by side with him while Calum and Hector tried to get Hamish to stop looking for treasures. Calum smiled when he saw that Hamish had dug up a leg from a pot-bellied stove. Neither Calum nor Hector wanted it, so Hamish knelt and reburied it in the sand.

Alex was relying on his whiskey tongue to start up the conversation. He was going to tell Benny to stay out of the army. To serve on the home front. He had it all planned in his head. What he thought Benny should hear. "You are not cut out to be a soldier, Benny. You are a composer. A great fiddler. You can turn a scrap of wind into poetry with those strings."

But it had been a long afternoon, and he could feel the effects of the liquor wearing thin. He tried to cough up the words but ended up spitting on the side of the road. He said nothing. He cursed his weakness as he watched Benny, with his fiddle under his arm, walk slowly over the hill towards the woods.

Now, Alex could feel the rain soaking through his jacket. The wind had turned to the southeast. The sea was a torn grey blanket of mist and fog, stitched together with seagulls. He stirred more puddles with the toe of his boot. There was nothing he could do now to bring Benny home. To bring any of them back. What could he say in a letter to Calum that would not make him the coward that he was?

> I am here in Beinn Barra, as safe and well as before. I hope you are all fit and able for the run. I hear there is quite a bit of that involved in your training. I'd love to be with you all, under different circumstances. The reason I didn't enlist is that I have something here I must conquer first. It's a long story from the ankles up. I can't explain it on paper. Things could very well be resolved by the time you return. I will be the first to greet you when you come home again. Hamish is as robust as ever. We meet every day on our journeys. I will take great care of him. He seems to want to take care of me as well.

He would never pen these words to Calum. He had never told them why he didn't want to serve. They probably already knew. They had never questioned him. He suspected that Calum had asked the others not to question him. Or Gunner, maybe. They left him alone with his decision, the way he had been left alone when his father died. They had protected him, taken him everywhere, everywhere but back to his father's memory. Cassie MacGregor had laid out her warning to his friends.

He did not want them to know that he was as cowardly about love as he was about war. That even at his young age he suspected that love and war could have the same ending. And how could he tell Moira that he had fallen in love with her the day he saw her licking the stamp?

Eight

1942

Benny Doucet's first letter arrived shortly after the new year had come to Beinn Barra in a quiet white flurry on a Monday morning. Flora and Napoleon sat over a cup of tea and devoured every word.

Dear Mother and Father,

I hope all is well with you. We are fog-bound at the moment and can see very little from where we are stationed. Hector said he can't figure out how the Germans can see anything to bomb, with all this fog in England. Our training is rigorous, but Calum, Hector and I have passed the test so far. It's our Cape Breton spirit. We live by the bugle, in the cold, the damp, and the fog. Daily, the bugler plays reveille. We have a call to the cookhouse, thirty minutes to parade, a call for dinner, for training, for lights out. You name it, we are called by the bugler. Hector calls him the "Tin Throat" and has threatened to fill his bugle with sand.

We did get to London to see the destruction. The people have not lost their spirit and go about their day with renewed optimism. I suppose that is what all of us must do, despite the circumstances that face us today.

I keep Beinn Barra alive in music with my old fiddle when the drills and training are over for the day. The boys keep their feet tapping and their hearts longing, as I do, for our return. Hector says he wishes we had the three widows here. They would keep the dancing going. I often think of the dance at the parish hall, when Hamish invited the widows from the kitchen to partner up with us in the square set. Hector still maintains that I put Hamish up to it.

We are a closely knit group here, the majority of us from Cape Breton. And the stories are funny no matter how often they are told. One soldier from New Waterford told us his uncle drank so much moonshine that his aunt placed a jug of shine at his elbow before they closed the lid on his coffin. Everyone called him Uncle Jug. They are great sports, these soldiers from the mining areas.

I am dismayed at the age of some of the soldiers here. They should be in a schoolyard rather than in training. I don't know how they made it this far.

I hope you are still going out to the dances on Saturday night and having a good time. I will keep you posted on what is happening here in Europe. Keep well!

Until,

Benny

Flora folded her son's letter neatly and took it upstairs. She opened her old Bible to tuck the letter away. She read slowly from the page she had opened, from the book of the prophet Isaiah. Chapter 2, verse 4:

> And he shall judge the Gentiles, and rebuke many people.
> And they shall turn their swords into ploughshares, and their spears into sickles.
> Nation shall not lift up sword against nation, neither shall they be exercised any more to war.

Flora heard her husband call her from the kitchen.

He was standing at the stove, fitting a piece of hardwood into the open cover. A large flame jutted above the lid. Napoleon stared into the flame like a man staring directly into hell. Into all its fire and brimstone. Into its collection of the damned. Napoleon was not without sin himself. But he had never turned on a man in pure hatred. He did not like the feeling brewing in him. With this war no closer to a conclusion, he felt a draft of damnation escaping from his veins.

"Are you trying to burn down the kitchen, Napoleon?" He heard his wife's voice coming from the hallway.

She came into the kitchen to survey the soot that had reached her spotless white ceiling and the back wall. Napoleon looked into her sweet face. On its smooth surface there was no anger. She did not fester over mishaps. When a woman truly loved a man, as Flora did, she included pipe smoke, thick mud, wet boots, sawdust, and horse shit tracked into the kitchen as part of "for better or worse." A good scrubbing with lye soap and warm water would take care of it. Flora went out to the porch and returned with a galvanized bucket of water to heat on the stove.

"You, dear woman, are to go upstairs and rest!" said Napoleon, taking the bucket from his wife. A man should clean up his own dirt, or he is not worth the rubble he stands on.

He listened to her soft footfalls on each step and heard the door to their bedroom close. Napoleon poured himself a cup of tea as the water heated. He pulled the bucket of hot water off the stove and placed it on the floor mat to cool.

Up in the bedroom, Flora removed Benny's letter from the Bible and reread it, imagining his voice with each word. She was happy that he could keep up his music for the soldiers, that the music was not put to rest. But how could he be so far from home when there was so much for him to do here? Napoleon missed Benny's help with the ship-building. Napoleon was getting on in years, and he had relied on his son's skill.

There was a smudge on the envelope. She had noticed it when she picked it up at the post office. She had time now to remove it. She could do that much on the home front to help them clean the mud they were caught in overseas.

Nine

1942

Cassie MacGregor relied on an omen to protect her son from the horrors of war. It wasn't much to go by. A flock of crows tearing their lungs out in the back woods. She had listened to them for days, bawling and screeching. They had started up at dawn, coming together for the funeral of one of their own. She believed in these things. Could feel the rage of their sorrow. She had felt it herself after her husband, Alexander, drowned. But she couldn't make a sound in front of her four children.

"There was no way you'd hear me bawling and screeching," said Cassie. "Had to keep it locked up somewhere." She swore to Christ that widows had two hearts. One that kept them going for everyday living. And the one they tried to settle at night when they felt themselves take leave of their senses. Light as a feather on her pillow, she felt her husband come to her. Ask her to dance in the dark. Later, he made love to her as peacefully as snowflakes falling on a waiting tongue. Afterwards, he took a handful of snowflakes and sprinkled them over the bed. One night he sang her to sleep. She had tried to sing along with him, but was too drained. There was no oxygen left in her night heart. The next morning, her day heart full of energy, she sang the song to her children while making their porridge.

"I hear they are calling up men for the home front," she said to her son, Alex, a week after the crow omen. He was standing at the mirror, shaving.

"They'll never get to leave another footprint on Beinn Barra. The other three," she said.

Alex caught a reflection of his mother's face in the mirror. She looked older than her years. Strands of silver hair fell on her thin shoulders, making her appear shorter than her tall frame. Mauve eyes, burdened with omens, sank heavily under her thick lashes. There was nothing left of the beautiful woman in the wedding photo with his father. A chill had set her mouth and refused to thaw. The old smile had decayed.

"I can't understand for the life of me why anyone would want to get up and go over there," Cassie continued, and her shoulders heaved.

"There's a war on, Ma," her daughter, Joan, shouted from the pantry.

"It's that Churchill," Cassie replied. "It's him looking to get our men over there. I'll bet Churchill wouldn't come to Cape Breton to settle a fight if they asked him."

Alex hung his shaving towel on a hook behind the stove and went out the back door without saying a word.

"They wanted to go, Calum, Benny, and Hector," said Joan, dishpan in hand, coming out of the pantry.

"Hector's father is a return man. Why in the hell would he want his son over there after what he saw?" said Cassie.

"What are you going to do, Ma? They' re all his friends. You can't tie him down forever. I'd go myself if they'd take me," laughed Joan.

Cassie left her daughter standing in the kitchen and climbed the back stairs to the attic. She moved boxes and an old wooden trunk out of her path until she stood directly in front of the seam in the far wall. She had not used the hide-away in years, since her children were little and her husband had hid their Christmas toys there. She removed the strip of wood covering the seam and slid the wall open with two hands. It slid with a rattle into the adjoining wall. *Perfect*, Cassie thought, as she entered the small space. *They'll never find him in here. Let them search all they want.* There wasn't a soul who could find the slit in this wall, by God. Santa Claus himself would have been mystified, her husband had often said. *All it needs is a good cleaning and a cot.* Cassie went out, slid the wall closed, and sat down on the old trunk.

She had heard stories of men being hidden in attics and barns and even dug-out crawls in the ground to avoid the bloody First World War. During conscription, the Mounties had come hunting the young men like hounds. She was grateful that she had this false wall, as her husband had called it, built by his uncle to hide illegal liquor from the Mounties. The house creaked as she sat in the attic. Making noises like an old voice that had forgotten its song. It was not a place she wanted to put her handsome, gentle son, but it was all she had.

She mentioned the false wall to Alex one evening after his sister had gone out.

"You know, the place your father hid your Christmas toys when you were kids."

Alex listened to his mother speak without saying a word. His father had rarely made it into any of their conversations since his death.

Finally, he spoke. "Are we planning a game of hide and seek, Mother?"

"I'm talking about the bloody war, Alex." Her voice was both annoyed and frightened. "You know it will be only a few months till the fighting starts for our boys. They won't keep them in England forever, and they'll be looking for more recruits to send overseas. The Mounties will be out in full force in the name of conscription. They'll drag them off by the scruff of the neck, like skinned rabbits. I'm warning you. You'll need a safe hiding place. I hear what people are saying. They'll never find you behind that wall, Alex," she stated matter-of-factly.

Alex left his mother standing in the kitchen and walked out the back door. He swore to himself as he made his way along the path to the shore. Thinking of life and death in bright, crisp air, the spaces between poems that let him breathe, let him believe that the whole damn world would be different if his father were still living. His father would have given him clear directions.

He had read about the enormous pressure for total mobilization. Prime Minister Mackenzie King had introduced the National Resources Mobilization Act, which called for a national registration of eligible young men, and authorized conscription for home defence. From April 1941, the young men called up were required to serve for the rest of the war on home defence duties. Conscription for overseas would follow. He knew this was coming. He knew his mother was right.

Nobody had bothered him yet. He would stay put and pursue his secret love like some tormented monk forced to feed from his own flesh. For his penance. What had he done? In the beginning it was her ankles that caught his attention, then the rest of her had fallen into place. He had done nothing more than fall for a woman from the ankles up. She never once changed colours. Pink and white. White and pink. *She is at her most beautiful when she moves*, he thought. Once, a sudden breeze from an open window had hidden under her skirt and let him in on a delicious secret. She was wearing pink underwear.

Ten

1942

Winter buried Beinn Barra deep in early December. White drifts rode through the open fields like high waves, stranding cattle in their stalls, chickens in their pens, school children in their homes. Behind panes of frosted glass, Hamish MacPherson created art with his tongue on the frozen easels. Harried housewives stared out their windows and prayed for anything that would melt the frozen misery of their lives in time for Christmas.

Joachim bundled up against the cold to make his way to the barn. He could see his neighbour, Gunner MacDonald, shovelling a path to the road.

The silence of the snow disturbed Joachim. His own silence disturbed his wife. She had always been able to turn to him in the past. Hold him against her fears. At night, under quilts. That was where he waited best.

"It's alright, Joachim, to mention his name," Ona had said, in the cold dawn.

"His name is not what I miss, Ona."

"You never say anything about him any more."

"What do you want me to say?"

"Say the same things that I say about him," she'd replied.

"I hear what you say; you know I feel the same way."

"I don't know what you're feeling. You've changed since Calum left."

"We have all changed, Ona. The whole bloody village has changed since the boys left for war."

"We are not alone, Joachim. Everyone is waiting for an end to this. The Doucets, Gunner MacDonald. Their sons are at war. And many more. You can't take this on alone. Speak to them. They are not strangers."

He had turned from her and buried his face in the white pillow. Ona was right. Everything had changed, but what could he say to anyone? They already felt what he felt. Gunner would understand this loneliness. But he, more than anyone, would know that knowledge could not take away the pain.

In the far distance he thought he could hear the sound of pounding guns. Joachim drove the shovel into the snow, and white powder flew back into his face. He heard a tap from the kitchen window and turned to see Hamish smiling at him. He had melted a space big enough to fit a smile. The rest of his face was a blur behind the frost. Joachim stopped and looked in at the smile. Behind frost, the boy appeared perfect, beatific, with cupid-bowed lips like his mother's. Joachim longed for conversations with the boy. He wanted to teach him what every father should teach his son. He wanted to tell him what he could not tell Calum. He wanted a verbal response. Understanding. How could a man talk to a smile behind frost?

He turned back to his shovelling and cut a deep path towards the barn to tend to the animals. Brown Butter looked at him with the round, sad eyes of a rejected lover and bowed her head into the straw as he milked her. Happy Herman, the black stallion, grew restless in his stall, kicked at the gate with his back hoof for attention. Angus the bull snorted indifferently. Raised the gold ring in his nose to prove a point. Robert the Bruiser came up behind Joachim and bunted his head against Joachim's back. The cold, hard eyes of the ram scoured him, a boxer ready for blood. From the chicken coop he could hear Murdock the rooster calling. The morning bugler didn't like to be kept waiting.

A few hours later, Joachim left the barn and walked towards the house for his first meal of the day. The frost had melted from the kitchen pane. Hamish stood with his full face in the window. Still smiling broadly at his father. Joachim looked in at the boy.

His wife wanted him to talk. The boy wanted him to smile. What was he supposed to do? He was trapped between the house and the barn, between Hamish's demanding smile and his wife's demanding heart. He turned and walked back to the barn as the boy tapped gently on the window. He could hear Hamish call out. He walked along in uneven steps, preferring not to look back at the happiness that lived behind the tapping.

Gunner MacDonald warmed himself by the fire in his kitchen after shovelling the path to the road. It had stopped snowing, and now a softer breeze blew snow like dust from window ledges. The sun finally appeared from behind a cloud and toasted the day. Gunner made a pot of tea and watched as the snowplow sliced open the road. He dressed warmly and made his way to MacSween's General Store and the post office.

At the store, four or five men stood around the pot-bellied stove in conversation. One old man sat beside the stove, his face partially covered by a newspaper. Two of the widows had made it out and were complaining about the snowplow blocking up their shovelled paths.

"I tell you," said the old man without looking up, "things would be different if I were over there with the troops." He dropped the paper when he saw Gunner standing at the counter. Spit from his chewing tobacco ran down the corners of his mouth; his pale poppy blue eyes looked like two marbles ready to fall over an edge.

"What in the hell could you do—teach the troops how to spit straight?" one of the widows asked him.

"Madam," replied the old man, "it is quite obvious that your tongue is more advanced than your intelligence."

The men gathered around the stove laughed heartily as the two widows walked out of the store, slamming the door hard.

Gunner proceeded to the post office and smiled when a letter from Hector was handed to him along with his newspaper. He walked home between the high snowbanks, the letter tucked safely in his jacket pocket. Gunner opened the Christmas greeting from Hector and hung it above the kitchen table. He hoped Hector had received his parcel, although there was no mention of it in his wishes for a good Christmas and a happy new year.

From his kitchen window Gunner could see the white blanket of snow that covered Beinn Barra. Spring was still beneath the snowbanks, he thought, allowing himself the luxury of thinking about the first spring buds popping their heads up in the Barra fields, and the green spreading throughout the village under his feet in just a few months.

Gunner picked up the Halifax *Mail-Star*. He wanted to read something about peace to begin this day. But Churchill had declared, "The ordeal which we have to pass will be fomenting and protracted, but if everyone bends to the task with unrelenting effort and unconquerable resolve, if we do not weary by the way or fall out among ourselves or fail our Allies we have the right to look forward across a good many months of sorrow and suffering to a sober and reasonable prospect of complete and final victory."

Hitler had said, "The great masses of the people will more easily fall victim to a big lie than to a small one."

In a world of declaring men, Gunner found nothing to give him hope that he would see his son anytime soon.

Eleven

1943

Some of the men declared unsuitable for combat after their training in England were sent home to serve in other capacities. Gunner wished that Hector would return. How fit does a man have to be to die, he mused? Or live under such conditions? How ironic that what an aging soldier remembers most about peace is war.

They had passed all their tests, Hector, Calum, and Benny. They would be moving on soon into the thick of things. So soft a word, "thick," for what was to come. Combat eventually destroys even the strongest, the fittest of men. If the hide is spared, the conscience is not. Something will find him sooner or later if he is left in it too long.

Gunner knew they had not been told where they were going when, twenty-three months after arriving in Liverpool, they left England in October 1943. The Cape Breton Highlanders boarded an American ship, the ss *Monterey*, for a destination unknown. Gunner reread his son's description of that journey:

Dear Da,

We have landed in Naples, Italy, after an unforgettable journey. It was a delight aboard ship to have plenty of good food and a good card game. The Pipes and Drums performed on deck for hours at a time. It was great to see the lights of Tangiers and Gibraltar, the first lighted cities we have seen since we left Canada. We didn't know for sure where we were headed. We were first told we were going to Ireland. After days of sailing, we were told we were headed for the Mediterranean. At one point, after we were given Mepacrine pills for malaria, I thought we were headed for the jungle.

Near Phillipeville, Africa, we were attacked by German Dornier bombers. Some of the boys were ordered to go up on deck and fire at the planes. They emptied twelve or fifteen 20-round magazines from their Bren guns at the planes from the roof of the captain's cabin. The bombers were flying very low, using aerial torpedoes. Let me tell you, I was wishing I had a couple of bottles of holy water with me, the kind my grandmother threw in the air during a thunderstorm. It was fierce. The *Santa Elena* was hit, and we had to take the survivors aboard the *Monterey*. When it finally ended, the boys were bawled out by the captain for the damage they had done to the wires and towers. I don't get it. It's like cursing your feet for wearing out the soles of your shoes.

And here we are, no worse for wear. God knows what is to follow. And He, too, at this moment, is not revealing his plan.

Regards,
Hector

Hamish gathered hen feathers to mail across the sea to his brother, Calum. Examined them carefully as he held them up for inspection. Groomed them like warriors. Among the brown feathers, Hamish added one white feather from Little Rachel. The hen watched with her one good eye as Hamish picked up her feather and held it up to the light of the sun. He ran it through his fat fingers and smiled into the cool November breeze.

Hamish stopped at the barn door to speak to his father. Little Rachel clucked as if to protest this delay with the enemy so close. She had grown accustomed to safety and salty sea air.

Joachim stood in the barn door, looking at the boy. He had not noticed it before. The same curve in the chin. The thick eyebrows almost joined at the bridge of the nose. How the boy and Calum smiled alike, setting off a quiet rumpus in their eyes. A smile he hadn't seen in two years from Calum.

"Look me dot, Da," squealed Hamish, holding up the white feather close to his glasses. Little Rachel ruffled her wings and settled back on her mound.

"This for Lum. Him gonna get me horse."

Joachim watched as Hamish approached with the feather in his hand. He wanted to say something nice to Hamish. Something like, *It's kind of you to think of your brother overseas.*

Instead, he warned, "Don't you go down on the breakwater with that wagon. It's too dangerous! You'll fall in. What will happen then?" He tapped the smiling boy on the head.

Hamish replied with a grin, "Me drown dead." He left a wet smudge on his father's cheek as he walked towards the house, the warning floating like a sweet breeze inside his head, his glasses hanging on the end of his nose.

Joachim saw no need to comment on the horse, to keep the fairy tale going as his wife did. Hamish would forget about it soon enough. He would be a child forever. He had never been to school. He could not read or write. They couldn't trust him around the animals. The big stallion was too contrary and swift, the cows too big and awkward for slow hands. He had warned the boy to stay away from the barn when he was not around.

His mother would not permit him to take in wood since the day the boy had opened the oven door and thrown the wood on her cake.

"That's enough, Hamish," she'd said, pulling the cake out from under the wood. "Let your father do that work!" She had taught him to sweep the floors instead, like a woman, and scatter dust from the mats. His white, chubby hands grew soft from dandelions and dust, and mixing delicate cakes. His feet grew dusty from outdoor dancing.

There would be no horse arriving from anywhere. That was something his departing brother had used to keep Hamish waiting for his return.

Joachim had built the red wagon for Hamish. He didn't mind making things for him. But now that flighty hen sat perched in it like royalty, as if to mock him, and kept a cold eye on him whenever he approached. The damn hen would look better in a pot than it did in the wagon, with its one eye beaming on him like a searchlight.

Joachim had the look in his eye of a man who knows how to protect his children but not love them in public. He left that to the boy's mother. She could do a better job of it.

Ona had cradled her second son at his birth, when the doctor said he was not sure the baby would make it. That the child was handicapped. Mongoloid. Ona held what looked like a string of limbs gasping for air and stroked him into human form. Sang him to sleep with a Gaelic lullaby tucked in his ear. The boy thrived. Ona paid little attention, a few months later, when the doctor told them that Hamish would be fragile. She paid no attention to the pitfalls of a wounded child. That was something adults imposed on them. As a mother, she would hear nothing of this.

"If he can love, he can live," she snapped, as she kissed the round cherub face of her beautiful child.

Joachim had looked down at the baby destined for soft winds and prayers and his mother's hand leading him through life. He had picked up his strong, healthy son, Calum, and gone out to feed the spring lambs. Calum was destined for great things. He could see it in the child's eyes. The way he examined things. Took them apart, studied them with interest, then put them back together again. Nothing would stop Calum from going forward on a sure foot. There was nothing lame about this child.

Hamish walked towards the house with Little Rachel in tow. Smiling and determined, Hamish drew the white feather from his pocket and blew on it as if it were a candle. He placed it on the table with the brown feathers and watched as his mother tied them with a piece of string. They would mail the parcel to Europe in the afternoon, filled with candy and fudge and fruitcake along with the feathers.

Hamish carried the parcel to the post office like a man on a mission. He made his way to the front of the line and placed it on the counter. Gunner MacDonald smiled at Hamish as he posted his own letter overseas.

"For budder," Hamish announced.

Moira weighed the parcel.

"This is heavy, Hamish. What have you got in it?"

"Hen, me put hen in partel," answered a proud, smiling Hamish.

Twelve

1943

Alex MacGregor lay with his eyes closed on his bed, listening to the rain falling on the roof on this dreary November afternoon. *Rain, rain, go away,* he chanted to himself.

He swore. For once in his life, rain was getting on his nerves. He felt it was responsible for the pistol at his head, shooting rounds of pain into the back of his skull. He was sure people were calling him a zombie, the term they used for men who did not go overseas into battle. For many reasons, but the suspected one being that they were too cowardly.

His friends had been shipped to Italy in October of this year. Things were heating up. The march of fire had begun.

Nothing moved in him but his own imagination under a mackerel sky. The moon was in its rest period, a dead planet above his head. No stars came out to brush the darkness. Moira came to him in a dream, not for comfort, but for directions. She could not find her way home. He walked beside her. Her smooth ankles danced lightly over a puddle along the road. Then one ankle was swallowed up by the puddle. It was drowning slowly. She allowed him to rescue it. To pull it back to safety with a fisherman's hand. She could feel the knots tied in his knuckles from years of kneading the waves. He was rewarded with a kiss on the cheek that slid down towards his mouth.

Nothing happened.

She knew what he was thinking. He could see it in her eyes when he went to the post office. There was something there. Hidden from him like the messages in the love letters that arrived from overseas for wives and lovers.

Something happened.

She smiled at him differently at the post office the next day. There was something urgent in her open request. "Alex," she asked, "what do you do to keep yourself happy?"

He lifted his head and slowly met her eyes. "Excuse me?" he stammered, but he wanted to run with his stupidity. He couldn't even answer a question without appearing deaf as well as dumb.

"You always look so forlorn. I was just wondering what you do besides fishing and waiting for your magazines and books to arrive? How do you keep yourself busy? You don't even go to the dances any more."

"I read and do some writing." He cleared his throat as if someone had just released him from a strangle hold. He couldn't tell her he had dreamt of rescuing her drowning ankle from a puddle the night before.

"What do you read?" she asked.

"I read Shelley's poetry."

"Shelley who? Do I know her?"

"He was a British poet."

"Oh. I'd die with just paper people for company," said Moira.

He could tell by the look on her puzzled face that she did not read too much of the living or the dead.

"I don't know why I even have to ask. You were always reading one book or another at school. Myself, before this bloody war started up, I wanted to take off to the States and get into the movies."

She was smiling at him again. But he couldn't tell her she would make a wonderful actress, poetry readings excluded, for fear she might leave Beinn Barra after the war. She was flirting with him, loosening his tongue for words she has not heard him speak, unhinging his limbs.

"Don't you wish you had other things to do with your time, Alex?" Her face was flushed. Her blood was part of the conversation. Part of the seduction. His body relaxed. He could feel a connection between them, not by words, but some sort of tension. This was his chance to ask her out to a dance. To forget about Shelley. He could interest her in poetry at some later date. He was about to ask when the door opened.

Someone entered.

Alex left the post office and walked down to the shore. In his hand was an official-looking envelope from the Defence Department. He knew what it contained before he tore it open. He had been requested to register for war duties on the home front. He tucked the letter into his pocket and walked towards home.

Later that night he watched the moon. In its first quarter. A fraction of itself. A comma over Beinn Barra. He wondered where the other pieces of the moon were hiding. Science had never been his strong point. Calum would know. He knew all about these things. Perhaps he should have let Calum in on his secret love life.

"Science is as philological as it is logical. Especially physics. It's quite simple. Logic is a mere equation. I read it somewhere," Calum had said once.

"How is that?"

"Everything is relative, Alex. Just think of it as, you can't do one without the other."

He'd wanted to ask Calum if love were relative to anything. *Does love really equate to war, as the poets suggest?* But he knew Calum better than that. If he asked Calum one question, Calum would ask him three in return. He would ask him for details. Make him give an equation. Make him equate thick ankles with the heart. What was it about her thick ankles that attracted you, Alex? Was it their shape? Their flexibility? Their softness? Are they relative to the girl's personality? Do they have a strong pulse? Are they a symbol of something else out of reach?

Jesus, he'd be so confused after all these questions he'd forget there was a woman above the ankles. No, he was glad he had never mentioned anything to Calum. Calum would have confused Shelley, had the two met face to face. *How can I understand anything about love when I could barely make a pass-*

ing grade? thought Alex. He pulled his blind down on the moon. He didn't need to know where the other pieces were. He could never make them fit, even if he found them.

Something remembered.

He had been with his father and his friend, old George, that day. His father had been promising for months to take Alex out fishing with him. His father had pulled him from sleep at four in the morning, had put a bowl of hot porridge in him and a strong cup of tea.

"It's time to go, son, old George will be at the shore, waiting for us." Nine-year-old Alex walked to the shore quietly behind his father, his dog, Hinna, at his heels. His rubber boots squeaked as he trailed along, carrying a Thermos of tea. He felt like a man following in his father's footsteps. His father sang an old sea shanty and encouraged him to join in at the chorus.

His father rowed the small dory out to the fishing boat. Alex held on tightly to the dog's collar as *The Sandy Moor* set sail to Dipper's Point to drop the mackerel nets. They had not been out long when the sea convulsed. Spouted anger from every wave. The morning sky turned the colour of steel, whipped the sun under an easterly cloud and left a grey smear.

He watched his father roll over the stern of the boat as he tangled with the net he been trying to haul back onboard. The dog was spinning in circles and barking savagely. Then it jumped over the side to join his father. Old George frantically threw out the lifeline, a long piece of rope. But his father had drifted too far to reach it. He heard his father's voice riding over the waves, ordering old George to sail *The Sandy Moor* in before they all went down.

How clear his voice had been, with just his head and hands above water. Alex tore savagely at old George's hands, trying to stop him from heading back to the harbour. He could feel the old man's blood under his fingernails as he tore at his flesh, and old George wept as his torn hands kept a firm grip on the wheel. Alex ran to the stern and looked out to where he had last seen his father. The dog was swimming in blind circles. His father was practically underwater now, just his hands above. Alex called out to him, but all he could see were his father's thick, white hands sinking beneath a wave.

The body washed ashore three days later. Alex stayed in his room all through his father's wake. He listened to the sounds of life going on below him, doors opening and closing, mourners coming and going. Muffled prayers slipped in under his blind. *Amen, Amen, Amen.* The delicate rattling of his mother's good china, special-occasion china, summoned to the table by death. A wreath of dead roses and leaves identified the house and fed its sweetly sickening smell to the wind. Why did people bother with these things? People already knew where they lived, and that his father had drowned, Alex told himself as he slammed the window down on the smell of dead roses.

The dog was never found. Alex lay in the dark, wondering what the sea had done with him. Had Hinna swum to another island and been claimed by a stranger?

On the second night of the wake, he lay in his bed, trying to trace his father's face. All around him he could see water. Wet hair. Wet hands. Thick white wrists. His father's remains were in the room directly below his bedroom. He wanted to sneak down and see what his father looked like. He didn't understand why he couldn't recall his face. To have something to remember between the sobs and the smells. All the women were gone. There were only a few fishermen in the room at this hour of the morning. He could hear their voices recalling old Gaelic yarns as he stood on the landing, but he could go no further. His bare feet pulled him backwards. He did not realize he was in motion until he reached his bedroom door. Under the darkness of his quilt, he spoke to his father. "I was too scared to look down and see that your hands and hair were still wet, Da. That's why I didn't come to see you."

He allowed only porridge to be brought to him. Porridge and tea. Three weeks later, he heard his mother's stern warning to his sister. "Don't you go asking Alex one word about that day, or you will be sorry you ever owned a pair of teeth. Don't mention your father to him!"

Cassie herself never mentioned his father, as if death had taken Alexander's name with him.

And what would he say to his father after all these years, if he asked, "What have you been doing, my son?"

"I have spent my time wondering what my life would be like had you not drowned. At night, I stir up dead poets and whisper their words back to them. I am a fishermen, like you, and someday I will sing all the verses to the sea shanty we began so long ago."

The morning sun came in under the blind like a hot rumour, the north wind roughing things up throughout his room. Tearing at the teeth of something. *Listen*, it whispered.

For the first time in years, Alex remembered exactly what his beloved father had looked like that day. The curly mass of blond hair tangling down over a wide brow. So coarse it felt like twine. The square chin. The soft blue eyes. He envisioned the sun lines settling in his brow, the laugh lines framing his deep grin. Every wrinkle came back to him. Every smile. His heavy Gaelic brogue breaking like static through the dark air.

"Get my son back to safety before we all go down!" his father had shouted to old George.

How safe was his son now? He whispered his dead father's name out loud for the first time in twelve years. "Alexander Louis MacGregor." *My father. The last time I saw him, I wanted to sing and die on the same day.* Gunner MacDonald had asked Alex to fish with him on his boat. He said he knew it was in Alex's blood. And what's in a man's blood will turn sour if he lets it idle too long.

Alex rose slowly from his bed and closed the window. He caught an image of himself in the old mirror above the commode. How much like his father he had become. The wide shoulders. The tangled curls. The blue in his eyes. The image looking back at him was a splendid specimen of a man beginning to age from blistering agony. Who was he kidding? His father was not a coward. Alexander Louis MacGregor was never afraid of anything.

Something moved him.

He shaved carefully. He did not need any visible scars on this day. The post office would open at nine o'clock. He would walk up to her and ask the question. As his father would have done. He took his time walking to the post office. To the small room in the corner of her house that could deliver both joy and sorrow on the same day.

Two small boys, fishing poles in hand, stopped him along the road.

"You got any worms, mister?"

"Just fried the last two up for breakfast," said Alex.

The boys looked at each other and grinned. "You're making that up." They ran quickly into the field where Alex pointed, and began to dig under the earth with their hands, like small terriers.

He paused before he pressed the latch. Listened to the wild screams of laughter from a group of young women behind the door. Perhaps four or five. He couldn't be sure. And then the words he knew by page number, had known for years, knew by heart, smothered out through the laughter. The women were sharing Shelley's words:

When a lover clasps his fairest,
Then be our dread sport the rarest.
Their caresses were like the chaff
In the tempest, and be our laugh
His despair—her epitaph!

Tossing them out between their insidious laughter. Their mock English accents adding to the assassination of the words he loved. He did not hear Moira's voice among the others. His fury wanted to tear at their throats, rip the words from their cruel tongues, and spit on their broken ignorance of the drowned poet.

Something stopped him.

The absence of her voice. Where was she in all of this? She would have been the one to tell them about the poems he read. He had told no other woman. Why was her voice silent while the assassination went on?

They went on to other things when they ran out of poems. Something lacy. Slingbacks. Penny loafers. He left between the footwear. Pulled his hand from the latch of a door he would never touch again. He already knew that. He glanced at the calendar beside the door in the small porch. November 1943, circled in black ink. He tore the month from the calendar and put it into his pocket. Above the calendar hung a picture of a house set back in a field. A dog lay sprawled on the verandah, its head between its paws as if it were trying to drown out something it didn't want to hear. It reminded Alex of his drowned dog. He swiped the picture off the wall and slipped it under his shirt.

Gunner was not at home when Alex arrived. A few hens scattered like dust as he opened the gate. The smell of burnt fudge sharpened the air. He wanted to tell Gunner his plans and ask for his advice. He could trust this man the way he would have trusted his father. The morning sun followed like a runaway flame above his head. Panic set in, stirring up the flame. He suddenly changed direction, the words still inside him. Words Gunner would never get to hear because Alex was walking through the field towards home. He stopped long enough to take in the green surrounding him. The mountain's trees waltzed in unison. Then pulled back, straightened their spines, and like aged lovers refused to dance in the heat.

He entered the house when the trees stopped dancing, walked up the stairs and behind the wall. The room was set up as if it were expecting company. The cot was freshly made, the floor just scrubbed with lye soap. He hung the picture of the dog where he could keep it in view. He was not concerned with time or dates.

Something had escaped him.

The time it took Moira to usher the girls out of the post office. The anger in her voice at their teasing. "You're itching for Alex MacGregor," they accused. The many times she went to the window, watching for the poet to appear. The distilled panic in her voice when she asked his sister where Alex had gone.

Joan avoided her eyes when she answered. "Gone out west to join something or other. Said he has no plans of returning to Beinn Barra any time soon."

Joan and Cassie collected his mail until everything stopped, months later. Nothing appeared in the post office ever again that could bring Moira close to the name of Alex MacGregor.

Thirteen

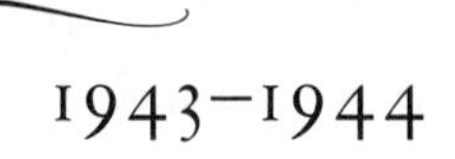

1943–1944

"Silent Night" was a soft and lingering trill in the throat. A slice of sweet foxberry pie going down easy, grooming the pallet for the grand finale. They sang with such graceful harmony at this Christmas Eve Mass in Altamura, Italy, that to many of the soldiers of the Cape Breton Highlanders, war seemed to be just the sound of a little drummer boy thumping to get in. *All is calm, all is bright.*

On Christmas Day, Calum, Hector, and Benny ate a turkey dinner and all the trimmings, shared smokes, and swapped stories about Cape Breton Island with their fellow soldiers. Fruit and chocolate bars were there for the taking. Hector wrapped his hands around a quart of Canadian beer and declared in a rather loud voice: "Now this I would go to battle for any day of the week."

An enthusiastic crowd shouted, "Here, here."

Despite the merry tempo of the day, the Highlanders knew what lay ahead in the coming weeks. It was written on the face of the stern but well-fed division commander, Major General Simonds, as he wished them merriments of the season.

On December 27, in his special order of the day, Simonds wrote:

> For shortly in the New Year, we can expect to make our first encounter with our enemies and this season must be for each of us a time of thorough preparation for battle. In the short time that I have been in command of the 5th Canadian Armoured Division, I have seen enough to know that when our opportunity comes we can "hand it out" in the best traditions of the Canadian Army. So with the prospect of action in 1944 I say to you all, "Let'em have it, a Happy New Year in the progress and Good Luck to you.

Deep into the night, Benny awoke from a light sleep. A foreign river floated nearby. He could hear the sound of walking feet. *There is always someone awake here*, he thought, on guard, waiting to "hand it out." The new year was three days away. The old was falling into memory. *Memories and rifles make a dangerous duo.* A couple of the soldiers had already pulled triggers on their own limbs. One young fellow had shot his foot after singing a searing lament his grandfather had taken from the highlands of Scotland. As they carried the soldier away, he began to sing and call out to his grandfather in Gaelic. And then listened, as though his grandfather were answering him. He was barely seventeen. Old enough to sing, but too young to "let'em have it."

Calum said he could tell the underage by their movements and their reactions to their superiors. They held their heads down when an insult was thrown at them, like small boys dodging rocks in a ditch, covering their heads, crouching down, and looking out between crossed arms to see if the coast was clear. They'd been trained to throw a grenade, but some of them had not gotten the hang of it, or were afraid of it and swung wildly at the target. They were still boys in a ditch fight and would not last a full day in real combat.

Whatever had sent them here was beckoning them back. Another young soldier had been returned to England this week with trigger wounds. Some of them stuck close to the older soldiers, like small dogs at their master's heels. They offered to light their smokes. Offered up pieces of chocolate bars left over from the Christmas meal. They kept candy in their pockets like schoolboys at recess. They were no match for the thirsty soldiers who wanted to get on with it. To get out of this boredom and get back home.

Many officers and soldiers deemed unfit to go into action were returned to Canada or sent to administrative posts in the U.K. It was survival-of-the-fittest time. And the lean, hard arms of the young boys slid their grenades onto their belts to guard their lives, and their hands into their pockets to guard their candy.

On January 13, the Cape Breton Highlanders entered the front line north of Ortona, Italy. The well-prepared Germans had been warned that the Highlanders wore skirts and had hands as wide as shovels. "They fight like mad dogs," said their German commanders.

Benny felt as if his bones were breaking through his skin. He wrapped his arms around his shoulders, shuffled his feet into the cold ground, and looked up at the stars. He could hear the muffled song of a small bird. He envied it its freedom, how it could bless a sombre world with one note. A multitude of white dots choked out the black sky. Left nothing but a smear above his head. A fractured breeze came from somewhere in the dark valley. He heard a voice beside him speak.

"What part of the Island are you from?"

Benny turned to face the young soldier. "Benny Doucet, two miles from where the crow flies near Beinn Barra," he answered.

"Aw, be Jesus, you're Strings Doucet, the fiddler himself! I'm from Sydney Mines, meself. Danny Steele. Crawled up from the pit and joined up with the boys on me nineteenth birthday. Wish to Sweet Jesus I was anywhere but here."

Benny smiled in the dark. "I know how you feel. I can't wait to get back."

"I signed over half me pay to me mother to save for me wedding. Getting married as soon as I get out of this hellhole." The soldier was in a talking mood.

"Marriage can't be any worse than this," joked Benny.

"You married yourself?"

"No, married to the fiddle; that's what some people claim musicians are, married to their instrument. I hid Carmen—that's what I named her—so nobody could get to her while I'm gone. My father would have lent it to people to keep it warm until I return. So I hid it in a safe place. God knows, I could play at your wedding."

Danny laughed. "Can't say I hid me woman, but I know she's waiting for me."

"I don't suppose we'll be here long. Just occupying defence positions for a few days," said Benny.

"Relieving for the West Nova Scotia Regiment," said the soldier, his voice wavering. "I don't know, bye, it's like asking the rabbits to guard the hounds. I don't trust anything here. Probably be court-marshalled for saying it. Sweet Jesus, I think them Germans are more ready for this than we are. Me, I fired at a rabbit once and missed. It laughed at me when it ran away."

"This will all be history someday," Benny replied.

"I hope we'll be alive to read it, bye, when she comes." Danny shrugged. "What made ya sign up?"

"Friends, I suppose," replied Benny, noting to himself the physical resemblance of this soldier to Hamish MacGregor, the round soft face. The gentle eyes.

"My friends thought it would all be over before we got to England," Benny explained.

"I don't think ya believed them."

"No, I can't say I did."

"I wish ta Sweet Jesus I would of run. Hid out in Bras d'Or or somewhere. I know a couple of fellas who planned on it."

"A good friend of ours stayed behind. The last we heard, he had not been seen for some time."

"It's not that different from here, is it, Benny? Somebody is still on the goddamn hunt for ya."

For the next couple of days the Highlanders settled in, conducted patrols, and were trained to recognize the difference between incoming German mortars and artillery and their own.

On January 15, around 1100 hours, heavy mortar fire struck an observation post occupied by a lance corporal and a young private. A sizzling cut like underground lightning. Benny and Danny watched from a slit trench as the Germans ranged in on the post. Benny could smell the sweat and fear of the young soldier beside him, like a schoolboy at recess waiting to be attacked by a posse of bullies armed with bare knuckles and snowballs laden with stones.

The Germans heaved round one to the front. Underground thunder exploded. Round two on the observation post came from the back. Round three up close and fatal. The lance corporal lay mortally wounded, but he made an effort to alert his comrades to the position of the enemy. The badly wounded private was dragged back to A Company headquarters, one foot a pound of crushed flesh and shrapnel, etching a red ribbon on the ground.

The young lance corporal was the first Highlander fatality of the war. News of his death spread quickly around the unit. The boys had lost one of their own.

"This is war, bye—we're not going to get out of here," said Private Steele to Private Doucet. His limbs trembled. In the trench, he had stayed very close to Benny, who could feel heavy despair linger on Danny's every "Sweet Jesus."

"Did you see how they can manoeuvre those goddamn mortars? They could snip the ashes off a butt." His voice dipped into silence.

Benny stared at the likable young soldier beside him, saw the vulnerable crust of homesickness swell in his eyes and stall on the pretty things in his head.

"When I pine for her, it's always in the dark," Danny whispered. "In the light, I'm scared it will kill the two of us."

In the distance, the muffled sounds of shelling echoed through the valley, a choir rehearsing all through the night. Everyone moved with bowed heads as if they were in some sanctuary of the damned. The first star of the night appeared. Dull and dusty-looking, laden with wishes, it sank beneath a cloud and died.

Benny sat under the dead star. He imagined the feel of rosin on the bow. One, two, three soft strokes. Another for good luck. He wondered how Carmen was holding up in her hiding place, a secret lover waiting in the woods for him to warm her up. He thought of the squirrel he had met on the path the afternoon he had hidden the fiddle. He could smell the juniper he and his father had planed down for the ribs of the last boat they'd worked on together. It felt like silk under his hands. "It fits like a glove," his father had said. "Like a glove." He could hear the soft steps of the kitchen dancers, his parents, when he played the waltz for them, and the hiss of the old cat, Jigs, coming from under the bed. He could feel the Beinn Barra rain on the young woman's skin after a dance.

She'd said she was going to change her name to Evol. "That's love spelled backwards, Benny, until you return," she had whispered into a handful of rain, then asked him to taste it. He remembers the sweet taste of music in her step.

The night barked in his head. Sleep tore at his lids like wire. In his head, a piece of unfinished music was being erased by shelling from the German guns.

On January 17, the lieutenant colonel gave the order for the first Cape Breton Highlander attack. Benny caught something in the lieutenant colonel's eyes. He was a man on the lookout for sorrow. He was new to this game, like the rest of them.

Every soldier took his position on a full belly. Their objective, a piece of high ground across the Ricco River, close to the Arielli River.

The Arielli River flowed with the clouds and residue from a hide-and-seek sun. A cool January breeze stirred its surface. A bird flew above the ripples, disappeared into a gully with its own song.

At midday, with the breeze at their backs, the Highlanders were ordered to redirect. Battle plans had been changed. The Perths had not succeeded in warding off the enemy. The Highlanders advanced down one of the gullies with their major. They soon realized that the smoke that had been promised to screen their attack was not coming. A few minutes later, the platoon crossed the river. Thirty-five yards from their initial target they were pinned down by soldiers of the 1st Parachute Division, the most highly skilled and effective German division in Italy.

Enemy machine guns whined in the gullies, enemy mortar fire. Moaning Minnies.

Three feet from Private Benny Doucet, death emerged from a stream. Even the dead must look for safety. Benny watched as the soldier fell face first on the ground. For a second his hands dug violently into the earth as if he were searching for his missing grave. A piece of bone jutted out of the gaping hole in his back. Another soldier lay beside him, motionless, one hand partially covering his face, the other sleeping on his chest. His right eyeball was dangling to his chin. Staring upward, as shiny as a fresh nickel.

Benny crawled slowly past the staring eye, past the digging hands. He could hear water running. A hand tugged at his arm. Its owner was gurgling something. He turned and came face to face with another soldier, the insult of death on his young face. Benny tried to whisper something, but nothing would come. He had seen this soldier before. "Where, dear Jesus, where?" he mumbled to himself, then remembered. At the dances. This man was from down north. "I should know his name," Benny scolded himself. "If only I knew his name. What can I say to a dying man without a name?"

The soldier was trying desperately to tell him something. The shelling moved closer. Benny crawled on, aware that the eyes were still on him. Turned after a few feet. The soldier was weeping. Benny crawled back and put his arm around him. "I remember you, soldier. You never missed a dance."

Benny's arms were bleeding. He did not feel any pain because he was bleeding the soldier's blood. But, oh, how a dying man's blood could taste like your own. Above the gully the sun was shining. A spasm of fear contracted in his chest. His whole body hurt. He was drowning in his own sweat and vomit.

Familiar voices took cover in his head, calmed him. He called to them. "Calum, is that you? Hector, answer me. I'm over here." He forgot that he had been sent up before them.

The sun looked like an out-of-control blaze in the afternoon sky. He heard someone shouting to "stay low." He crawled away from his own vomit. Wiped his mouth with his hand. He could taste the soldier's blood on his lips.

"To hell with the training," he told himself. "How can you fake death with another man's blood on your lips?" He kept crawling on the belly of the gulley. Something stung the side of his head. He heard another voice, but this time he was not mistaken: it was the voice of Private Danny Steele. Benny lifted his stinging head. He could see Danny clearly. Coming closer to him. His arms flagging wildly. From under his helmet, blood streamed in jagged lines down Danny's face. A Christ-like figure carrying a rifle, one boot still on his foot, the other foot a dangling mass of flesh and cloth cut off above the ankle. Here in this gulley, under the fire of man and sun, where men pranced about without limbs to support them, Private Benny Doucet was being summoned. He stood and moved towards the wounded private.

"Get down, soldier, get down. What in the hell do you think you're doing!" The shout came from behind. The shelling grew heavier. Something split the air. Broke it in two. Separated then from now. When life shifted into death there was a mechanical lull. Private Danny Steele's helmet hit the ground and spun in a circle before coming to a stop. His head veered to the left, a broken puppet, before he fell.

Benny was screaming now. "Jesus, Jesus Christ, help me, get me out of here!" Running towards his fallen comrade. His hands in the air. A sharp snap above his head knocked him down on one knee. From his left wrist something took flight. Three feet behind, his left hand lay in the river. Palm up.

Two days after sitting under a dead star, Benny woke up in a hospital bed, his left arm cradled in white bandages. Another bandage was tied securely around his head. A dark crust of dried blood on the edge of the arm bandage resembled a dead daisy.

He stared past the two forlorn privates calling his name. They had brought him a piece of Beinn Barra fudge, chocolate. He ignored the sweet. He watched Hector's mouth move. He watched Calum hold up a white feather from under his headdress. Sounds fell out and dissolved. They had been warned to speak softly. Their eyes watched him the way children's eyes are drawn to the dead.

A nursing sister came in and inserted a needle above the dead daisy. She idled beside the bed until slowly there was no pain, no sounds, no war, no sweets left of the day. Only darkness pecking at his lids.

A week later, he was returned to England, where a surgeon scraped the left wrist bone clean. "Congratulations on being alive," the surgeon said. "There are worse things in life than madness."

Benny watched the man's mouth open and close. He felt cold and hungry. But not the hunger that gnaws at the belly. This was different, a hunger of the senses. Like a man would feel when lost in a storm, returning again and again to the same spot, only to realize he was still lost. He was hungry for sound. The sound of what? Nothing came to him. Mouths opened and closed like mousetraps. "Snap. Snap. Snap. Snap."

Shadows crawled up the wall beside his bed. Waving to him. Several hands waving at once. Waving hands are silent. They make no sound.

"Who waveth there?"

A nursing sister offered him some bread pudding at the end of a spoon. She chased the waving hands away when she stood beside the wall, spitting out words from under a pair of loose teeth. The pudding was dry and sour, but he managed to swallow it.

When she left, the hands left with her. Took them away in the empty bowl, she did. All but one. Alone on the wall, it waved. Up and down. A flip-flop wave. A spreading-out wave. It waved to the young woman who entered the room and smiled as she passed Benny's bed. She stopped beside another bed and spoke softly with an Irish accent to her sleeping brother. A nursing sister walked in briskly, spoke to the young woman, then proceeded to change the bandages on her brother's leg. The soldier awoke and howled like a mad dog at the nursing sister. The young woman opened a small case and removed a shiny object. The sister said something to her.

The hand on the wall stopped waving. There was a small sound at the back of the room. It was not a voice. Not a cry. The young woman played a flute for her brother. A note above a whisper. A travelling whisper. The beautiful whisper settled above Benny's bed.

The pain danced itself down Benny's arm and out through his wrist. The dancing hand picked it up and danced on the wall in slow, rhythmic steps. Danced it across the wall.

> "Dance, dance, wherever you may be,
> I am the Lord of the dance," said He.

He had heard this music a long time ago. Where? Where had the flute found it? Where was it hidden, this music the hand was dancing to in perfect harmony with his pain?

> "Dance, dance, wherever you may be."

Suddenly, there were too many voices beside his bed. Screaming out orders. Stopping the music. Sliding the dancing hand off the wall.

"This soldier started weeping like a banshee when he heard that flute. I told her to keep it down. This is not a bloody concert hall. You have to tell the Irish twice before they hear it once. She said she'd play only to her brother's ears," a plump supervisor grumbled.

"He must be in great pain, but for some reason he doesn't want the needle. He's trying to fight it off like a raging bull. Why would he want to put up with the pain?" cried a nursing sister.

"He can't explain anything to you. He's Canadian. Maybe they like pain over there," said the nursing sister with the loose teeth. "A musician, we're told. He could speak French, English, and the Gaelic at one time. He couldn't find a word to save his tongue today. He just stares at you like a lost dog. This one's too far gone."

Another sister dabbed his arm with some cold liquid and shoved a needle into his vein. Gave him back his pain. It ran up and down his arm, slowed, then danced down his arm and settled in his wrist. On a wild terror it went looking for the hand. *Where is the hand? The dancing hand?*

They left the room, with their flat, sweaty faces, taking with them their trays and the used needle and the cold liquid.

"Dance, dance, wherever you may be,
I am the Lord of the sound...come with me..."

Benny could still hear the music. It whispered along the pillow and settled in his ear.

"Dance, dance, wherever you may be."

But the pain was still close, and it followed him into a dark, altered sleep where sounds were strictly forbidden.

Fourteen

1944

The news about Benny Doucet had spread throughout Beinn Barra long before Gunner MacDonald saw the words that fell out of Hector's letter. Reading it now, Gunner could see the mortar severing the first piece of the man. How he must have paid homage, on his knees, to his dead hand lying in the river. Gunner had witnessed soldiers searching for their blown limbs as they would their missing children, the fear in their eyes as hard as stone. Had watched grown men crying like children over the bodies of dead horses and mules to which they had given pet names.

> Jesus, Da, when they let me and Calum in to see him, it was like looking at a corpse they had propped up in a coffin, with its eyes wide open. He was as white as spit. He just kept looking past us, as if he was expecting someone to come and get him. I thought he was going to say something when we

called him by name. But he just kept looking straight ahead. His right hand was all bandaged up. A dry stain of blood was showing through. They told us he was shell-shocked as well as having been hit in the head. Calum gave him a piece of fudge. He didn't seem to notice what was going on. I don't know if he recognized us or not.

This is hell. This should never have happened to Benny. Some of the boys said he just stood up and ran towards the young miner. The sergeant hollered at him to stay low, but he paid no attention. He wanted to help the miner, who died anyway. Why did he do it? Didn't he know he was going to get nailed? There was nothing he could do to help the other one at that point. Some of the boys think he had already been hit in the head before he ran to him.

The boys say he knelt by the river, looking down at his hand, before he lost consciousness. I wish to God he'd stayed home with Alex. These fields are not for everyone. What a waste, all that talent. My God, think of the boats and the tunes that will never sail from his hands ever again. We heard he'll be shipped home to Camp Hill and then back to Beinn Barra, hopefully. I know the Doucets will be happy to have him back home, no matter what. Calum and I are hoping he'll get something back from life, but Calum says he doesn't think he will remember much of what happened to him here. We can do nothing at this point but hope that our friend and comrade will find some kind of peace back in Beinn Barra.

Gunner folded the letter and put it in his pocket as he walked. In the distance, a dog barked. The wind was panting, in short painstaking heaves, from the southwest. The sun drifted behind a black cloud. In a few months, spring would open its mouth and let the brooks sing again in Beinn Barra. Let the wildflowers appear like rainbows in the fields. Pull people from their gloom. Colour is an agent of the mind. A reminder of lighter times. But the mountain before him remained the same in its summer or winter shades, its vanity undiminished. Like some forms of religion, that mountain insinuated itself into a man's mind and wouldn't let go. The infinity of it now, snow-capped and silent, as if a cloister of monks were spilling their prayers down over it. If he were a praying man, instead of an angry one, he would stop at its feet and collect its spills to dull the anger.

He could see someone in the distance, at the foot of the mountain, on his knees, praying. What do you say to a man at the end of his prayer? Napoleon Doucet's face was cold and grey, as if the weather of the day had settled on it. Tears bled from the craters of his eyes.

"What's this all about?" he asked Gunner, without looking up. For a second, Gunner believed Napoleon was questioning his faith.

"My wife was right. She said Benny wasn't cut out for combat. She is at home, making plans for what is left of our son when he returns to Beinn Barra. I never said a word to him when he joined up. I didn't ask him to stay here, tell him he was leaving something great behind."

He looked at Gunner beseechingly, than continued, "Should I have said something to him, Gunner, should I have asked him to stay home? I left the decision up to him.

From one man to another, I know you cannot direct another man's conscience. One minute he is a man, and then comes a piece of paper telling you that half of him is gone. What will become of our son without his music? You take this from a man, and what do you give him to replace the missing half? I should have known better, as you yourself know. How can you become a whole man with a gun pointed at another man's heart?"

But Gunner had no answers for him. Gunner had nothing to offer but his own sorrow. He was careful not to preach about the line of duty to a man of Napoleon Doucet's intelligence. He looked at Napoleon and held out his hand.

Gunner looked up towards the top of the mountain. The white heads were bowed, humbled, but he was not sure if it was in prayer, or in shame.

Fifteen

1944

A SCOTCH MIST COMING DOWN over the mountain provided distraction for the crowd gathered around the front of MacSween's General Store on the day Private Benny Doucet returned to Beinn Barra.

The three widows had elbowed their way to the front and, as the truck came to a stop, they stared in at the small figure wedged between the two husky fishermen who had volunteered to bring him home from the hospital in Halifax. Benny moved his head in slow, unconscious movements, making no attempt to rise from the seat. Three young girls wept and looked away. One older man, who had accompanied the fiddler on the piano at the dances, turned and walked away with his head bowed.

"Jesus, Mary, and Joseph," cried one of the widows, "the poor bugger looks like death warmed over."

The men were taken aback by the pallor of Benny's skin. The soft, white hue that traced the sunken cheekbones. The yellow teeth, too large now for the thin face. Hair shaved to the skull, as if to make it easier to see what would come from his mind. Eyes that stared past them.

Benny looked through the truck's open window. He had in his focus a tidy stretch of grey sand with white seagulls in flight. The birds dipped down and became noisy as they landed on the shore. A few feet away, a figure in a dark cap raised his arms. Behind the figure something stirred in a red wagon. The figure hovered over the wagon, then disappeared from sight.

Someone offered Benny a bottle of cold pop. His right hand, taking some kind of confused directions, reached out and gripped the dashboard. The driver gently guided his hand towards the bottle. Benny drank the orange liquid in fast suckling gulps, then dropped the empty bottle at his feet. The driver motioned for the other fisherman to open his door.

"You can get out and give your legs a good stretch, Benny." He spoke heartily. "You'll be back home soon, just a couple of miles to go."

And then Benny Doucet stood again on Beinn Barra soil, a young man in an army uniform, a long khaki greatcoat hanging from his shoulders as if draped on a crooked hanger. His black army boots curled at the toes, their laces perfectly tied. Tilted to the back of his head, his cap bore the Gaelic motto of the Cape Breton Highlanders: *Siol na Fear Fearail.* The Breed of Manly Men.

Benny stood beside the truck and urinated in mid-air. Children playing at a distance stopped and watched the man in the long coat. They were fascinated by this public spectacle. Only dogs marked their territory like this. They moved closer just as the man in the coat held up his arm, revealing only a stump where a hand should be. A crooked line of flesh ran above his wrist like an uneven hem. They stopped abruptly and moved back towards the fence they had just climbed. They had heard about the fiddler soldier whose hand was missing, but they could not believe the performance in front of them.

The men in the group lowered their eyes and shook their heads, sighed deeply for their own loss, as well as Benny's. One of the men spoke to Benny, who did not respond. A blond woman loomed, made her way rather daringly to Benny, and wrapped her arms around him in a flirtatious gesture.

"You might as well grab a dead goose by the neck," one of the widows advised the blond woman in a kind voice. "That man will never be what he used to be." Benny turned away from the woman. Evol ran off in tears without even thinking of changing back to her old name.

Benny watched as Hamish and Little Rachel appeared. The hen flapped her wings when the wagon hit a bump. Benny lowered his arms and stood at attention as Hamish and Little Rachel approached the truck. Hamish offered his right hand to the man in the long, dark coat.

"Hawoo, Enny," said Hamish with a wide grin. One of the men spoke softly to Hamish in Gaelic. Benny stared at the boy in front of him. At the small, fat hand whipping the wind. The good eye of the white hen looked frozen in their direction. Hamish mumbled something to the hen in Gaelic, and Little Rachel responded with a long, gravelled sound.

Benny's eyes levelled with the face of the boy. Eyed the smile that never ran from the face. The deep dimples imprisoned in clouds of flesh. Soft green eyes smeared with joy. *Where? Where?* He had seen this smile before.

The sun poked its yellow rim out from behind a dark cloud and chased the tail end of the Scotch mist up over the mountain. The children sat along the fence, their voices still as sleeping dogs. Too bold to leave, too timid to come any closer to the man in the long coat who had marked his territory.

The driver walked along the side of the truck. "It's time to go, Benny. Your folks are waiting for you." He spoke quietly.

Benny slipped his wounded arm out of his sleeve and held it straight out towards the boy. Hamish shook the stump as if this were a ritual he performed daily. Gently pumping the dead limb back to life, a friendly greeting between friends. Little Rachel stretched her wings and stood unsteadily on her foot and a half, then settled back on her mound.

On Benny's face recognition flickered, and then burnt out like a candle in a dark church. But something had sparked, stroked a smear of bright colour on his cheeks. Unnoticed, except by the frozen eye of the hen, who had stood to applaud.

Flora Doucet wanted three things to go well when their son arrived home. Her Benny to remember her and Napoleon. Her tea biscuits to be light and fluffy. Her buttermilk to be cold and fresh, the way he liked it.

Flora had suggested that they ask someone to pick Benny up and bring him home. Napoleon's back was bad, and the stress of the long drive, along with the return itself, would, she thought, be too difficult on them.

They had already been to Halifax to visit him. Flora had her doubts that Benny would ever recognize anyone again. He had not even turned around when she called his name. It was Napoleon who believed that music still lived in Benny. "It's alive in there somewhere," he'd said to Flora. The doctors had not yet finished their tests. Weeks later, Flora and Napoleon would receive a letter stating that Benny was not capable of any intellectual interactions and, unfortunately, would not recognize anyone. That he would have flashbacks in times of stress, but that he could be medicated when necessary. That he might, in familiar settings, be able to follow simple commands.

They were standing at the gate when the truck drove up. Flora looked in at Benny's sombre face and knew that two of three things would go well. She wrapped her arms around her son when he exited the truck.

Benny looked down at the smiling woman. She smelled like tea biscuits and buttermilk. Her hands were cold, but her eyes were as warm as summer puddles. The woman squeezed the stump gently, as if she were kneading soft dough into a sculpture, a hand. He watched her mouth. It was whispering. It kept whispering. On and on. It whispered a kiss on his face, another on the stump. She held it up and whispered to it. The whispers moved up and down as if the hand were still there. Benny felt a tingling warmth in his arm. The woman was remembering where the fingers and thumb once lived, and fit into her hand when Benny played his first jig for her, "The Squirrel in the Kitchen," at the age of five. She'd taken both his hands in hers and kissed them over and over again. Napoleon had beamed with joy at Benny's ability to play so well at his young age.

Napoleon had said to his wife, "I can't believe how he can tune that fiddle and rosin the bow just like a professional."

"Old Rory the fiddler has taught him well," said Flora of the man who had shown her child the fine art of finding his own vibes on the strings. She added, "And you will teach your son to be a boat builder like yourself."

Now Flora wrapped her arm around her husband's shoulder. "Our son is home, Napoleon. We have something to be grateful for."

Napoleon shook Benny's left hand and welcomed him home. Benny stood at attention. They stood eye to eye.

Terror was a new feeling for Napoleon Doucet. He had never before encountered it in the eyes of any man. He wanted to make his son whole again. To give something of himself, if need be. Napoleon waited for a word to come from the silent mouth. He wanted to know that Benny's voice had been saved, that whatever else the war had taken from him, it had at least left him a voice.

But he waited three days, and then the voice that came was old and stale, and it said in an agitated tone that it must find the fiddle.

The fiddle that Benny had made himself. The stump of the old maple tree that had formed the back of the fiddle still stood a half-mile from the house. Napoleon had gone with Benny to pick out the perfect hardwood for the fiddle when Benny was seventeen years old.

"I'll take the one that bends gracefully with the breeze," Benny had said, looking up at the tree in front of him. "She will hold the greatest sounds."

For the front of the fiddle, he had chosen a soft fir. "This one," he said, tapping the tree firmly, "will let the music run gently through her veins."

When the wood had cured, he scaled the front and back of the fiddle to one-eighth of an inch in thickness. He softened the strips of wood for the ribs in boiling water and moulded them in three sections. With a steel knife, he carved the neck in hardwood from the maple tree. Gently he pared the front of the fiddle from the fir tree and watched the shavings spiral to the floor like cut blond locks. He fashioned the bow from the same maple tree. Napoleon plucked fifty or more black strands of hair from their old horse, Casey, for the bow. Then Benny removed the strings from an old fiddle and attached them to the new one.

"There, sweet lady." Benny ran his hand gently over the curves of the fiddle and bow. "I will name you Carmen, from the great opera, and you will keep men dancing until dawn."

Sixteen

1944

Gunner MacDonald stopped at the side of the road when he saw Benny approach. It was their first meeting since Benny's return to Beinn Barra. April wind wheezed as the two men stood on the barren road, in dirty, melting snow, eye to eye, soldier to soldier, brothers in arms.

"How are you, Benny?" Gunner asked quietly. "It's nice to see you again."

Benny listened as if he'd understood the question, but did not answer.

"Benny, do you remember Hector?"

The elder man watched Benny as he began to move in quick, awkward circles, his eyes those of a stranger in a gaunt, pleated face. Gunner did not want to look down at the dark sleeve, at what could easily have been his own wounded son in front of him, at what still could be.

At forty-seven years of age, Gunner could still dig up

parts of men he had seen at the front. Convoys of maggots where a soldier's heart once beat. Orphaned limbs dying in the mud. The odour of death penetrating the grub. Once, at Vimy Ridge, he had come across a German soldier, belly down on the ground, his hand still on the trigger of his rifle. One eye staring straight ahead. One foot blown off. It lay on the ground a short distance from his body. On the barrel of the rifle, a bird fluttered on a broken yellow wing, then landed on the severed foot. All around him a chorus of split and dying men cried out fragments of names. This was what he remembered most vividly, the famished voices of the dying, even now, crying out to their loved ones. Names that interrupted his sleep, after all those years.

"Monday, Monday, Monday, gonna find the fiddle," Benny mumbled.

"Benny, your friend Hector, my son, do you remember him?"

"Monday... Monday," Benny grunted.

"Calum and Hector, remember, Benny? They left here with you. You all went overseas together."

"*Lundi, lundi*," Benny whispered.

"Today is Tuesday, Benny. It is nearing the end of April 1944. You left for overseas on a Thursday, in 1941. What do you remember about Monday, Benny? What is it about Monday that you remember?"

"Tuesday, Tuesday, *mardi*, *mardi*, gonna find the fiddle."

"Where's the fiddle, Benny?"

"Gonna find it, gonna find the fiddle."

"I'll help you find your fiddle, Benny. I will do anything

I can to help you find your fiddle. Do you remember anything about Hector?"

"*Samedi*, *samedi*, Saturday, Saturday. Find the fiddle."

Benny scratched his head as if to annoy a thought that was festering there. He held a steady gaze on the older man. The man's mouth was moving faster than Benny could follow. A lonely mouth with a worried frown living in it. Benny watched it curl its bottom lip. It shivered. It caught a tear. Swallowed it. Then ate two more. A big hand swiped at the eyes and hid the tears in its fist. The name swarmed like a fly in Benny's head. Where did the name go? It had to be there in the man's fist.

The mouth was still moving. After swallowing the tears, the name too perhaps, it moved up and down and then closed. The man's eyes, dark and round, were looking for something.

Gunner watched as Benny turned away and rambled on down the road, his head weaving from side to side, the flaps of his coat outstretched, the beak of his cap pulled down over his brow. Benny stopped and looked back, then scurried off into the ditch. Almost waved, but then put his hand to work searching the debris in front of him. Wisps of brown grass flew in the air. Broken glass from a beer bottle. A piece of driftwood. Three or four boulders. A child's red mitten, then the other, fully frozen.

Gunner wanted to go to him, to question him once more, but he decided against it. He was not a man who added pain to pain. He carried Benny's pain with him. Took it to his bed at night. Everything hurt more in the dark. He could sense what lay beneath the surface. It would erupt. War still heated his veins. Kept him ready for the explosion.

He watched as Benny climbed out of the ditch and walked further down the road towards the shore. A flock of seagulls lifted up around him. Benny stood in the middle of the gulls, his dark sleeves held high as if he had just released them, one by one, from inside his coat.

Joachim MacPherson thought he might find something in Benny's eyes when they met at the crossing a few days later. Something that might have lingered from a leftover conversation between Benny and Calum. A tangible word or deed that would not leave him.

"Hello, Benny," he said quietly. "I am Calum's father. You remember Calum."

A crazy mix of loss and fear was what Joachim saw. A carrier pigeon without messages.

Benny stared into Joachim's eyes. *Calum*. He had heard this name before. He wanted to smile inside out at the sound. "Gonna find the fiddle," he said, before letting the smile out.

Joachim remembered the sturdy young man who had walked up the gangplank of the ss *Orcades*. Beside Hector and Calum, he'd stood in defiance. Joachim looked at the man he had watched grow from boyhood. He knew what war could do to the inside of a man. But Benny was an old man on the outside as well. His eyes were clouded over like two dead puddles. Skin ran loosely from his bones, stopped dead by the jagged flesh at his wrist. He used it as a child would a stick. Swinging and swaying it in mid-air. Stretching it out full length when he played his imaginary fiddle. Tuning it to a precise sound before he played. Benny had forgotten everything but the fiddle, for which he continued to search.

Ona MacPherson said Benny remembered something else: their son Hamish. She said she could tell by the way Benny looked at Hamish. By how gentle he was with him.

"He knows Hamish," she said to Joachim.

"How can you tell?"

"Just watch them together."

"Benny plays with the wind, the boy jumps in it. What is it you see?" asked her husband.

"He can sense that Hamish is no threat to him."

"The boy is no threat to anyone, Ona."

"And Benny knows that. He is always calm around Hamish."

"Why would he remember the boy over the others? Benny knew a lot of people from far and near. He played all over the island."

"Because he plays *to* Hamish. He played *for* the others. He still understands his music," Ona insisted. "There is a difference when you love someone. And he knows Hamish loves music."

"They say he cannot recognize anyone, Ona. That part of his mind is totally erased. What music comes out of an imaginary fiddle?"

"I don't care what they say, he definitely knows who Hamish is, and he certainly remembers his fiddle. I honestly believe he understands what you say to him, but has forgotten how to respond." Ona's face was blotched with anger, her voice agitated.

"He is a child at heart, just like the boy. You should not read any more than that into it. He does not even remember his parents by name. They are just figures to him."

Joachim's foot throbbed. Anger lived in his lame foot. Came out like the old woman in the weathervane when a storm was predicted. He could not come to terms with his wife's perceptions. Ona reminded Joachim of his own mother when she got something in her head. His mother had always believed he would catch up to the faster kids in time.

"It's all right," his mother had said to him. "You will catch up with them. I know you will. Sometimes they let you play tag."

When he got older, he had watched his two brothers shine their dancing shoes with lard and prance out the door on Saturday nights. Like cats, they avoided puddles and light rain. Steered their soles into soft grass. Swiped stains away with the quick kiss of a hanky.

On Sunday morning, he checked their shoes while they slept. Found a smudge on one pair. A woman's print. He met the owner of the print a month later. She sat across from him at Sunday dinner. Her green eyes watched his every move. Her hands felt light and knowledgeable. In her handshake, he felt Saturday night's pulse.

"I haven't seen you at the dances," her mouth said. Everyone remained silent.

"I can't dance," said Joachim, his eyes watching his hands look for work at his plate.

"Everyone can dance," she offered with a smooth drawl.

"Joachim would rather farm than dance," his mother said, as though she were offering up seconds.

He excused himself at that point and walked away from the table. Three weeks later, milking in the barn, he felt a tap on his shoulder. Ona stood behind him with a pair of black shoes in her hands.

"These were my brother's. He forgot them when he left," she announced. "I know they will fit you."

"Fit me for what?" inquired Joachim.

"For your first dance," she quipped, "and I'll not take no for an answer."

"My brother still has his dancing shoes." His voice was as delighted as a woman's at the thought of it.

"Stop feeling sorry for yourself," she snapped. "To heck with your brother. I'm not in love with him. Maybe it's you I want."

They were married a year later. He was wearing his dancing shoes the Sunday Calum was born. In his last letter home from overseas, Calum had mentioned a dance he and Hector had been to.

Joachim pushed open the screen door and walked towards the woodpile. He had an urgent desire to kill something. The hens scattered. In the distance, the church bell began to peal. This daily recital of ringing church bells had become a custom since the war. At the sound, people stopped to remember their loved ones who had made the supreme sacrifice. Women pulled their hands from flour bins and blessed themselves in white dust. Children played dead in the fields and in the schoolyard. They were carried off by their friends and placed up against a wooden fence. Some children prayed over their alive-dead bodies, while others walked away, annoyed. The dead, with their eyes closed, were caught smiling up at them. It was a violation of war to smile. Even on a mock battlefield. They had all seen Benny Doucet come and go with never a smile circling his teeth. One young boy, who had spelled "patriotism" correctly in a spelling bee, stopped to ponder. Maybe Benny's smile had been shot off along with his hand, and they both drowned in the Arielli River.

Hamish stopped along the road and listened to the ringing of the bell. He hushed Little Rachel into silence. He removed his cap and gave the great sounds an awkward salute. He did not have to ponder anything. He just listened. He would wait for the sounds to disappear before he moved on with a smile.

Joachim picked up his axe and swung it wildly into the chopping block. Into the twisted maple he had uprooted. The bell kept ringing. The axe fell again into the same wound. Rose again in a fury. The bell kept ringing. Another swing. And then silence.

Benny stopped playing and stared at the church steeple. Birds hid deep in the trees with their songs. Ona buried her face in her hands. Joachim weaned a small sound from his throat and fed it to the open air. Beinn Barra did not respond. In the silence he had created, Joachim wanted noise. Lots of noise. He lifted the axe high above his head and circled it around and around. He was not sure how long it would take a man to kill silence.

Seventeen

1944

Some people did not look up when Benny Doucet appeared on the spring roads of Beinn Barra in his long, dark army coat and cap. One of a breed of manly men, now half dead and half alive, half mad and half brimmed with joy, half full of music and half drained of a simple note, half longed for and half feared. He had been ruined by what defined him best. His honour.

Overseas, their husbands and sons and grandsons darted in and out of the enemy scope. The young women feared that their men would return like Benny Doucet. Without limbs to cradle them in their arms. Without the sense to know why they should be held. Some of the women wept when Benny passed by. They had known him personally. A couple of them intimately.

He did pause when one young women walked by. She did not speak to him, but walked close enough to touch his hand. Held it for a moment and looked directly into his eyes. There was something about her that Benny felt he should have known. Something that did not require a name, perhaps, but a feeling. He turned and watched her walk away. He did not connect her to music, but to rain. When he listened to his heart, he could hear rain.

It had rained on something soft. The scarf on her head. And the rain had fallen along her skin, she remembered, and drowned her passion. But Benny had found a dry place that night after the dance. Under the big maple near the graveyard. There is nothing like nearby death to make a man feel alive and needed by a woman with rain on her skin. She remembered that the rain had stopped by the time they left. They took a shortcut home through the graveyard. A half-moon illuminated the tombstones as they strolled by. They read an inscription: *Jesus Is Watching over Thee*. The name had been corroded by time and weather. She ran along the path. Pale as frost when they stepped out of the consecrated grounds, she had wrapped Benny in her arms. She had the same look in her eyes as she walked by today.

There was no rain on her skin, but to Benny she looked cold and scared, like everyone else without a name.

The storm came with hard rain clawing at the roof of the Doucet house and a slow, blue flickering fire behind glass brightening up what was stolen from the light of day.

"It won't last too long," Flora cried out, as two visitors sat themselves down in the Doucets' kitchen and talked about the weather.

Benny hovered in the stairwell, rocking back and forth like a child trying to pump a swing into full flight. Thunder growled like anger at the clawing rain. Jagged fingers of fire selected an object to uproot, claimed a large maple to the west of the barn. Limb by limb, the branches were raped of their golden leaves. The naked tree split down the middle, two ragged arms left to collect its loss.

Benny closed his eyes like a blind man, his arms flying in mad, unmapped directions. He pounded at the walls and the floor with his one hand and his two feet. The men wrestled him to the floor, and his father pried open his mouth and dropped one round white pill on his tongue. *Corpus Christi, Body of Christ.* A solace for the man who had forgotten his name, but not his storms. Napoleon rocked his son in his arms until this storm had passed.

It was soon over. The fire was diminished. The split maple would become fuel for winter's crust. Benny lay quietly on the kitchen cot. He watched the grey cat as it came out from under the bed, its eyes like wheels, listening carefully for the sounds it could pick up faster than humans. Flora opened the kitchen door and shooed the cat outdoors. This cat had no use for gossip and went out happily, meowing along the path.

One of the men who had appeared in the storm was the bearer of news. There would be a wedding this coming summer, to be held on a Tuesday, the day everyone in Beinn Barra seemed to be joined in wedlock, and he was the groom-to-be. Everyone was invited, as was the custom in most country villages. The bride was the postmistress, Moira, who had had her wedding gown sent to her from the United States.

"The biggest regret is not having Benny to play at the wedding." The man's voice was deep and seemed to crawl out from his chest instead of his throat when he spoke.

Flora swiped at her eyes as she pulled an apple pie from the oven. The other visitor reached under the table, pulled out a fiddle case and opened it carefully. He rosined the bow in slow, awkward strokes. White dust fell like dandruff to the floor. He knew that Benny was watching him. He began to play. A light jig set the heavy feet of the men in motion under the table. One of the men dipped his fork into the thick apple pie. Drank his tea in gulps. Animated victims of strings and storms.

Benny listened carefully to the missed notes, the off-key cries from the strings, the out-of-tune amateur with his eye on the apple pie raising steam in front of him.

The fiddler noticed that Benny was weeping, his gaze not moving off the fiddle. He was happy he had brought along his fiddle to soothe Benny after the storm. He was not aware, nor would he ever be, that Benny wept for the piece of music he was trying to play. The fiddler was killing "Neil Gow's Lament for the Death of His Second Wife" in the off-key of D major. He kept playing off-key as Benny stood, swayed a little, then walked to the door and went out into the field. He moved his arms into position. Nestled his stump gently on his left shoulder. Tuned up. Swung his right hand across the mouth of his fiddle.

Key of D major, key of D major, something whispered in his head, as he looked out at the carnage near the barn. The grey cat was perched on one of the arms of the split maple, looking down at the golden leaves that lay dying on the ground.

Eighteen

1944

EARLY SUMMER, *1944. It is only a matter of time, or does time matter anymore?* Alex MacGregor wrote slowly. His scribbler placed firmly on his knees. His head bent over the trail of words. Reading them back to himself.

> I didn't expect that Benny would survive this war, or that he would return with his shattered madness. I saw him for the first time as he made his way down to the sea this morning. Got a slit's eye view of his ragged sleeves. His careless posture alerts the village that he is on a quest. Uprooting things keeps him alive. Even madness has its strange sense of direction. He knows what he is searching for here in Beinn Barra. Play on, play for me, play softly. I can hear you. Play swiftly! I will catch up to you, Benny, my friend.

Alex folded his scribbler and let his eyes circle his surroundings. He cursed the four walls he thought of as the Wooden Trench, the slanted ceiling that hung above his head like a storm cloud. He sucked in the malignant odour of the place as he picked up his pocket knife and stabbed another slit in the flimsy wall beside his cot. Outdoor air feasted his tongue. The wind brought with it a gift from the sea. Salty and cool. It slid off his tongue like a lie.

He envied Benny Doucet his madness. He was armed with it. He had worked for it. Earned it. Mission man. Nobody got in his way. People stood back and bestowed on his madness first-class privileges, to the roads, the open fields. The ditches of Beinn Barra were his to explore, the shoreline his stage. Who would dare to stop him or his agent, Hamish? Benny's madness was not a performance. It was real. He sought what every man wanted in his life. Honour. Alex picked up the scribbler and continued to write.

> I wish I could speak with Gunner. To hear what he has to say to a man dying in wood. "Man can drown a thousand deaths, if not by the elements, then by the fury of life itself." These were his words to me. Gunner, too, read Shelley's words before falling deeply in love with his beloved Iseabal. He knows I am here. I am sure of this.

There is someone I could see. Someone as silent and hidden as himself. Alex pondered but did not write this down in his scribbler. His sister could bring Benny to him. Too dangerous to bring Hamish along. Hamish remembered names. He would have to play it safe. Make sure nobody was around to see it happen. A foggy day would be best to bring Benny to the MacGregor house.

He appeared on a Friday, just after the church bells stopped ringing, when the fog hid Beinn Barra from itself while fish suppers boiled in fat pots and children played games in the fields like small ghosts. He stood at the top of the stairs and looked around like a harried stranger in a foreign land. A rush of voices spoke at once behind him.

"Don't keep him too long, Alex. His father is probably looking for him." Joan's voice was edgy, as if she had just stolen a child.

"Dear Jesus, I would never have known the poor bugger, in the fog or under the sun. The look of him." Cassie's voice was laced with congestion and anxiety.

"Don't rile him up, for God's sake; he could go foolish in the attic!" Joan warned.

Alex shooed them down the stairs, turned to his friend, and extended a trembling hand. "Hello, Benny."

Benny stared at the pale young man in front of him. The man who came out of the wood to shake his hand. *The pale man is crying. Why? His hands are jumping.*

"Jesus, Jesus, what have they done to you? You are a shadow of yourself."

The man's eyes are big. He rubs them with his fists.

"Do you remember anything, Benny? Anything at all?" Alex looked directly at Benny as he spoke, his voice trembling like that of a man being held upside down.

"Find the fiddle, gonna find the fiddle." Benny's voice wavered.

"You do remember something, Benny. Where did you put the fiddle?"

"Monday, Monday. Wall. Wall."

"Did you hide your fiddle in a wall, Benny? Is that where you hid your fiddle?"

The pale man is crying. Crying. Crying.

"Do you remember your music, Benny? You knew so much music. Did they rob you of that, too?"

"Tuesday, Tuesday," said Benny. He crossed the floor and approached the seam in the wall, which Alex had left open. Benny moved in slowly, like a fly through an open door. Saw it as a place where things could be hidden. Under a cot, maybe. But there was nothing here except a scribbler hiding words. A little table for dirty china, prayer beads, holding a man already crucified on wood. A brown dog with no desire to see any of it. The girl in the picture looked interesting. Above the cot. Her bare feet almost touched the blue quilt. Her toes dangled over the patch of blue as if it were water.

The pale man picks up the girl. Puts her in his pocket.

"Do you remember her, Benny, the girl at the post office? Her name is Moira. I saw you looking at her."

The man is crying. The man with the girl in his pocket.

"I wish you could remember, Benny. I have so much to tell you. Where are Hector and Calum at this moment? You were the last person to see them. I am afraid for them. Do you understand any of this, Benny? I believe you do, but I wish to God I knew for sure."

The pale man is rocking on the cot.

"There is not much difference between you and me, Benny. I tell you this because I believe a part of you understands that a part of us is missing. We are like puzzles now, with a few missing pieces."

Alex studied Benny to see if he understood. Benny's eyes were fixed on Alex's face, watching every muscle, like a child looking into a dark well.

The man is making a noise.

"The girl in the picture, Benny, I loved her the way you love music. Maybe she loved me too, because she keeps asking about me. I stir her up in my mind the way you stir up your music."

"Gonna find the fiddle. Tuesday, Tuesday." Benny, anxious that nothing had been found, began to move about in small circles, reaching out to touch the walls. He knocked gently on the walls as if he expected someone to answer.

"Benny, would you like something to drink?"

Benny did not respond, but moved out into the attic. His stump dropped down onto the window ledge, thumped the old trunk, swiped at a rack of old clothes. Found a cloud of dust that gave his lonely hand something to play in. Through the dust he could see the figure of the pale man. How slowly he moved, as if he had evolved from the dust and taken on a human form.

Through the window behind Benny, the fog curled and a brassy sun festered on the ledge, like a small blister. Alex could hear his sister's voice growing louder as she neared.

"I'll have to get him back now. He's been here too long. I know his father will be looking for him. They keep a close eye on him wherever he goes."

Benny stopped circling the dust and listened to the voice. He looked towards Alex, who stood in front of him.

The pale man is smiling and crying.

Alex's smile cracked like broken china. Blood trickled on the borders of his mouth and collapsed like a wayward sentence.

"Christ, did he hit you?" cried his sister.

"No, he didn't hit me—he's as gentle as a lamb. I bit into my own lip."

"I've got to get him back to the crossroads."

"Let him stay for a while longer. Maybe he doesn't want to leave."

"No, I probably shouldn't have brought him here in the first place. Somebody could be watching the house."

"He likes it here," said Alex.

"How can you tell, did he tell you that himself?"

"I know him better than anyone. He likes being with me."

"You're starting to sound like Hamish. Why don't I bring you a hen for company? I have to take him back. Now."

"Will you bring him here another day?"

"I'll see. I have to be careful, I don't want people asking any questions. His father keeps a close eye on him."

"I want to see him again. I believe he understands what people say to him."

"I told you I'll see, Alex. I have to get going with him now."

"You have to go now, Benny." Alex put his arm around Benny's shoulder, then watched as he disappeared down the stairs, the hem of his long coat stealing the dust as he descended. He could hear Benny thumping the walls on the way down. A long reap of sound escaped Benny's throat at the foot of the stairs. A bird who had come home to an empty nest. It echoed back up the walls and into the wood. It lived for days on the cot. In the quilt. On the walls. On the rim of the china. In the old prayers decaying on the prayer beads. And in the picture of the girl with the dangling feet. Alex heard it whisper from under his pillow.

Nineteen

1944

Alex rose slowly from his cot at six a.m. and coaxed something green from his lungs into a dirty rag. Exhaled "Jesus Christ" from a parched throat. His fever had lingered for a couple of days now, made him more thirsty than ever as dawn filtered into the cracks of the Wooden Trench. He stared at the wall two feet to his left. Yellow fingers of light, without a thumb, reached down, crossed over each other, and settled back into position. He continued to stare as the light criss-crossed the wall like searchlights. He watched a bold black spider darting between the fingers, sunning itself in gold, taking advantage of the long reach of each limb. And then it disappeared, making its escape through the crack that had let the fingers in.

He sat back down and dropped his head between his hands. Everything about the day was too hot. His hands burned his flesh through the stubble on his face. He walked on his knees to the galvanized bucket in the corner and relieved himself. A hot steam whistled up his nostrils. Everything in this six-by-eight trench of wood tasted of himself. Smelled of himself. Crawled on himself.

Alex flipped the cap off a medicine bottle and sipped its contents. It tasted bitter as it struggled in his dry throat on its way down. He stretched out on the cot. The fingers had left in the wink of a piss. The walls were as grey as rain clouds. The ache in his chest kept rhythm with his heartbeat. With his tongue, he traced the outline of his dry lips. He could not tell anyone that, as a grown man, he missed the taste of rain and a pair of thick white ankles. He knew she still asked his sister about him. What did that mean? It sent an ugly rumour to his heart. What right did she have to inquire about him?

It had rained for seven nights and seven days the previous week. He kept track of the elements with a blunt lead pencil. The rain began to fall at 11:47 p.m. on Friday, April 10, 1944. A silent lull followed. It came down harder at 12:38 a.m. He heard a truck approaching along the dirt road at that hour. The driver shifted gears. Put the truck into low gear as it came down over the hill. Doors slammed as voices milled together. One female and one male. The woman swore at the flat tire. Nineteen minutes later, the engine turned over. The sound travelled north towards the Devil's Lung. It would take the damp lovers fourteen minutes to reach their embrace.

Alex had been to the Devil's Lung. But only once. He and Calum were twelve years old when another more worldly twelve-year-old told them about the Devil's Lung and introduced them to the word "adultery." He told them he had heard about it at a wake. The boy said it was more exciting than a raid on a bootlegger. It involved a man and a woman. But one of them had to be married, or it would have another name. It was usually the married one that started things going by getting buck naked. It looked easier and was much faster than churning butter or splitting wood. The boy told them that the Devil's Lung got its name from all the noise it made, like the devil breathing hard. "Adultery," he said, "could make a goddamn racket in no time."

Alex and Calum had hurried home from school that Friday to get their chores done. They met along the road at dusk and ran up over the hill. The Devil's Lung was full of wind and birds when they arrived. They hid in a windy tree and waited.

"Can you see anything yet?" whispered Calum.

"Nah," said Alex. "He was probably lying."

"No, he wasn't. Everybody tells the truth at a wake."

"How are we going to see them in the dark?" Alex wondered.

"We don't have to see, we just have to wait for all the noise, then we can sneak up on them."

"Then what do we do, Calum?"

"We'll watch to see if it's true."

"What if the man sees us and chases us?"

"He can't if he's buck naked."

"What if the woman is buck naked? He can chase us then."

"Be quiet, Alex, I hear something!"

"What?"

"Listen!"

"It's rain, Calum. Maybe adultery sounds just like rain."

A heavy rain chased them out of the tree and sent them home. Alex stuck out his tongue when he reached his back step. He was twelve years old when he acquired a taste for rain.

The blunt lead pencil was Alex's memory. It kept for him what his own memory could not. What it had written would slip a smile on his face for a moment or two. Take it back suddenly. He had broken the lead pencil twice on the day Benny returned to Beinn Barra. He did not have to question his sister or his mother for old information. It was tucked away under his cot in his scribbler. He warned them not to open it. It was a mouth he wanted closed. He wanted new stories from them. News from overseas. Had they heard anything about Calum and Hector? Were they still in Italy? When he had enough information, he wanted them to leave. He did not require visitors. He was never alone with his pencil and scribbler nearby, he told himself.

They disinfected his room in five minutes and left again with the dirty dishes. Sometimes he walked lightly around the attic while they scrubbed out the Wooden Trench. He leapt like a cat over the old trunks. Hung like an antique coat near the open window. There was always a chance he might catch a glimpse of her coming or going to the post office.

His sister and mother took care of the land like men did. The ground had been tilled. The potatoes planted. Frills of green ran beyond the naked eye.

"It's going to rain tonight, Alex," his mother whispered. "Are you warm enough with that beast in your lungs?" Alex did not answer the question with words. He nodded, indicating that in this trench he had all he needed to fight any beast. It was not the first fever he'd had to deal with in the Wooden Trench.

He had what he wanted and needed in here. Moira's picture. His lead pencil, a thick scribbler, a pocket knife, a few books, an alarm clock, three stones that Hamish had given him, rosary beads that had belonged to his father, a galvanized bucket, a calendar, an oil lamp. He no longer went down into the main part of the house, even for a smoke. His mother did not want him to leave trails of smoke in the attic.

"They sniff like hound dogs, those Mounties," his mother had warned him. "Even when you're in bed, they're probably crawling around the shingles like spiders."

"Ma has the house shut tighter than a bull's arse in fly time," his sister announced.

His mother always whispered when she was in the Wooden Trench. She could never be too careful. She didn't know whose ears could be sneaking around the house.

"Ma, there's nothing but a couple of old hens and a friggin' deaf rooster out by the door," her daughter argued.

Cassie shook her head and descended the stairs to the kitchen. She could not argue in whispers. Joan laughed out loud and followed her mother downstairs.

Cassie soaked the dirty dishes in the pantry. She insisted on doing them herself. Alex was served his meals on her good china, like a privileged prisoner waiting for someone to name his crime. Cassie stroked the delicate rim on the edge of the cup. Clovers in Gold was the pattern. Tiny four-leaf clovers surrounded by gold. A wedding gift from an old aunt in Boston. Her husband had said they cost more than the boat from which he fished. The last time they'd been put into service, she recalled, was at her husband's wake. She had placed them carefully on the table. The six rugged pallbearers had watched the steam rise from the hot tea as if they were waiting for something to explode. Their fingers were too big for the handles, shaped like dark green leaves. They wrapped their hands around the cups and drank to their fishing mate from what appeared to be an opening in their bare-knuckled flesh.

Cassie carefully dried the dishes Alex now ate from. She had good reason for putting them back into service, she told herself. Her departed men deserved nothing less.

When Alex woke in the afternoon, the fever had run out of him. His skin was damp and clammy. He stroked his right hand into the silence of the space. Creating figures. The shape of Moira's ankles. The map of Italy. A snow angel. The shape of Benny's missing hand. The wheels on a bicycle. A raven's wing. He stopped and leapt off the cot. He could hear voices, muffled but getting closer, one followed by another.

"If there's a zombie in here, we'll flush him out." The voice was sharp and shrill, as if it spoke from inside a tin whistle. They had been here before. Five or six times. The same voices, the same fists. Uttering the same threats.

His mother's voice followed. "I told you already. Alex left early one morning and said he was headed west. I have not heard a word from him since."

Words he could not hear clearly followed the shrill voice.

"Go ahead and search with a bulldozer, you're not going to find him in this attic." His mother's voice was steady, unflinching. "Take a look at what the war did for poor Benny Doucet!"

The men ignored her. Alex could hear footsteps moving closer to the seam in the wall. The hard taps of fists along the boards. And finally, silence once again.

Alex tiptoed to the wall. Pressed his face to the crack, closed his left eye. His friends appeared in slices of his world. Hamish first, in his delirium of motion. Arms swinging freely. A dot of red and white beside the blue sea a few feet away. The hen's wings folded in leisure. Benny stood near the wharf in his long, dark coat. Full of wind, it ballooned out, shaping the man into a musical giant. He raised his dead stump, dropped his head onto his left shoulder. His right hand moved in short, quick strokes. The man and his imaginary fiddle played wildly. *If only I could hear what Benny plays to himself*, thought Alex.

What Hamish heard was recorded in his soft limbs, now exploding in pure joy with each vibrating note. Benny's music was sealed into one mute, solitary cell of his being. Inside its beautiful, fragile wall were delicate slow airs, sweet strathspeys, pounding reels, one last march. No one would hear them again because nothing was recorded. Alex was certain of this. No one would hear "Farewell to Beinn Barra" because no one, except the composer himself, knew for sure if it was ever set down.

Alex opened his eyes again. Hamish and Benny were standing close together now. He wondered what had caught their eye. Hamish pointed to something across the water. Perhaps an eagle fishing. Or a flock of gulls. Alex could not see anything at his angle. He kept watching. But there was nothing to see when they walked away, just the flat sea with its blue spread unruffled like a freshly made bed. In his scribbler he wrote short pieces of incomplete sentences: *Spider escaped. It is free. Fists pounded at four p.m. Followed by voices. Low tide. Heard the music. Sweet and low. Heard it all as Benny played to me.*

TWENTY

1944

TERROR ROSE ON ONE KNEE in the mud, eyes flaring, nostrils bathing in steam, mouth honking like an old horn.

"Can anybody shut that bastard up before I feed a bullet down its throat?"

The mule balked before moving on, as if it understood the officer. Calum felt the barrel of his rifle in his hand. Shifted the load he carried. A pick and shovel. A couple of mortars. Everything cold for a hot battle carried on his back. The mules were loaded down with heavy equipment.

They had started their long, tiresome climb up the muddy mountain trail to the village of Orsogna at dusk. Daytime movement was impossible here. The Germans were everywhere.

"Hanging in the trees like acorns," Hector said to Calum in Gaelic.

Calum swiped at the branch of a tree. A broken twig rested in his hand. He popped it between his lips like a smoke. Swore to himself that he could taste Jerry powder. Spat it on the ground and kept moving.

Hector patted the lead mule between the ears to comfort the poor creature. It turned its crazed eyes on him. They reminded Hector of the eyes of his beloved dog when he found him caught in a trap, his eyes pleading to be rescued. Hector had closed the eyes before pulling the trigger on the dying animal.

"How is the mule supposed to know we're trying to sneak up on the enemy without a sound?" he mumbled. He was determined to battle with anyone who insulted this mule. It had the sense to protest its agony.

After three hours of climbing they reached the top. Level ground was solid under their tired feet. The Gurkha Rifles, an Indian battalion of the 4th Indian Division, were happy for the relief. It was visible on their worn, hungry faces. Few of them spoke English. They could not relay much information to the Highlanders. It was hard to fight a war in another language.

A hundred yards away the enemy played hide and seek. Close enough to smell the mule with the bad temper. The slightest movement brought forth a roar from the mouth of a machine gun, letting the breed of manly men know that the enemy was within firing distance. That it could kill a man as quickly as it could kill a mule. Impending mortality in the eye of a scope. Every path and roadway was guarded. The platoon crawled about at night in these hills, like nocturnal creatures, sliding in and out of slit trenches.

Three weeks in Orsogna and there was little to quell the appetite. Mules for waiters, honking and balking in mud up to their bellies, bringing insulated hayboxes with fresh stew, hardtack biscuits, and tea.

"I swear to Jesus, if I see another hardtack when I get back to Cape Breton, I'm gonna shoot it to hell," said Hector, spitting out crumbs.

"I'd shoot Hitler between the goddamn eyes for a tea biscuit," someone snarled, spitting his cold tea into the air like chewing tobacco.

Four days later, wind and fog colliding above their heads, Calum and Hector were singled out for contact patrol.

The burly commander from mainland Nova Scotia, Jentor, pointed to them. "You two, MacPherson and MacDonald, make sure your goddamn rifles are hot when you return from patrol should you encounter the enemy. I'm not sending you off to pick blueberries!"

Hector clenched a tight fist behind his back. He had seen Jentor kicking at the mule, cursing its hide. "Good-for-nothing skinny foreign bastards. They don't breed 'em like they do back home. Their Jesus horses die from fright."

The son of a bitch was here only temporarily or Hector would toss him down the mountain, head over heels.

After a two-mile patrol up the hills, Calum and Hector made their way to an old farmhouse in the distance. Spandau fire was cracking like splitting ice drifting in their direction. The enemy was on their trail. They entered the kitchen door as quietly as fog. A woman's whisper came from another room. Two women were in what looked like a parlour. Part of the side window had been shattered by bullets. The elderly woman was seated on a padded chair. A doily was strung to the chair's back like a dull web pulling her into its fray. The younger woman was standing in front of her. As a shield. She turned and spoke quietly to the woman who could have been her grandmother. "Canadians."

The old woman, wrinkled and wrapped unevenly in her own skin, shivered. Her swollen feet were propped up on a wooden stool. Blue veins like a pattern of loose threads gathered at her heels. Her face pulled back in terror. Her voice stuttered with fear. "Canadians? Canadians?" she moaned. Both Calum and Hector nodded yes. The old woman did not take her black eyes off them.

Calum looked down at the mud they had brought in under their feet, without knocking, as if they had insulted the culture of this home. The young woman noticed it too. Gave a half-smile as her eyes wandered from the mud up his pant legs, past his loins, up over his chest to his eyes. She said something to the old woman, then left the room. Returned with a few hard biscuits on a plate. The old woman gnawed along the rough edge of the biscuit and looked at the scalloped pattern she had created, then swallowed the remainder in two bites. The young woman offered a biscuit to Calum and Hector. Both declined. Nodded their thanks to their host. She was trying to explain something to them. Something about a brother who was coming to get them. To bring them to a safer place. Her mouth moved rapidly, like someone out of breath. She was not without her own fear, was quelling it for the old woman's sake. But her eyes were eloquent. Calum examined every move her lovely face made. Her high cheekbones danced behind her smile. It was her mouth that betrayed her. Quivered when she looked at the old woman. At what she would become someday, if she lived long enough.

Hector saluted a goodbye as he made his way to the kitchen door. Nuzzled the door with his rifle. It whined and opened slightly. The fog had thinned, unveiling lines of blue, like those in an old scribbler. He could hear nothing in the distance except the sound of a bird.

An old moon waited for daylight to go out. Hector returned to the parlour and spoke to Calum. "The shelling has died down." They left under a patch of blue. Crouching slowly on their knees towards the field. Calum turned to glance over his shoulder. He could see her shadow in the jagged window. Tracing their movements in the open field. He had motioned to the two women to stay low when he left the house. To wait quietly for the brother's return. But she was standing firmly and defiantly in the shattered window. She had something in her hand. A goodbye. Her fingers were spread openly above the bullet holes. Waving.

They moved on another hundred yards until they reached an apple orchard. They rested their backs against the largest tree, hoping it was not spiked with land mines. Their rifles pointed at the moon.

"They're sitting ducks," Hector half whispered. "What the hell could we do? The old woman couldn't walk on her own." From where they sat they could see only the outline of the old farmhouse. They heard the first volley of bullets rain down on the house. Followed by grenades.

"Jesus," Calum whistled under his breath. "Jesus." They saw two German soldiers in silhouette as they moved from the house and disappeared into the back woods.

"I'm going back." Calum's voice was weary.

"Are you crazy? That's just what they want us to do."

"I don't care, Hector, I'm going back."

"You want to get yourself killed? They'll be waiting for us. Probably have us in their scope this minute."

"I'm going back. They may think they blew us to bits in the house."

Calum was in the lead, his jaw locked in defiance, his voice floating back to Hector as if from underwater. Crawling under a moon that could be their traitor. Clouds running into it like driftwood. A spotlight running on weak batteries. An on-and-off-again moon. They halted a few feet from the house. Listened for voices. Heard the soft wind claim its last breath. Moved a few more feet towards the front door, closer to the parlour. And up to the window. The old woman was slumped in her chair, her head slanted forward as if in heavy sleep. One foot on the floor from her attempt to run for cover. Blood dripped to the floor from one exposed hand. The young woman was caught in the on-again moon. The good-bye hand rested against the wall, spread open into a silver fan. She was lying on her back, her knees drawn up slightly like a child who has succumbed to a lullaby. The other hand extended under the old woman's chair, its white palm delicately formed in a soft curve, ready to catch the spills.

Calum motioned for Hector to move slowly from the window. They crawled backwards to the corner of the house as the shots rang out.

"They're firing from the west side of the house," Calum whispered. "Get ready to fire!" A small porch gave them some protection from the shells.

"Jesus, they're in the trees," Hector whispered. "I can see the reflection of the barrels in the moonlight."

"Get in position, Hector!"

"I'll cover the tree on the left."

Silhouettes flew like bats from the trees. One with an arm outstretched as if reaching for his rifle. Calum and Hector lay low, watching for any sign of movement from the arm. They crawled slowly towards the bodies, then Calum noticed the arm go up. He was two feet from the barrel of a German Schmeisser. A wheezing sound stuttered, followed by a quick shot. A searing sound of metal feasting on bone. Like a thousand cracking twigs. A body lifting in air. Whistling. Relieving its lungs of their last duty. The smell of blood seasoning the earth.

"Are you hit?" Hector cried in a choking rasp.

"No, you got him first," Calum wheezed. "You saved my life."

"Bless me, Father, for I have sinned." Private Hector MacDonald curled the plea on his lips as he rose from his knees like a schoolboy after a lengthy confession. He looked down at the two slumped Germans. They were no more than twenty years old. He remembered his father telling him that some soldiers removed things from the enemy dead. Old coins, unsmiling faces in photos, brittle four-leaf clovers, medals engraved with bearded saints, four-holed buttons, a piece of material from a women's dress, a child's scrawl on a ragged piece of paper, an empty enemy shell. Gunner could never figure out why these useless remnants were of any interest. Perhaps, he'd told Hector, they were part of the penance.

Hector wanted no tokens.

They walked away slowly, after removing the bolts from the German rifles, and made their way back to camp. A bright moon bit at their heels. They had followed orders. Warmed their rifles on two dead men who had warmed their rifles on two dead women.

When sleep came, hours later, Calum could hear no sounds. He could be dead now. Buried in a makeshift grave under a scab of foreign turf. Something inside his head begged to be stilled. It was her voice he did not want to hear. To remember. Or the sound made by the hard, uneaten biscuit when it fell a few feet from her hand.

Hector felt a cold chill break along his spine. He had started a letter to his father two or three times. His hand shook. The words on the page were scribbled like a child's writing.

> Da, how is it I could kill a man with the comic strips you sent me in my back pocket? Red Ryder, Mickey Mouse, Little Annie Rooney, Alley Oop, Joe Palooka, Blondie…

Hours earlier he had killed a young soldier. He wanted his father to know. His father would understand. It had been the soldier or his best friend, Calum.

He wanted to go home. He wished to God he had never signed up, that he had heeded the signals in his father's eyes when he'd told him he was signing up for this war.

Twenty-One

1944

They were in the direct line of fire. Benny, Hamish, and Little Rachel. Standing still, halted by the sounds around them.

"Get away from the fence, you fools!" A young boy called out a warning.

There were three other boys, besides the warning voice. Twelve to thirteen years old. A row of tin cans lay sprawled on the ground. The shooter stopped and dropped his BB gun to his side. He was stocky, with a hill of freckles across the bridge of his nose.

Little Rachel ruffled her feathers. She could sense danger. Her wings spread as if she was about to take flight. Hamish looked over towards the young boys and smiled, with a wave of his hand. Two of the boys approached. They were smaller than the one with the hill of freckles.

"We told you to get away from the fence before we start shooting again," screamed the bigger of the two boys. His eyes were cold and calculating as he looked down at the hen. "What happened to her other eye?" he asked with a smirk. "Did she get hit with a BB?"

Hamish smiled and patted Little Rachel's head. He didn't know what a BB was.

Benny was silent as the boys walked around the wagon with their guns at their sides, contemplating their next move on the enemy.

The smaller boy, who had two broken front teeth, kicked at the wagon. A shower of hen feed caused a small riot in the air. Little Rachel squawked and dipped her beak into the empty bowl. The bigger boy let out a cruel laugh. Spit slid down the corner of his mouth, and he caught it with his finger and flung it at the agitated hen. He ordered the others to join in the fun. They moved in and circled the wagon.

Benny and Hamish stood side by side until Benny began to move about, pacing back and forth, his eyes like flames. The boys laughed out loud at a performance they had not anticipated.

"He's war crazy," cried the loudest of the pack. "My father said he went like that when they shot his hand off over there in the war."

"What's wrong with the other man? He's always smiling," observed the smallest boy.

"He's just a simpleton. Born like that. He doesn't know a snake from a piece of string," said the boy with the smirk.

"He just loves to dance." The cruel one pointed to Hamish's feet and ordered him to dance. "Dance for us, simpleton. Dance!" Hamish smiled and twirled in the air to a feast of laughter. He kept twirling to the laughter as his glasses went flying through the air.

One of the boys poked Little Rachel with the butt of his BB gun. "Are you crazy too, little hen?" he yelled, as the others broke into fits of laughter. Little Rachel flapped her wings. With a smile, Hamish watched them through his dusty glasses, now hanging at an awkward angle from his round face. Hamish believed they were playing a game with him.

"Can you dance for me, little hen, can you dance for your dinner?" cried the loudest boy, with his gun pointed at the wagon.

The hen was agitated and stumbled up on her good foot.

"You're not gonna shoot the hen, are you?" asked the smallest boy, alarm in his voice. "The hen wasn't in our way."

"No, you fool, I'm just going to make her dance because they interrupted our game."

Two shots rang out in a swirl of dust. Little Rachel flew two or three feet in the air before settling back down on her mound, her wings flapping like a door on a broken hinge. The boys' laughter rose with the dust, scattering in the thin wind. This was even better than killing cans.

They turned when they heard the loud moan, saw Benny outstretched on the ground, trying to unravel himself from his long, dark army coat. His stump pounding the ground. Benny cried out again in a haunting, holy tone, like some tormented cantor at the latch of heaven's gate.

"Jesus, did you shoot him?" cried the terrified voice of the smallest boy. The other three stood together, paralyzed by fear.

"I wasn't even near him," the shooter whispered. "Somebody else must have shot him." They all looked around the empty field.

Hamish was kneeling over Benny on the ground. Trying to pick him up. Mumbling something nobody could understand. On the ground, Benny looked like a savage beast fighting its tangled way out of a scrap of cloth. His knees were tucked under his chin. The back of his coat moved about slowly, like a twisted, battered tail. His voice was one continuous hymn of agony.

"Let's get going!" the smallest boy cried. "I think we shot him." But they did not move, could not move from their positions, as if they were waiting to be arrested.

The shooter had dropped his gun at his feet, its barrel pointing directly at the tattered tail a few feet away. "I didn't hit him, honest to God. I don't know what's wrong with him." His voice was a sob.

They did not hear or see the man walking up behind them, but they watched as this man bent over, picked Benny up, and cradled him as if he were a child. The man's voice was steady and gentle. "You're okay, soldier. It's all over. I'll take you home," he said to Benny.

Then, in a voice that cut like a knife, Gunner MacDonald said to the boy with the pointing gun, "If I ever catch you interfering with my platoon again, you will answer to me."

Gunner waited for a reply from the instigator, the one in the made-up army fatigues. The boys huddled together in fear, the one with the broken teeth creating half-moons over his bottom lip. The hill of freckles choked out a frightened, "Yes, sir."

They watched as the man, with the now silent Benny Doucet in his arms, and Hamish, pulling behind him a disgruntled hen in a red wagon, descended over the hill. They stood close together, with their guns at their sides. They were weary of the day. They were out of ammunition. And hungry. They looked at the scattered ground where the outline of Benny's movements were visible, but nobody spoke.

The church bell sounded in the distance. The chime coming closer as if it rode on the dark cloud that drifted above their heads. They moved in single file towards their kill. The smallest boy dug into the earth with the end of a stick and listened to the cling-clang of the cans as they fell one by one into their open grave.

Twenty-Two

1944

"Sheer illusion and lace and white nylon stockings for Moira," quipped Joan in a mocking tone, as if Moira were a member of European royalty shipped to Beinn Barra, where it was relatively safe and peaceful to be married.

Alex's heart cracked under the weight of his sister's words. He could ignore it no longer. He had heard his sister mention the wedding months ago, name the groom as some older MacInnis, from a nearby village, who had returned from Ontario to teach here in Barra. Alex had blocked it from his mind like a bad dream.

He thought of Moira pouring her ankles into the form-fitting nylon stockings. Fitting her white shoes carefully over them so as not to cause a run.

It rained. He could smell it before daybreak, closing in on him like a shadow over a clam. A heavy downpour by seven a.m. He could hear the tide from the centre of nature's womb, tossing and turning like a baby jockeying into position for birth. Thunder above the black clouds hammered for an opening. Lightning hissed at the towering steeple of the church. People ran inside. A blue car pulled up as close as possible to the double doors. A white illusion holding a speck of pink entered.

It was ten a.m., and she was about to become another man's wife. An older man's wife. He closed his eyes when the bells stopped ringing, and lay on his cot. They would start up again when it was all over. He waited for the sound of cow-bells and car horns and, finally, the blast from the shotguns. It was the end of June. People needed something to celebrate. And Moira was offering it up, American-style, in a storm.

Alex did not eat for weeks following Moira's wedding. He lay awake, fantasizing about the night that should have been his. Was she not still asking his sisters about him? Indeed, she had never stopped. He folded her stockings neatly and unravelled them again and again in his mind. They became the fabric of adultery to his imagination. He tied them into knots and hung them from a tree in the Devil's Lung.

It always rained. Water became the supplement of his nourishment. He no longer cared to wash or shave the coarse stubble that clouded his face. He wanted to hide inside his own flesh. He would drink most of a glass of water, then sprinkle the remainder into the air and catch the raindrops on his tongue. He was delirious in these storms.

His mother and sister complained when he refused to let them clean the Wooden Trench. He knew chaos, and chaos knew him. Why invite order in? He began to eat one meal a day. He preferred his tea strong and black. He saw his future at the bottom of the cup. The leaves were always against him. Cold and scattered.

He recorded details of everyday events with great accuracy. He paid close attention to the tides. Water lived in his soul. He felt he was yet to be born. He belonged to the sea, like his father and the faithful dog. He wrote poems. The darkness was his audience. Whispering his words back to him. *I thought I heard your footsteps on the stairs, and watched as silence, the thief, left only dust in your absence.*

Her name filled his mind. He took Moira down with him in his dreams. Watched as the waves unravelled her sheer illusion. Someone with arms and hands much stronger than his always rescued her. Out of the waves, she came fully unravelled. A stripped illusion. Waves flowing gently through satin. Like angel hair, her bangs uncurled. But not her stockings. They floated, wrinkle-free, white as a dove's back, before his eyes. Moving slowly. Moira turned and watched them go with one hand outstretched. He tried to rescue them, but they slipped away. Dividing the delicate membrane that was his grief into two separate waves. One for life. One for death. One for her. One for him. It was too late. Too, too late. He wept as they floated out to sea, becoming a blur on a soft ripple.

Twenty-Three

1944

Private Hector MacDonald's smile was noisy, a deep chant of broken breaths and misplaced words on the field where he lay among the dead and the dying. He thought he could hear the swirl of the pipes. His own words bathed in the music. He tried to turn towards them, but could not move his head. His hands were empty. His Bren gun lay three feet from where he had fallen. The barrel of the gun pointed in his direction. *Perhaps it is a snake*, he thought, shivering in the sunlight. The glory of speckled gold riding on its back.

He wondered where the others were. He had started out with Company B under a full moon. But now the sun was sneaking up under a blue sky and a leftover moon. When did it begin and when did it end?

He could feel nothing now, but he remembered the tanks firing the day before until their guns were angry hot. Ahead in the moonlight, he had seen the dark, humped body of Hill 120. All around him he could see the Highlanders coming back and going forward, dragging their wounded back with them. Stumbling past their dead, calling out to one another in Gaelic and English. How had they missed him? Someone was sobbing close to him. He wandered if Calum, who had been following close behind, had made it out. He tried again to turn his head to the right, to see whose still body lay four feet away from him. He caught a glimpse of a ragged sleeve and something that had spilled out from under it. Something dark and alarming. He had heard a voice coming from the direction of the sleeve for hours during the night. At one point, he thought he heard it humming an old tune. But now the sleeve was as silent as the dust that swirled around it. It lay there, unwilling to do anything. Unable to sing, or hum, or cry out, or disclose its name.

Someone else moaned. A long, drawn-out, agonized cry like that of the lynx he had once heard beside the lake near his home in Beinn Barra. The mournful sounds of the lynx had been bothering his father so much these last few months that, in his last letter to Hector, he had threatened to shoot the agony out of it.

War is all sounds. The cracking of a tender twig, footsteps in an abandoned house, a deep sigh, a whisper falling off a leaf. A death hymn. A woman asking your name in a foreign language. Oh God, how he had wanted to scoop her up into his arms and kiss his name on her mouth. That young woman standing at the train station. At that moment, time was his enemy, and possibly hers the way she had smiled at him, letting him know she was waiting for someone else.

The lynx would not stand a chance against his father's aim. In pursuit, his father would be soundless. Would level him with one shot. In the light of day.

Hector closed his eyes to bar the August sun from his vision. In this darkness, he composed a letter to his father.

> We started out to bust through the Gothic Line, but the CBH met very strong resistance from Hill 120 here in Montecchio. The Germans have the place loaded with barbed wire, ditches, and mine fields. I have been hit and am waiting for the stretcher bearers to come along. I don't think my injuries are too bad, but I am lying low in case the Germans are watching. I am surrounded by the dead and the dying. At this moment, I do not know where Calum is. Let's hope he is not down. There are too many dying here. Too young. We were with Company B on this mission. I hope to God you killed that agony with one shot.

Hector opened his eyes. He could hear a soft cry to his left. He tried once again to turn his head, slowly. The face he saw was out of focus. He blinked his eyes to clear his vision and saw a white hand twitching on the ground like a nervous kid playing a piano. The fingers stirred up little clouds of dust. "Calum," he whispered. "Is that you, Calum?"

No reply. The hand was still twitching. Now the face came into focus. The German soldier was about seventeen or eighteen years old, his dark eyes insane with fear, his front teeth sunk deep into his bottom lip, giving him the appearance of a crazed pumpkin put out to terrorize children at

Halloween. Little rivulets of blood formed crooked lines down his chin.

Hector closed his eyes. He forgot where his own pain was coming from. During the night he had thought it was in his right side, but then it had moved to his back and taken over his legs. He could hear voices in the distance. Something or someone was moving closer to him, standing now over the young German soldier. There were two of them. Their German voices commanding and sharp.

Hector heard the click of a Luger, one lonely shot, somewhat muffled but close enough for him to feel the body of the young soldier shift position. They walked around Hector as he held his breath. One of them kicked at his boot, which had fallen off, and he felt it fall beside his elbow. The other one kicked his back. He swallowed the pain. In a few minutes they were gone, believing he was dead. He waited for a time before turning his head. The white hand had stopped playing. Hector could smell the blood coming from the hideous pumpkin smile. One of the eyes lay open in what seemed like a half-wink.

Pain and time can move at the same pace. Hector had felt relief when they had taken the agony from the dying soldier. But now...he had taken some comfort from the hand uprooting the dust. Perhaps it had been recalling a tune. He had even wished for a moment that his father would let the lynx howl. There was still some kind of life in agony. The impact of the bullet had moved the hand closer to him. He could reach out and touch it if he wanted to. Feel if it had ever held a jigger. Thrown a line and hook into a stream. Stood up and lofted a silver trophy. What colour were the eyes of the young girl with whom he may have left intimate secrets?

Oh, my God, I am heartily sorry for having offended thee. Hector felt the prayer slip from his tongue into the mud. He could not remember the rest of it. Could not remember whom he or the kid beside him had offended. Perhaps he himself had hit the kid. Or the kid had hit him. The German officers had taken the agony out of the young man with one clean shot. In the light of day.

His father had never mentioned killing another soul in his life, his war life. Hector remembered asking him how deep were the trenches. And his father had answered, "as deep as your fear."

Hector could feel a new kind of pain growing in his leg. The kind that breaks into bones as suddenly as a toothache breaks into your jaw and sends your whole body into a panic. He knew he had to remove the shrapnel from his leg, but he would have to move slowly. He had seen that he was close to a pathway on his left. He reached over and grabbed his helmet. He propped himself up on his elbows and looked around at the bodies that lay on the hill. He would have to move towards the path to take cover in the trees. He could hear the sound of distant shelling as he crawled. Finally, reaching the dense brush, Hector reached down, cut open his pants leg, saw the shrapnel lodged in the bone of his left calf. *This is nothing*, he thought. *Imagine you're on your father's fishing boat with a fish hook in your calf.* Biting down hard on a twig, Hector pulled the shrapnel out carefully and wrapped the wound with the gauze he carried under his helmet.

Sweet Jesus, don't ask me to step-dance at this moment! He tried to smile, to prepare himself to follow the path to find his platoon.

He stood, weary and cold and alone, holding onto the branches as he moved forward into no man's land. He knew he must not call out to anyone in the platoon. He reached into his pocket for a biscuit he had stashed there.

"Well, I'll be Jesus," he whispered to himself. "I never thought I'd be so damned happy to see a hardtack. Wait until Calum hears this story."

Hector had limped only a short distance when he heard voices. He turned and faced three German soldiers with their guns pointed directly at him. "*Vo sind sie?* Where are you from?"

At close range, men from his own platoon began to fire at the Germans, and they hit the ground, pulling Hector down with them. He could not remember what happened next. When he came to, he was lying beside dozens of Canadian soldiers in a makeshift German camp. His leg was numb, but he could feel the heavy bandage someone had wrapped around it. From somewhere came the notes of a familiar Scottish tune, a low whimpering hum borne of pain and longing. Hector turned and saw a soldier in a West Nova uniform, a division from the mainland of Nova Scotia. He was a fellow Cape Bretoner. The soldier wept as he hummed "The Flowers of Edinburgh" in a low voice.

Twenty-Four

1944

Calum spit against the wind and cursed its return with his mind racing. Three soldiers from his platoon had fired at the Germans when they saw Hector being led away. Calum knew before it was officially recorded that his friend was now a prisoner of war.

The battle for Hill 120 was one of the worse encounters of the whole bloody war, comparable only to the fight for Coriano Ridge. The Highlanders had gone to the top of Hill 120 but were overcome by the fiercest fighting the Germans could offer. Deep bomb shelters, well-sited MG positions, shoemines planted underground to blow your legs to hell once you stepped off them. Disappointed with their failure to capture the hill, the Highlanders nevertheless knew they were better soldiers for it.

Calum sat off by himself and lit up a smoke. Blue circles clogged the air. Through the billows he could see an older soldier rocking back and forth on the ground, his eyes motionless, his shoulders folding under his chin. Someone had taken his rifle from him and handed him a drink. It fell between his legs and leaked along the ground, making it looked as if he had relieved himself on the spot. The soldier did not notice the water forming a pool around him, the white cloud stretched like sheep's wool hung out to dry above his sunken head.

Calum watched as two medics pulled the soldier to his feet and led him away. This was the end of the external war for him. The internal war, that was different. Horror could live out its life in a man's cells. Keep the battle going a long distance from the bullets. A servant of madness off the playing field, it could erupt anywhere. Between the sheets. In the arms of a woman. There were only two ways a man could really leave this goddamn war. Silent or dead. Hector was missing and Benny was silent. And Alex was out of touch. Calum hadn't heard from Alex in a long while. He firmly believed that Alex was still in Beinn Barra, not too far from the sea.

Someone would be sent in to work on the morale of the soldiers. This was as necessary as their next battle. As sharp as a landmine, as biting as shrapnel, this was how the soldiers must be kept. Or they might stall in their boots. Might listen for sounds and recollect faces they might never hear or see again. The swish of a breeze in a woman's skirt must be kept near, whispering a name in the folds. Every child's smile kept alive on the canvas of the mind. Every mother's and father's words heard above a heartbeat. These were the things that improved a man's morale. Let him sink into the mud with dignity. Let him go hungry for one more round of fire. Let him witness death's hand as it rose from the earth to claim its seeds, to take him down, using his own blood as fertilizer.

Sometimes a soldier would die with serenity on his face. Without a trace of mechanical interference. These were the soldiers who "died clean."

Private Calum MacPherson had been sent with a detail to prepare the dead for burial. They had taken several extra G1098 blankets to wrap the dead, and a spool of telephone wire. The G1098 blanket was, in effect, every infantryman's coffin, carried on his own back.

Shattered men give no resistance. Calum felt an urgent need to close their eyes. When he was twelve years old, his father had asked if he wished to close his grandfather's eyes as they prepared him for burial. The old man had died during the night from pneumonia. Calum remembered looking up at the wall where his grandfather's last gaze must have rested. A picture of women gathering pieces of wood and twigs in their arms and aprons. Plump, sturdy women picking up the pieces of a dead fall under the sweep of Van Gogh's brush. He could not remember what his grandfather had liked most about the picture. Perhaps it was the nourishing effect, the need for comfort and warmth, the eternal need for survival exemplified by these women.

The first soldier Calum wrapped had died clean. There were no visible signs of bullets or penetration. In this theatre of war, each soldier was but one solitary player, supported by a cast of friends. And in turn he wanted to support them.

Calum stared into the young face before he covered it with the blanket. It looked neither grotesque nor surprised. Rather, it looked satisfied in death's serene sculpture. He reached up and sealed the eyes shut.

Two dark stains of flesh and blood filled the eye sockets of the next body. Part of the nose was missing. Several teeth were shattered. The lips formed a perfect "O."

"Oh my God, my God," the soldier sent with him on detail half whispered. "I never knew a man could come apart like this."

"Keep going," Calum said, his voice steady and sharp, but surprised at the soft tone in the other man's voice.

"There's two bodies left," said the soldier, looking over at Calum. "I believe this one was a friend of yours." Calum turned and looked down at the outstretched body. "No, I don't recognize him, but I'll wrap him," he said quietly.

The soldier walked towards the other body and stretched out a piece of telephone wire. "Christ Almighty!" he cried. "This fellow is ready to explode—he's turning black."

"Wrap him quickly!" Calum ordered. He looked over his shoulder to see the young soldier retching a few feet from the body.

"You can do it, get him wrapped!" Calum shouted as the man wiped his sour mouth with a dirty sleeve, then threw the blanket over the disfigured face and proceeded to wrap the body quickly. There was a an old white scar running from under the dead man's left ear to the back of his neck. He wore a wedding band.

There was only the whiteness of death under the coarse beard of the soldier Calum prepared to wrap. A few razor scars zigzagged on the skin, just below the smile that lay deep above the chin. Almost wilful. His last farewell. Even in death he was grinning wildly. His face was a mask of rapture and expectancy. Like a young boy watching his own image shining back up at him as he took his first dive into deep water.

"We'd better be getting back! It's starting to rain." The young soldier sent on detail with Calum was standing over him.

"What did you say?" Calum looked up.

"I said we should be getting back. Our job is finished here." Calum looked down at the body. He had wrapped it neatly.

"How long have I been sitting here?" he asked.

"It's been awhile. We better get going before it rains too heavily."

Calum got up slowly and placed the remains beside the others. They had positioned them in a straight line. Calum noticed that the body beside the last one he had wrapped had exploded, and was making soft, gurgling sounds. The dead spilling a secret among the dead.

Twenty-Five

1944

Two wailing women clawed at the seam in the wall, their voices scorched with panic.

"Alex, open the goddamned seam, there's a fire bruising up the kitchen wall!"

Behind the wall, Alex lay on his cot. A warm kiss tickled his knuckles. He opened his hand and the kiss expanded. Up to his neck, his mouth. Dripped to his shoulder. Then slid away. He tried to catch it with an open hand. To give it directions, to lead it back to him.

She had never been this close to him in a dream. Flesh to flesh. He reached up and felt her ankles. Her stockings. Dove white. The seams perfectly straight. His fingers circled the red hat she held in her hand. It was easier to ruffle her bangs with her hat off. To trespass with his fingers along her neck. She was trying to tell him something, but he hushed her into silence. He didn't not want anyone to know she was there.

"How did you get in here, Moira?"

She did not answer. She held up her right foot. He could feel her muscles talk. "Aren't you glad I'm here?" they said. He laughed and pressed his smile on her face. Adultery was possible under moonlight. Rain was not always required. He didn't need an equation. Love was greater than hate. He had passed the test. She had come to him, finally. On a poetry-free night, she was at his side, looking for gladness.

Something was hurting his chest when he woke up. He could hear shouts, and fists pounding on the wall. A rough hand seemed to be pulling at the fibre of his lungs. Stitch by stitch. He tried to take a deep breath. When he did, he could taste smoke in his mouth. The pain stomped inside his chest like an angry bull's hoof.

He was fully awake now, but he could see nothing except a dull light from the lamp. Above the light, he could make out the picture of the dog. Smoke burned his eyes. His hands searched blindly in the dim light. He crawled along the floor. His blind hands looking for, searching for, the seam in the wall.

"Jesus, Jesus," his mother and sister heard him wail. "I can't find the seam."

He pulled himself up against the wall and peered out through the slit. Something stared in at him. Silver. Half cooked. "Oh God, the moon is on fire." Half of it was already gone, dropping its cinders into his lungs. He sank to the floor and tried to take a long, deep breath. He could see nothing now as he tried once again to find the seam in the wall. He crawled towards the wall, felt the picture of the dog and held it safely in his arms.

He did not hear the last of their panic, his mother's collapse, the breaking sound of the attic window as his sister suspended their mother, wrapped in a sheet, from the window. Cassie dangled like a icicle ready to topple.

"Christ Almighty," cried a young man on his way home with two friends from a dance, as they came within view of the MacGregor house. "It's a ghost," he shouted, as he tore at his zipper and ran towards the woods, then back again, forgetting what he had intended to do.

"You won't scare it away with that," cried his friend. They watched as someone jumped from the window and pulled the sheet to the ground. Then ran towards the house when they saw the flames shooting up from the back, near the chimney, just as Cassie's daughter pulled her mother away from the wall and placed her on the ground. Joan huddled in cold silence beside the soaring flames.

Everyone watched as Cassie unravelled from the ground. In ragged swirls. In torn edges. A magnificent, tattered dance of dirt and gravel and cloth exploded in the air in front of them. And the dancer raced for the rising fury of the flames as if she had rehearsed this role for years. There was no stopping Cassie MacGregor as she lunged towards the burning inferno. Tearing at the shingles like a crazed animal. Openly calling his name. His full name.

"Alexander Pius MacGregor. Alexander Pius MacGregor."

As though she were introducing him to someone. Naming him for heaven. A crowd had gathered but, sensing futility, they stood back and watched as the flames consumed the moon.

From the black debris of the MacGregor house, neighbourhood men gathered the charred remains of Alex MacGregor and placed them in a pine box.

Cassie attended her son's funeral with soot in her hair and dried blood under her nails. Her mouth moved, but no sounds escaped as she approached the grave and stared down into the ground that would be womb to his ashes. She wore a plain black dress and a dark scarf that kept sliding to the back of her head. Her daughter stood as still as a frozen twig. Gunner MacDonald stood against the wind and read the words of Percy Bysshe Shelley from an open book:

> I offer a calm habitation to thee,
> Say, victim of grief, wilt thou slumber with me?

Some of the mourners, thinking MacDonald was reading from a prayer book, bowed their heads and made the sign of the cross.

Cassie was never certain that they had found remains. She had never asked. Perhaps Alex had vanished from the flames by some mystical twist. Perhaps he was now watching his own burial with wry amusement. She had never really understood the heart of her only son.

At the gate of the graveyard, the postmistress leaned heavily against the fence. Moira, in the family way, had walked slowly from the gravesite when she saw Gunner open the book. Her husband said it was her condition that caused her to weep at the thought of a poem.

"Cassie MacGregor hasn't had a straight thought in her head to call her own since her husband drowned. Kept young Alex too close to her. He might have been better off if he had gone overseas," one of the mourners remarked to his wife.

"Christ knows, the Germans couldn't have done any worse to him than that fire did. He died in hell."

It had long been rumoured that Alex was still in Beinn Barra, even though his mother claimed he had gone out west. Gunner had been convinced of it. But he had remained silent to protect Alex. *Protect him from what?* he now asked himself as he walked up the path. How does one protect a man from his own hell?

A neighbour housed the MacGregors in his grandparents' old home two miles down the road. They settled in and sank into sorrow. For weeks, no clothes were hung out to dry. Not even a dishrag was put out for a breath of fresh air. Flour and potatoes were left on their step. The curtains were kept drawn. The radio voiceless.

Then, one Monday morning, a few weeks later, a full line of clothes ran like a frill of rhubarb lace in the breeze. White sheets bloomed in the sun. Pillowcases were fattened by salty air.

Hamish, Little Rachel, and Benny stood on the side of the road and watched the parade of laundry in front of them. Benny made his way towards the clothes, Hamish and Little Rachel in tow. He dove his stump into the first sheet and swung it like a pendulum. He moved from sheet to sheet with his stump held high like a sword.

"Gonna find the fiddle," cried Benny, a delirious look in his eyes. Hamish smiled as he dipped his nose into a pillowcase.

"Fittle not here, Enny," Hamish said, moving towards a pair of bloomers on the line. Two swollen legs, full of sunshine, flew in his face before he wrestled them to the ground. Hamish slung them back on the line. They were too skinny now to be hiding a fiddle. Hamish dipped his nose into a brassiere and pulled it off the line. He attacked a pillowcase head on. He roamed around in circles with the white pillowcase on his head. They left empty-handed and walked on down the road.

Benny was in the lead when they came to the old MacGregor property. A woman with soot in her hair stood among the ruins. She did not look up as Benny and Hamish arrived. Hamish knew he had seen this woman before, but he couldn't remember her name. She was searching for something near a burnt-out old trunk, her white hands diving into the ground. When the woman looked up Benny could see a circle of soot around her mouth. She was holding something in her hand. "Look what I found!"

Hamish stood beside Benny and studied the four-leaf clover the woman was holding in her hand. Blood trickled out from between her fingers. Cassie MacGregor held the broken piece of a cup and laughed hysterically.

"Alex, my son, sent me this four-leaf clover," she said between laughs, holding out the piece of china for Hamish and Benny to see. "Come and see the four-leaf clover he left here for me to find!"

She walked over to them and held up the broken handle.

"Wat colour that?" asked Hamish, admiring the treasure the woman was presenting. Cassie did not answer. Little Rachel stood and flapped her wings. Benny looked solemnly at the broken woman, beautiful with sorrow. A statue he had seen somewhere. *Where?* At the mauve in her eyes like two bruises. At the opening in her black mouth, where her pain comes from. She called out a name he had heard before: "Alex."

He believed she had a name too. But it had disappeared from his head. Her body moved like a wave being teased by the wind. She had the rhythm of a dancer. Her bones flowed under her skin. He could hear music as she spoke. Her voice came from the back of her throat and sneaked out of her mouth like a piece of fresh gossip. She wanted to share her joy.

Benny knew how music could move a woman. The quiet passion that built up in the limbs and startled the feet into action, abandoning all shyness and trampling danger with a light touch. But this woman was not dancing today. Her feet had forgotten how to dance, because they were bare, and cold, and moulded in soot.

Twenty-Six

1945

Gunner MacDonald drank weak tea from a cracked mug for months following the capture of his son, Hector, and the death of Alex MacGregor. He watched as swirls swam to the ridge of the mug and disappeared. Voices came and went out again. He asked no questions and gave no answers. The priest came to the house and blessed his darkness. Food was placed in front of him and was removed untouched. How could he eat when his own son and thousands of others lived on rations? He realized that Red Cross care packages would be shared among the prisoners of war. But little else would be provided. He knew what shape Hector would be in now. Physically and mentally. Gunner dreaded the long nights alone on the cliff, yet he wanted no visitors.

He watched from his kitchen window as Benny and Hamish, with Little Rachel behind, journeyed down to the shore in the mornings. How eagerly they set off each day, meeting at the crossroads. What waited for them was often a raging sea. Angry gulls with wings twisted out of shape, like torn shingles ready to topple into the waves. Beside the wharf, Benny tuned up his fiddle and began to play. What lunacy composed, the wind awaited and drowned out, into oblivion, into freedom.

Hamish danced like a spring colt with a wind-whipped mane. Little Rachel, ruffled and sea-sprayed, pulled in her wings and dipped her beak into the straw as if willing herself to sleep out the storm. Gunner waited daily for Benny and Hamish and Little Rachel to appear in his kitchen window. He sipped at the world through illusions. His only solace. He ran his dancing fingers along the window ledge as Benny played. Fed the music to his feet. They moved in sequenced shuffles in the dust under the kitchen table. Scared the cat out from under the table with a jig. The cat hid out for weeks in the barn, emerging only to eat and retreating quickly from the thumping inside the big house. Gunner tried to avoid the shadow of Cassie MacGregor, which roamed through the cemetery of Beinn Barra.

Shadows danced in his nightly dreams. Feet and hands blazing. Faces invisible. A new dream presented marching feet and hands saluting wildly. Pipers swirling in the dust. Six pounding feet on his pillow. Scattering the feathers. Saluting in unison. The owners of the feet and hands emerged one by one. Hector grinned broadly. How happy he looked, the gap in his front teeth giving him the appearance of a younger schoolboy. His reddish hair cropped short. His tall frame poised by discipline. His army uniform an inch too short at the sleeves, exposing thin but rugged hands. He began to say something but retreated into silence and looked down at his highly polished boots. Danced up a white storm of feathers.

Behind him stood Benny, in full uniform, except for his cap. Sturdy, nearing six feet in height. His light brown hair grown down over his collar in wild waves. His blue eyes casting off an electric stare. A fiddle was tucked under his left arm. The broken neck of the fiddle dangled by the strings against his thigh, a dead duck carried gently to the feast after a savage killing. His two strong hands were knotted into balls of flesh. He was angry that his fiddle was broken. Inside his fists he carried two new compositions.

Calum was the last to appear. Looking much older than his years. His brown eyes feverish. His six-foot frame bent. A deep furrow on his brow. His wrists were wrapped in dirty brown braided rags. An unanswered question on his lips. His uniform was neatly pressed, but his feet were bare. He was searching for his boots. He wanted to dance. He shouted as he searched. A scar was visible on his right foot, shaped like a star. The other foot was bleeding. Red stars appeared on the white sheet. Twinkled out. Leaving stains.

Gunner awoke early and sat at his kitchen table. The new year was three months old, and stained. He was not a superstitious man. He should have paid no attention to the poor widow with her forerunner story, told to anyone who would listen at MacSween's General Store. Three knocks came upon her door, but each time she opened the door, nobody stood there. Not a two- or four-legged creature in sight. And it was in broad daylight. Had it been someone who lived under the cork, with a tongue as dry as sawdust, she would have known, she claimed, for she could always tell those who favoured the drink to a crust of bread by the way they tapped at the door. People rolled their eyes when she predicted that death was tapping on Beinn Barra's door.

Perhaps, thought Gunner, he had never been spiritually healthy. Had never examined or witnessed the necessity of living between earth and sky with one eye on the supernatural forces. He had never been haunted by ghosts. He neither believed nor disbelieved in such things. Should they appear, what would he offer them?

If only he had gone to the MacGregor house and asked to speak with Alex, he might very well be alive today.

He dressed warmly and walked slowly to the top of the hill for the first time in months. The morning air rattled up a cough in his chest. A faint light glowed from the MacPhersons' kitchen window. A thin line of smoke rose in the air like a bird off course. A white, broken moon stamped in the pre-dawn sky. Songs of the wind come from the northwest. Winter was still visible and clean under the trees. Piles of dirty snow lay in ditches. The sea heaved like cracked plaster under ice. Groaned. He watched Joachim MacPherson walk towards the barn. Joachim's shoulders curved inward like a man who bore winter not only on his back, but in his heart.

A village could shape a man. Nourish him at its breast. Wean him to live out his intimacies under patched quilts. Pat him on the back for his integrity. But grief was another story. It would shadow you as it robbed you blind. Night and day. It would stalk you into submission. Offering up its palms of sore flesh. Everyone was hurting. Bleeding for change. It was coming. The carnage was coming to an end. Too late for himself and the man who had just disappeared into the barn.

Gunner moved his cold hand along his temple. Shook his head slowly to spill the dream from his head. It would not budge. Could not budge because it was part of the robbery. So he stood in this stained March, a man slapped raw by what he felt was coming and what he knew was gone forever.

A man could hurry death. Relieve it of its natural process. He had used a rifle on the old dog. Let it feast, in its arthritic sprawl, on a bowl of corned beef and pork. He had waited until the meal was diminished to a swish of the tongue to clean up the particles of food that had broken away. And then, with one shot to the back of its head, its snout lay in the middle of the bowl, its tongue dark and longing as if it had reached the centre of its own heart and drank to its own demise. His grief for that dog had lingered for weeks. More of a melancholy for something warm and constant at his side.

He had never fully focused on the death of his wife, his beloved Iseabal. It came and took her one spring, along with the stillborn child. There was no final meal for them. Just words. Her own. He had listened in silence to his beloved, practical Iseabal dying on the white sheet.

"Make sure Hector doesn't get carried away when you take him fishing!"

He smiled.

"I want you to dance for me forever."

He held her hand. "I will love you always." He kissed her damp cheek.

"I must leave you now."

He closed her eyes. He had no dialogue that could escort her into death. He was a man who dined lightly on religion. Never went to church. Claimed belief in himself was the only faith a man could fully contemplate.

For years after Iseabal's death, people brought him the names of widows who were great cooks, fussy housekeepers, delicate fudge makers, swift fish gutters, experienced snow shovellers, and fence menders as good as any man. He thanked them all for their interest. He had become proficient in all these skills, except for the fudge making. He still burned the pot.

He had commissioned his heart for one sorrow. He loved one woman. Had loved Iseabal from the moment he saw her red mane of curls bent over her father's fishing net.

"What are you doing?" he'd asked.

"I'm spinning for gold," she said, without looking up. "I'm just getting started."

"You're doing it all wrong. I'd never pay you for that job."

She looked up then and smiled. "Then what would you pay me for?"

"For leaving my nets alone," he said, grinning.

They left the nets that summer and walked along the dirt road, leaving their footprints in the sand. Once, she had looked back over her shoulder to see how far they had come. Or perhaps how far they could go together.

Hector possessed his mother's spirit and daring. She had not been afraid of death. Just the departure. A phase, she had called it. Just another phase of life. He felt comforted by the thought that his son might be thinking the same thing in the prison camp.

He was nearing the MacPherson gate before he realized he had walked farther than he'd intended. Joachim came out of the barn and saw Gunner's shadow. Gunner had not seen his neighbour since Joachim's visit when news arrived of Hector's capture. Joachim seemed surprised to see Gunner at this hour of the morning, under a white moon.

"How are you doing, Gunner?" Joachim offered his hand.

"Just out to inhale the morning air. The house gets pretty stale."

"Will you come in and have a cup of tea and a bite to eat?"

"You're a busy man, Joachim. Perhaps some other time."

Both men avoided the word "war." But the word was there between them. Joachim's face was a pattern. March had taken up shelter in it. His eyes, two beads of frost, lay marooned in their dark pools. His lids were like heavy icicles dangling off a thatched roof. He had not seen war the way Gunner had seen it. In his lameness, he would always stand by and wait helplessly.

Gunner watched as Joachim walked slowly back to his house, then stopped and turned, as if he had thought of a question. But neither man spoke. Joachim's left shoulder drooped, as if something too heavy had been placed on it. Perhaps death itself, Gunner thought, carrying its own weight. *Is this what people describe as a forerunner?* he wondered, then shuddered at the thought of becoming a believer in forerunners on a morning that had not yet fully come to life. A morning that was still dotted with fading stars.

Gunner had always fitted his life into pragmatic corners. When his wife died, he became a proficient homemaker. When he longed to hear her sweet voice, he asked Hector to sing the songs she had sung. When his son was captured, Gunner picked a corner of the house that gave him solace from the words and deeds of the professional grievers. People damage the bereaved with too many or too few words. They forget that the griever has been robbed.

They had meant well, the three widows barging in through Gunner's door with a pot of soup.

"Gunner, you're not to worry," one of them sobbed. "My cousin from Sydney was captured in the First World War and returned home looking like a badly skinned rabbit." She paused to blew her nose. "By the time the mean old bugger died, he wouldn't give a peeling to a crow because he said he had starved for too long to give anything away to man or beast. He was eighty years old and weighed three hundred pounds."

Gunner thanked them kindly for their visit and the pot of soup, and locked the door behind them. Gunner preferred music to words. He imagined that he could hear Benny play down by the sea as Hamish danced. But here, in the morning that had finally let go of its faded stars and white moon, he could hear nothing but the banter of a cranky rooster accompanying the thump of his own lonely heartbeat as a few drops of rain dampened the fields of Beinn Barra.

He turned and walked towards his house. He sat down with his collection of letters from overseas and reread the letter from Calum.

Dear Gunner,

I am writing today as one soldier to another. My heart sinks for your pain, as well as my own. Hector is not only a friend, he was my right hand, my vision, my path, my shadow, my laughter, my light in this darkness, and, God only knows, my "Amen" when sorrow fell heaviest, as with Benny. I know that if anyone can survive the peril that exists for those captured, he will.

I do not fear death today as much as I fear what is left of my life at this moment. I feel like a dead star in a lost galaxy without Hector and Benny at my side.

History, with mercy on our side, will someday tell the dirty truth. The Canadians have paid the worst price here in Italy. I feel we have been shipped here to learn the meaning of the word "mud." We live and die in it. It's in our boots. It's in our pores. It's in our dreams while we sleep in it. Every soldier here doubts that he will ever feel clean again. There are not enough Canadian reinforcements, so we do double duty in the mud and cold rain, without a morsel of food, sometimes for days. We were not trained well enough for this war. We have been hit hardest by leaders who abandoned advances that may have saved thousands of Canadian lives. We should never have been here in the first place.

Why were we dropped into such a poor state of affairs in a country that had been led by a dictator? The poor people here didn't need us tearing up their country. The enemy is secondary. It all seems so futile.

As I see it now, and you no doubt fully understand, it's not only what a man sees here, but what he feels that carries him forward. I go into battle with the instincts of a hungry dog. Otherwise, I could not go at all, but stand by idly and bark my bloody head off. There are times when I believe all is lost. But then something comes along, maybe the smile of a child when you give him a piece of fudge or a stick of gum that you received from home. I never realized the swirl of the pipes could pump freedom into your step as they do, for me and the rest of the boys. They are my mating call to Beinn Barra every time I hear them. And it is refreshing to meet up with the women from Canada. We are so grateful for their work here. Many of them are not that far from the front. I can't imagine the courage it took for them to cross the Atlantic in such turbulent waters.

The boys and I were insufficiently amused by Lady Astor's comments in the House of Commons on the D-Day Dodgers. Someone should have told her that the Canadians had been fighting in the southern theatre of war for almost a year before D-Day, and had been slaughtered by the thousands.

I rather doubt this is much comfort to you today. I remember Hector and Benny with great honour and a smile a day.

Sincerely,

Twenty-Seven

1945

The Cape Breton Highlanders had been in northwestern Europe for a month by the end of April. Cold rain scratched like cat claws at their flesh. Calum looked over his shoulder at the weary soldiers trailing behind him as they rounded up the German prisoners.

Smoke filtered through teeth as yellow as phlegm from the prisoner beside him. The German's stare was occupied by defiance. He was much younger than most of the soldiers who had surrendered after the Highlanders broke through the inner defensive ring of the town to the north of Delfzijl, Holland.

He was light-boned, his hands sharply defined by scars running like branches to his thin wrists. He examined them carefully, holding them out in front of him, and began to groom them like a cat. Licking them in short, slow strokes with his tongue. He defiantly bared his yellow teeth once again. There was an exquisite air about him, as if he had been pulled reluctantly from a Stradivarius and sent off to war. He rotated his head from side to side as if to balance out a tune or a piece of music that had settled there and grown cold.

A long line of prisoners huddled together, conversing in hushed, broken tones. *Not much difference between them and our own*, Calum thought, *except for the uniforms*.

Some of the prisoners inhaled deeply the smokes they were given by the Canadian troops. Others tore at sunken lids with their thin hands and looked out at their defeated world through bloodshot eyes. One older prisoner paced at the end of the line, taking quick, short puffs off the end of a smoke. A dirty rag tied to his left foot. He had removed his boot, and dragged his foot as he walked. Calum motioned for him to remove the cloth. Trembling, the soldier held his hands up, as if he had the need to surrender one more time. Calum removed the dirty rag. A deep, ugly bullet hole spouted blood. He called for a dressing and wrapped the wound himself.

Intelligent eyes followed Calum as he stood up. The prisoner was at least thirty. Looked as if he could have been an educator. Or a scientist who would have preferred to look through a microscope than through the scope of a rifle. He reached into his pocket, his gaze fixed on Calum, and pulled out a photo. The child's face was solemn, as if it had been captured in a moment of deep thought, too deep for the child to completely absorb. Two or three years of age. Calum stared at the picture and turned away from the soldier. He could feel the man's eyes still on him. The soldier held the picture in his hand as he continued to pace. A friend threw an arm around him, steadied him towards the edge of the line, and sat him down. Another soldier offered him his cigarette.

Calum walked slowly along the line of prisoners. Many of them paid no attention to their captors as they conversed back and forth. One soldier sang in a deep, gravelled voice, as if to buoy the spirits of his fellow countrymen, then raised a hand for the others to join in the chorus. Another prisoner kept ducking down and crawling along the ground. Somebody pulled him to his feet, but he again hit the ground and crawled in and out of various legs, like a friendly dog. He had a long, pointed face, and the stubble clung to it like barbed wire.

Calum returned to the end where the wounded soldier sat, still holding the picture of the boy in a tight fist. His face was paler now, and his head rested on the shoulder of his friend. Calum could see only the eyes of the child, as if they were deliberately seeking him out. To guard his father. Calum felt the outline of wood in his left pocket as his hand reached in for a cigarette. He withdrew the object, cupped it in his hand, looked down at the dog he himself had whittled.

Calum looked up to see the prisoner on his feet again, the picture still in his fist. Two medics were putting him on a stretcher when Calum reached down and offered him the wooden dog. The prisoner's hand shook violently as he accepted the gift.

"*Danke schön. Danke schön,*" he whispered in a low voice, through a row of broken, yellow teeth, as he was carried away, the dog held securely in his hand, along with the picture of his young son.

Twenty-Eight

1945

Spring was dirty in Delfzijl. Private Calum MacPherson stopped to pick up a muddy yellow flower. It spread between his fingers like a dead butterfly. He could not name the flower he had just killed with his bare hand. How was it possible that a man could weep for a dead flower? Perhaps it was the unexpected sight of beauty that moved him. His limbs trembled like a man rescued from a sinking ship.

A breeze escorted the tears down his face. Like a summer breeze back home in Beinn Barra. Playing hide and seek in the open field, frolicking down the side of Barra mountain. He heard Hamish's voice, as lingering as the echo fed to the cave they'd cut out of the mountain when they were kids. Hamish had found something. His arms were loaded down with dandelions, and he was passing them out to his friends. Alex and Benny and Hector were smiling and thanking

Hamish for his gifts. He had two flowers left, and he was looking for Calum.

In the distance, war called. The flower fell from sight. Small arms and mortar fire peppered Calum's thoughts. He looked over to where four of his comrades conversed with each other in an arena of blue smoke. How desperately they clung to words. One of them held up a letter and read from it. Calum was not close enough to hear the words. They motioned for him to join them. They were all hardened veterans like himself, tattooed with shrapnel and mortar bites. Born and raised near the crusty mountains of Beinn Barra, all. From the Valley of Death, to Cassino, to the crossing of the Melfa, to Hill 120 and Graveyard Hill, to Coriano Ridge, to the crossing of the Lamone, and into Holland, the quagmire of death stayed under their boots. The Cape Breton Highlanders sank into the mud and buried their dead all along the route. They witnessed the freedom marches when they liberated the first big town in Holland. Young women danced into their arms like sheets full of wild wind.

They paused when one of the boys mentioned Ortona, a seven-day marathon bloodbath that had ended the lives of almost two thousand Canadians in one week. They were as thrilled as schoolboys counting down to the end of the year when Calum joined them. The letter reader was recounting a late-winter snowstorm in Beinn Barra. How it had clogged the roads and buried the clotheslines and halted the potato planting for a week. The farmers were happy, he said, because snow was the poor man's fertilizer. And the potatoes would be plentiful for the dumpling stews. His letter ended, "*Tha blith e fad a nis.* It won't be long now."

Every face was set in deep concentration, aroused by the thought of a potato simmering beside white dumplings. Every craving here was a safeguard against the inevitable. The next bullet. The next mud hole. Food and rest were the soldier's sacraments. Calum smiled, thinking of Hamish, and that Hector would make it back to Beinn Barra.

For years Hamish had been put on pie patrol, stationed outside the kitchen window, armed with a smile, as the pies cooled on the ledge. The enemy loomed above his head. They cawed and flapped their shiny wings as they landed a few feet from the window, dangerously close to their objective, in attack mode, their beaks sharp. Hamish waved them off with flapping arms and a gentle warning: "Go 'way, crow!" He was congratulated for his preservation of all things good. Later, he got the first piece of the cooled pie. He rested in a rocking chair with a full belly and a keen eye. The enemy had returned. They stared at the empty ledge and flew off in a rage, leaving behind a trail of black feathers. General Hamish smiled and asked for another piece of pie.

The real enemy was still watching. The Highlanders knew the time had come for the decisive assault on Delfzijl. At 0100 hours on the first day of May, D Company advanced. The flooded roads were in such poor condition that the supporting arms vehicles could not advance. Private Calum MacPherson and the other Highlanders proceeded alone.

Private MacPherson was in the lead when they were attacked by a sudden flurry of German flares. Pinned down by snipers and the damned Spandau guns. Nothing short of murder. A young Highlander lay face down, mumbling into the earth, willing his grave to open up and swallow him whole. Another, sinking in mud, screamed for someone to catch him before he fell. In a few minutes he was silent. His hands lay folded on his chest, with his thumb wrapped around a small medal. He had not even sung the "Death Hymn," the soldiers' name for the gurgle heard before a man dies.

Artillery was called for by D Company and delivered. One platoon was pinned down in a German trench and running short of ammunition. C Company was ordered to send men back for ammunition from D Company's carrier. B Company was ordered to assist D Company, holed up in a Jerry trench under heavy fire from the top of a dyke and exhausted now of all ammunition.

Private MacPherson looked down at the yellow smudge that lingered between his fingers. How ironic, he thought, that the last thing he would kill in this war was a nameless flower. There were six soldiers and their sergeant in the trench. Two of them spoke Gaelic to one another. Another prayed out loud. Private MacPherson was quiet. Private Raven was the sound man. He had ears like a cat. They were within fifty yards of the 105mm gun positions, he told them.

The Highlanders dashed forward a further thirty-five yards and occupied another enemy trench, under direct fire from the bazooka and two machine guns and three hundred infantry. They were being fired at from all sides. The enemy entrenched on top of the dyke and threw their grenades directly into the trench. Two of the privates collapsed on their knees. Like altar boys in trained devotion, they went down quietly. One was a burly young man. His head fell backwards, exposing a deep gash to his throat. His eyes rolled and looked out at the riot of the morn. His lips moved without sound. The other soldier had been hit on the side of the head. His jaw was open, and closed slowly as he invited heaven's mercy into the fold. The air was dry with terror as the trench filled with muddy water, blood, and a broken prayer.

"Keep low! Stay down!" The good-natured sergeant offered up encouragement. Good humour. "Help is not far away." He had been in the trenches long enough to know the score. He didn't need a hole full of insane men mingling with the dead.

Another grenade.

Private Calum MacPherson went down on one knee, as if he, too, were genuflecting. Something warmed the inside of his ear, like a woman's breath. Who came to him in this early dawn? He pleaded with her for more light. "More light, more light, please! Oh, Jesus, Jesus, no, no. I can't see them."

"What is it, soldier? You've been hit." Someone was speaking to him. "Hang on! This war cannot go on much longer. It's coming to an end. Help is coming. You can hang on. What is it you can't see, soldier?"

"I... can't... see the... dandelions."

Twenty-Nine

1946

After almost five years abroad, the Cape Breton Highlanders would see their homeland once again. The 43,000-ton *Ile de France* was crowded with soldiers on their way home. Thousands of relatives and friends cheered from a distance as they watched the big ship approach Halifax Harbour in January 1946. They had been asked to stay away from the docks and join the reunion at the Halifax Armoury, where the main events were to be held. The Cape Breton Highlanders marched off the ship at 1830 hours, to the pipes and drums of their reserve battalion. It was a Saturday. Thousands in the crowd held up banners of tartans as the soldiers called out to loved ones from the deck of the big ship. Children waited in anticipation for gifts to be handed out. Women fainted in the arms of husbands and lovers. Others danced. Brown paper bags flew in the air. Corks popped. Bouquets of flowers wilted in the cold air.

Cape Breton Island held its breath four hours later as the trains rolled along through the long, white fields, past evergreens bundled down with snow. The returned men took in deep breaths of highland air as they called out to people lining the tracks. They reached out to touch the trees. Past chiming church bells, the soldiers tilted their head dress. Children stood along the tracks in their Sunday best. They had turned snowmen into soldiers. The snow soldiers held Union Jacks in their frozen arms.

Benny and Hamish and Little Rachel stood alone, farther back. Little Rachel peeked out from under a quilt. She felt at peace under the old quilt. Big Murdock the rooster was dead. Killed under the wheels of the neighbour's tractor. Hamish waved his arms high above his head. He could sense a celebration in the air. He felt he knew every soldier on the train by the way they smiled down at him. Waved to him as friends do. Benny stood beside Hamish and played softly as a crowd of soldiers called out his name. He did not look up as the trains advanced down the tracks.

In his barn, Joachim MacPherson could hear the slicing of the trains' wheels as they chipped away at the frost on the rails. Like the opening and closing of a winter grave. He did not look forward to this day. He intended to spend it working. Anything to keep busy. His hands trembled as he worked on the carving his wife had asked him to make for Hamish's birthday. She had insisted on a horse. He knew why. Didn't bother to argue. He would do whatever he could to please her. What difference would it make to the boy? A horse or a hen, the boy could not distinguish between the things that were given to him. Everything was a gift to him.

Joachim had abandoned the idea of whittling a horse that would fit on a shelf. He had cut down two large pines and planed them into blocks. He would need two blocks for the head and neck, and a large block for the body and the legs. By the time the trains passed, he had carved out the wild, sightless eyes of the horse. He blew bits of dust out of them. The large head cocked arrogantly. The nostrils flared. Its muscled body rippled under Joachim's touch.

He had made a roaring fire in the pot-bellied stove and stood now and watched the orange flames like stray bullets fire off their energy into the open air.

His wife, Ona, lay fully dressed on her son's bed, trying to remember what she and Calum had spoken about the last time they shared words. A strand of hair had fallen across her eye, and Calum had tucked it back into place. He seemed to know where everything fit in her life. He'd warmed her hands in his as they stood on the front step. He told her he felt he was doing the right thing. That he would be back. Everything would go well for him and his friends. They could rely on each other, no matter what. A light rain whispered through her hair. Her emotions were open to him. Had always been. She had not given him any warnings. She would provide all the safety he'd need just by loving him. That's what mothers did, she believed. That's why her beloved Hamish always returned unharmed when she let him roam freely through Beinn Barra. Perhaps if she had said something, asked him to stay home and go on to college, offered up some form of alert, he would have heeded her. "Remember to be careful" seemed a frivolous statement to make to someone going off to war.

Ona stood up, slipped into her warm coat, wrapped a scarf around her shoulders, and walked slowly towards the barn. Light snow curled at her feet like unravelled socks. Nothing on this day would relieve her pain.

Through a split in the shingles, the eyes of the wooden horse stared out at her. The animal looked alive. There was a gentleness in its eyes that lit little points of fire in her blood. Her husband turned the horse and placed its white mane, fashioned from the hair of their old mare Thunder, on its head. The large horse, with its magnificent mane, stood beside the roaring fire as if it were waiting for a regal coach to arrive.

Ona entered the barn and stood in front of the horse. She saw the distant look in Joachim's eyes, watched him turn his back. How much smaller he had become, his clothes hanging free of his once sturdy frame. He had turned on himself and invited in a shadow.

Gunner MacDonald stood alone on the hill near his home after the trains had passed and looked down at the blue sea. Soft waves trembled out on the sand. He knew it would be one of the first places his son would visit, should he return. He remembered Hector mentioning in a letter that he had left a message in a bottle and buried it in the sand. A treasure he would dig up for old times' sake when he returned.

Gunner now read the paper carefully and listened attentively to the overseas newscasts. The Americans had freed hundreds of prisoners of war in Germany. Many of the POWs had been flown to Brussels and France, and then on to England. But he had received no official word as yet that Hector was among them. He had been notified that several of the prisoners were Canadians, but that no names would be officially released until such time as the regiments and documentation were cleared. Hector had been a prisoner of war for thirteen months. In all this time, Gunner had received two postcards from Stalag 7A, in Moosberg, the largest of the POW camps in Germany.

In one card, Hector mentioned getting parcels from the Red Cross that were shared among the men. Gunner went up to his room and took out all the old letters he had received from his son. He had filed them by year. He reread a letter from the summer of 1942, while the troops were still in England.

Hector described a fight that had broken out in Aldershot between the Cape Breton Highlanders and the New Brunswick Hussars, an armoured regiment that had trained with the Highlanders at Camp Borden in New Brunswick. It started with two men, then the Hussars, some of them half-dressed, came over the walls of their ancient barracks, and the Highlanders joined the battle, knuckles up.

"She was fierce," Hector wrote.

We were going at it like hungry dogs on a sweet bone. MacPherson was beside me with a Hussar in a headlock. Then we looked up and saw Doucet in the crowd of people watching the fight. He had positioned himself on some makeshift stand and proceeded to rosin the bow of the old fiddle he'd brought along with him to Europe. I thought Doucet must be planning to poke a few eyes out. Why else would he bring his fiddle and bow to a brawl?

The fight kept getting meaner, then we spied the Provost Corps and the regional police trying to get her stopped. But the boys kept fighting. And then, through the crowd, comes the sweetest music you'd ever hear. There was a lull, and then half-naked men, bleeding from fist wounds, began to smile. Spectators clapped their hands. Someone behind me alerted me to the lieutenant colonel watching from the sidelines. Sure enough, there he was, with his shiny black boot tapping like a tomcat at a door trying to get in out of the rain. Someone spoke to him, but he brushed them aside. He was entranced by Doucet and his fiddle. All he could do was watch the swift and killer strokes of Benny Doucet on that old fiddle.

Nobody moved. Then I heard the shuffling of feet, and in jig time every torn and haggard man was dancing up a storm. It became a competition between dancers, and let me tell you, I let loose and joined the pack. We danced the rags off our backs. And Benny kept playing. When she was all over, the boys picked up their bloody rags and shook hands with their neighbours. We've been the best of buddies ever since.

The lieutenant colonel asked for the name of the great fiddle player. Then he posted this in the mess hall: "In a time of aggravation, common men living under uncommon conditions, due primarily one supposes to an overabundance of fog, crumpets, and blackouts, a Cape Breton soldier stood above the ranks to tame the savage beast of war with the greatest music one could ever hope to hear."

Love,

Ona left the barn and returned to the house alone. She had not read any of Calum's letters for a few days. She had circled the date on each envelope as it arrived. The final letter was postmarked in March. She held it in her hand a long time before she put it back and picked up a letter Calum had written while in Scotland, on a training mission. She traced each word for the warmth of Calum's hands.

Dear Folks,

I'm writing today from the Isle of Skye. I've had the pleasure of strolling along its mountains for a couple of hours. Sweet heather crawled up my boots, and I reached down and made up a bouquet to give to the first woman I met. The dear soul was in her seventies. She grinned flirtatiously and thanked me kindly. "Are ya still practising, lad?" she joked. "Ya ought to be careful, handsome like ya are, who ya pass the bouquet to, with me being a widow for years and me soul a clean slate and all, and waiting to scribble something on it at the wink of an eye." She was gone before I got her name, but she did tell me she was from Glasgow, visiting relatives here in Skye.

Ona did not realize that she was reading the letter out loud, nor that her husband had entered the house and was listening beside the bedroom door. She did not hear him leave or witness his closed fist strike the side of the house in one swift blow. She thought what she heard was Hamish banging along the side of the shingles. But there was no one to be seen when she looked out the bedroom window to call Hamish into the house.

Ona held her hand to her throat when she saw the spots of blood in the snow leading towards the barn. She dropped the letter and ran out to look for Hamish.

"Hamish, Hamish, are you in there?" She could hear the fear in her voice as she half ran towards the barn.

There was no reply as she swung open the barn door and stepped inside a wave of heat. The pot-bellied stove was a red ball of hell on four legs. The majestic head of the horse was turned in her direction. Looking directly at her with its wild eyes. Its mane ruffled as if it had made an attempt to flee and was stopped in its tracks. She could not see her husband, crouched down in the corner of the barn, weeping into his own blood.

The trains finally arrived in Sydney, where five thousand Cape Bretoners filled Dodd and Richie Streets and the area surrounding the CNR station. The pipes played as the soldiers stepped onto Cape Breton soil once again and strangers kissed the faces of the returning warriors. Mothers held their sons. Small children were lifted up into the arms of strange men, whom they were told to call "Daddy." In bright-coloured hats and muffs, wives and girlfriends were rounded up in a circle of public embrace. A group of men clicked bottles they slid out of their coat pockets and christened the air with moonshine. It fell like a shower of welcome rain over the crowd.

A week later, on the northern tip of the island, Beinn Barra was quiet. Snow in the fields and on the roads stilled the sounds of running schoolchildren and trailing dogs. They leapt into the snowbanks and reclaimed their Union Jacks from the frozen snow people. The church bells grew silent.

Gunner listened to the kitchen noises as he planned his day. The clock struck out eight rusty gongs. The log on the fire crackled and spit cinders into the grate. The porridge thickened in the pot, fat bubbles bursting in the air. The kettle hummed and sighed when he moved it to the back of the stove. Gunner did not hear the truck driving down his shovelled lane. Nor did he hear the man approach his door and knock quietly, not until the third rap. Gunner knew the young veteran who stood at his door, who asked if he should stay while Gunner read the letter.

"No, thank you," he replied politely.

Gunner opened the letter. He could hear the porridge bubbles exploding in the pot. The message was brief: Private Hector Neil MacDonald had been freed from Stalag 7A and flown to London, England.

"Due to the thousands of rescued prisoners and the varying degrees of their conditions at such time, many of them without any identification, we regret the delay in informing you of his release. After due medical treatment, Private MacDonald will be returned to Canada in the coming weeks."

Thirty

1946

TWO MONTHS AFTER THE TROOPS arrived back in Cape Breton, Gunner looked out his kitchen window and saw a lone figure on the road, watched it pass the graveyard and look in. Private Hector MacDonald was dressed in full uniform. An army duffle bag was slung over his shoulder. His emancipated body angled awkwardly. Hector collapsed into his father's arms when Gunner ran out to greet him.

Gunner asked that no one come to visit his son. There were no war conversations in the quiet house that kept a lamp burning throughout the night.

Hector travelled the rooms of the house like a stranger, studying pictures on the mantle, on the walls. His mother's face looked down on him as he stroked a note or two on the old piano and listened for the echo. His father's house was immaculate. Even the dead were dust-free. Hector watched outdoor shadows climb the walls. He studied them, looked for familiar shapes, the barrel of a rifle, the blade of a bayonet, the approach of the guards. He stayed in his own room for weeks, eating his small meals and looking down over the graveyard. He had no idea where Calum was buried in Europe. He didn't want to ask.

From his upstairs window, Hector watched Cassie MacGregor roam through the graveyard, a prisoner of light snow, moving like a speckled bird, now stilled by the magnificent silence that was spread over a pure white cemetery. In the Stalag, he and other prisoners had been driven to work on a farm near the camp. Along the route, Hector had watched one old woman, day after day, circle a grave in an unkempt cemetery. One hand on the tombstone, around and around she went, like the second hand on a clock. She was always alone, a shawl slung over her shoulders as if she'd left her house in a hurry. Then one day she was gone. She never appeared again. Now Cassie's daughter appeared, pulled her mother by the coat sleeve, and led her away.

Hector rarely visited the window that faced the road where Hamish and Benny passed.

Twenty-seven years old, Hector MacDonald looked out at the world from the upstairs hall window in his father's house on the cliff. He could see the frozen pond that had kept their winter games alive when he and his friends were kids. They held bobskate races and hockey games. And snowball fights, when boys from further along the mountain laid claim to their pond. Innocent battles, snow for ammunition.

The pond was empty today. The snow fighters had gone. Calum and Alex were dead, and Benny, the best snow ammunition maker of them all, roamed somewhere in between.

In MacSween's General Store and at the post office they inquired about Hector.

"Thank you for your concern," Gunner would reply politely. "Hector is resting."

"I don't think he wants anybody around, if you ask me," said one of the widows after Gunner left the post office. "Poor Hector is probably as crazy as Benny. Jesus knows, he might be dancing around, thinking he's Fred Astaire. That Hector could dance, you know that as well as me."

"The war never made anybody sane," another of the concerned widows stated.

"What war were you in?" one man asked. "That man has been to hell and back, and he should be left alone. It's going to take time, after what he's been through, for him to see the light of day."

The next morning, Gunner heard a slight tapping at his kitchen door. Believing it was the wind, he ignored it. Hearing it again, he went to the door and looked down at a smiling Hamish, who stood on the step with a crooked twig and two beer caps in his hand. Hamish was alone except for Little Rachel, who was snugged up under a quilt in her wagon. Gunner invited Hamish in, sat him by the fire to warm him.

"What brings you here, Hamish?" he inquired.

"Me knows you house."

"Where's your friend, Benny?"

"Him sick, him can't play."

"That's too bad," said Gunner, as he made a pot of tea for his visitor.

Hector stood at the top of the stairs and listened to their conversation. He descended the stairs quietly and stood by the kitchen door, out of Hamish's sight. Gunner noticed Hector, could see by the look on his son's face that he was happy Hamish had come to visit. Hector listened to Hamish's voice teetering on the edge of broken vowels coming through an ever-present smile. Hamish was eating molasses cookies and talking about a horse. Finally, Hector walked into the kitchen and faced Hamish for the first time since he'd left for overseas.

Hamish jumped to his feet and shook Hector's hand. "How you, Tor? Me got you present."

Hector wrapped his long, thin arms around Hamish and held him.

"Here you present, Tor," said Hamish, handing Hector the twig.

"This is quite a present, my friend. What is it?"

"That a bird."

"A bird," repeated Hector. Gunner smiled for the first time in months at the twig in Hector's hand. A long twig, with two small limbs on each side for wings.

"What kind of bird would you call this?" asked Hector.

"That a gull. Him like you."

"I like him too," said Hector. "I'll take good care of him. Thank you for the gull."

"Me got present for you," Hamish said to Gunner, and put the two beer caps in Gunner's hand.

"Thank you, Hamish. This is a good present. Were you down at the shore today?"

"Yeah, me see gull. Them fly by the boat."

"You didn't go on the breakwater, did you?" Gunner quizzed.

Hamish smiled and reached for another molasses cookie. "No, me not go there. Me not allowed."

"Good for you, Hamish."

"Me go home now," said Hamish, when he finished his tea. He shook hands with Hector and Gunner, and put two more molasses cookies into his pocket.

Hector stood in the kitchen window and watched Hamish, with Little Rachel, walk down the lane to the road.

"I never noticed before how much he and Calum smiled alike," Hector said.

Gunner watched as Hector disappeared up the stairs with the twig. It was the first time Hector had made reference to any of his friends since his return.

A grey sky filled Hector's bedroom window. He sat the gull on the window ledge and pulled up a chair. The stick gull sat on the ledge as if it waited to be named, to be acknowledged as something so important it could make a grown man cry. Hector held his head in his hands. He felt it was about to explode and he had to hold it together. His father knew for whom he wept, of course. Gunner always knew. His father was a wise man, a brilliant man. Hector wondered for whom his father had wept when he returned home from the first big war. He would ask him someday, between his beer caps and a batch of molasses cookies.

Hector carefully picked up the gull and named it "Someday." He placed Someday back on the ledge and watched as Cassie MacGregor appeared on the hill crest and stood as if she were waiting for someone.

A few weeks later, Gunner was busy on the back porch when he heard a rap at the kitchen door. Hector was sleeping in his room. Gunner went to the door, expecting Hamish. Instead, he stood face to face with the three widows. And a plate of fudge.

"We hope we are not intruding, but we thought you and Hector might like a taste of fudge," said the eldest. The other two looked over Gunner's shoulder for any sign of Hector.

"Please step in for a minute," said Gunner, thanking them. "I'm rather busy with my chores, but we can always spare a minute for kindness."

The widows sat together on the kitchen lounge, their eyes wide as saucers. "You do keep a clean house, I must say," offered the youngest.

"Yes, indeed," echoed the other two, eying the corners of the kitchen and the shelves for dust.

Gunner knew what they had come to see, and waited for one of them to inquire. Hector was awake now, listening at the top of the stairs. He had heard the rap on the door and had also assumed it was Hamish again.

"We hope Hector is doing well," two of them said, almost together. They looked at Gunner, hoping they had not overstepped their boundaries.

"Stay low, Calum, stay low!" They all heard it. Hector's voice ricocheted down the stairs and fell like a stone at their feet. The widows were up at once, tripping towards the door. They did not understand the intensity of a flashback. They spoke not one word until they reached the end of the lane, puffed and winded.

"I told you he was foolish, even crazier than poor Benny, who doesn't talk," cried the oldest.

"It's the war that's got him like that," said the youngest. "Keeps them ready to fight, with nothing on their minds but war."

They shook their heads as they retraced their steps along the road, hoping to mercy that no one in Beinn Barra had seen them try to sweeten the pitiful lives of the MacDonalds with kindness and fudge.

Thirty-One

1946

Joachim MacPherson kept the white wooden horse in the barn, under a cover, before he stabled it in the corner of the boy's bedroom, at the foot of the bed. Any bigger, he thought, and he would not be able to get the thing up the stairs without removing its legs.

"A little horse that fit on a shelf would have been just fine, Joachim," said his wife, but she smiled with pleasure and patted the mane of the great beast in admiration. "I know Hamish is going to love his horse."

Joachim did not comment. He knew she was acknowledging the work he had put into making the horse. The long, late hours in the barn. The miles he travelled to get the enamel paint. She wanted to fulfill the boy's wish for a white horse. Joachim did not tell Ona why he had made the horse so fine and grand. That he was fulfilling his own wish, a wish for Calum.

What difference would it make to the boy? He didn't understand where his brother had gone, or why he would never return. He had stopped talking about the horse when Benny came back. He would go for months without mentioning Calum's name.

Joachim stood back and looked at the animal when Ona left the room. It looked as if it would gallop on command. Its eyes seemed to follow him. To question him here in the boy's room, as they had in the barn.

"For whom did you create me, for Calum or the boy? What purpose am I to serve in your life?"

Joachim had never thought about how the boy would react to the horse. It would be the same way he reacted to anything. He loved everything, without judgement. Why couldn't Calum have promised him a whistle or a ball?

Ona had opened the window before she left the room. The spring wind from the northwest seeped in through the curtain, ran headlong into the horse's mane, causing it to stir. The horse bowed its head majestically. A light dust rose up from under its feet, like soft mist to join the wind. The horse frolicked.

Joachim slumped beside the bed and watched the performance. The head dipped, the mane fluttered, the tail swished. And yet the eyes would not let him go. They looked into his with mysterious defiance. Joachim stared past the eyes at the long, elegant neck, the sturdy flanks, the curved hoofs. There were no imperfections. This was as flawless a specimen as any man could create. He bowed his head and remembered Calum's tall sturdy frame in his uniform. The swiftness of his feet on parade. Like dancing steps falling into place. Left, right. Left, right. The alert eyes.

He looked up. The animal's eyes continued to question him. To stare through his bones. To hurt him. For what, admiring his son? He wanted to tear it apart with his bare hands. What right did it have to anger him so? He had done what was requested of him. What he thought Calum would have wanted. What else did this animal require from him? His wife was happy with the horse. The boy would be happy. Why did he have to feel so threatened by something so inanimate?

He rose to his feet when he heard Ona coming up the stairs with Hamish.

The wind had died down, and the horse stood still, as if it understood that its owner was approaching. Hamish stopped inside the door and looked at the beautiful wooden horse. He did not speak as he approached it. He ran his chubby fingers through its mane. He felt the smooth ripples on its back. Let his fingers get lost in the long tail.

Joachim and his wife looked at each other, puzzled. They had never seen Hamish speechless. Hamish walked in front of the horse and looked into its gentle eyes. Then his face cracked into a slice of sunlight. That's when the wind returned and the horse came to life again. It galloped. It flung its mane. It swatted its tail as if shooing away a fly.

Hamish heard his mother's voice, but he did not turn to look at her. He was applauding the horse's performance. Patting its rocking head. He nuzzled his face into the flying mane. He wrapped his arms around its thick neck and kissed it softly. The horse stopped rocking as its head came to rest on Hamish's shoulder.

Hamish stumbled awkwardly to the open window and looked out as if watching for someone. His arms rose in the air like those of a drunken preacher. He waved them frantically in the open window and cried out in a voice they rarely heard, a voice like that of a bewildered animal. His head turned from side to side. He beckoned with a closed hand. Begging the earth below him, the sky above him, the gate to his right to open up and let someone in. It wasn't until he turned and faced his mother that she knew he was crying.

Thirty-Two

1946

It was addressed to her. Ona held the brown envelope tightly in her hand as she walked home. Hamish was speaking Gaelic to Little Rachel, believing that the hen understood. She turned and spoke gently to her son. "*Bidh sambach*. Hamish, be quiet!" She needed to keep her mind clear.

She let her hand feel the contents of the envelope. It confirmed what she already knew. She gave the envelope to her husband when she entered the kitchen. He slid a sharp knife under the flap, as if he were gutting a fish. A small black leather case with a gold crown on the lid spilled out onto the kitchen table. Inside was the Silver Cross on a thin purple silk ribbon. And something else, attached to a blue card: the Birk's Memorial Bar, engraved with his name, regimental number, and date of death. Joachim left them on the table and walked away.

Ona collected the contents of the envelope and tucked them into the trunk in Calum's bedroom. Except for the Silver Cross, which she slipped into her pocket. She would place it around the horse's neck, she thought, as a special tribute to Calum. She removed a scrapbook. The photo of Calum, Hector, and Benny that appeared in the newspaper when they left had taken on a yellow tinge, an afterglow. She ran her open palm lightly over his letters, over his silent voice, over the names she had heard him speak. She read with interest his last letter home. It had arrived after his death. She had not opened this letter for months. The war was coming to an end when he wrote it. The troops were on their final mission, the Liberation of Holland.

She and Joachim had cautiously allowed little slivers of hope into their lives then. Touched each other differently. All day running into each other like blind bats against a house. One touch. Then another. One kiss. Then another. Till finally, with Hamish sleeping, they came together as wild as swirling snow. Laughing afterwards, as if they had escaped an avalanche. Had outpowered it by their strength and love for each other. By the hope that the world was ready to settle down.

"I've knit Calum a sweater," she told him that night.

"I'm sure he's lost a lot of weight."

"I'll fatten him into it," she said.

"I know you will." Joachim said, then added, "Things will be different for him, you know, with Hector still missing. And I doubt Benny will make many connections."

"He was very close to Alex," she said. "He'll have another battlefield to contend with there."

Now, she unfolded the last letter they had received from Calum and began to read it out loud.

Dear Family,

I can write with great certainty that all arms are ready to fall. Things are coming to an end, so we are told in this month of May where many of the flowers are in full bloom. I will leave with much sorrow, knowing that those who cannot return with me have paid the supreme price for their graves here in Europe. I keep the faith that Hector will be freed and will return home. You wouldn't believe the welcome the Highlanders received. These people were seeing Canadian soldiers for the first time. They were ecstatic. People filled the streets. Girls in red, white, and blue dresses. Most people wore a bit of orange for the royal family.

I watched as Dutch women who were reported to have had relations with German soldiers had their hair chopped off and were belted around by the other women. Dutch traitors, on their hands and knees, were marched down the main street to jail, where they were shot to death. Men and women paraded along the street, singing their national anthem over and over again. I stood among the crowd and finally understood why we were here. Happiness does not come without a price. I miss Hamish terribly. I know he will be my salvation. He understands life on a different plateau.

One I could never hope to reach. Keep the home fires burning until we meet again.

Love,

Calum

How foolish, how naive she had been to believe that the guns were empty. That all arms had been laid to rest on the breast of history. They had been so sure he could make it through those final weeks in Holland. *Who is tending his grave?* she wondered.

Ona looked around the downstairs room that had been Calum's bedroom. At the ceiling she had painted for his return. At the new quilt covering his bed. At the rug with four galloping white horses. She aired it out once a week to keep it fresh. She'd decided to leave it where it had stood for so many years. Where it rightfully belonged. He had grown up on this rug. Played on it. The room was energized with little comfort zones that she had claimed for her own. She smiled as she read his acceptance letter from Dalhousie University. She polished the picture of Babe Ruth. The picture of Calum and Hamish on that Sunday afternoon when all was right with the world. She could not put space between then and now. Except to claim it. This space was hers.

Joachim had not set foot in this room until eight months after Calum's death. He came to the doorway that day and looked in at her. Held his distance like a child scared there might be something under the bed. She asked him for a cup of weak tea, but someone else delivered it.

On Calum's last night home, a week before he sailed for Europe, she had tiptoed in to watch him sleep. She stood on the rug and looked down at him for a long time. He slept soundlessly, like a newborn. Hands folded on his chest. Had he known, figured it out already, that the mind was at times the noisiest place to be? Perhaps she knew then. Had been given clues. How many times had she met Gunner MacDonald and saw what was in his eyes? There is no room for hope behind a round of fire.

"Do you think they'll be home soon?" she had asked Gunner one day at the store.

"When everything is exhausted, Mrs. MacPherson. One side will have to surrender sooner or later. They are fighting for surrender now," he said. He had a way of staring at people directly when he spoke, this quiet man who kept his emotions to himself. She watched his face cloud over with concern. Or was it anger? She could see that he didn't want to alarm her. Whatever was on his mind didn't make it to his tongue. She watched his hand move slowly to his hat as he bid her good day.

"You must come over for dinner sometime," Ona said, but she wasn't sure whether he heard her.

She watched Gunner walk down towards the sea. The wind changed directions and unravelled the man into scraps of cloth. His coat flew open and clung to his back like a cape. His scarf flew from his neck and sailed in the wind like a kite. He made no effort to button his coat or retrieve his scarf. A ragged form of still life, he stood quietly, looking out over the sea. Above his head, a flock of eagles navigated in a circle, calling out to each other as if in alarm.

Thirty-Three

1947

Ona had no memory of the diary entry she was now reading, two years after Calum's death. It was her handwriting, she was sure of that, although it was not her best penmanship. Some of the letters were scrawled, not fully formed:

Monday, May 5/45

From under the wing of the white sheet being hung to dry, I watched the old priest walk through the gate. His fedora was angled to shade the sun from his eyes. He walked slowly through the wildflowers to the back porch door. In his right hand he carried the telegram. How neatly folded your death came to us, Calum, slipping in through the screen door.

She closed the diary and sat down in the chair near the window, stretching her feet out in front of her. A small cluster of veins nested along her ankles. The cluster on her right ankle resembled a daisy. She could not remember the last time she had identified what marked her as a woman.

Some people believed she kept her hair black from a bottle. But at forty-seven years of age, she had not greyed, not even around the edges. There was something new in her eyes. Sometimes she looked at the emptiness when she brushed her hair, and it stared back at her. Emptiness could stare outside in.

Naked in front of the full-length mirror, she saw other changes. She was surprised that her stretch marks had receded to white lines. They'd once been blue. Now they were thin waves that rippled when she stirred her skin with her hand. Motherhood was always in motion, she thought. A stamp of approval on the skin. She smiled at what comfort she would carry for the rest of her life.

She did not bother to dress. She was in no hurry to cover up her new comforts. She added an entry to the diary.

June 1947

My beloved Hamish on this day of blue patched skies and shifting winds has set out to rescue what was strewn about in last night's storm. He is collecting the sea's ruins and placing them gently in his wagon beside Little Rachel. His friend Benny has joined him. Dear, wounded Benny. I would love to hear what he and Hamish can hear. Hector has not made a public appearance as yet. I know how painful it must be for him. But it is a joy to have him back here in Beinn Barra, especially for his father. He still has to visit Camp Hill for treatment, but Gunner says he can see signs of hope in his eyes. If only I could collect the fallen and give them wings.

Still naked, she noticed a shadow dance along the back wall of the house, dance along the shingles as she moved closer to the window. She watched it perform through the lace curtains.

While the dog barked to interrupt it, it danced. When the hens clucked at a distance, it danced. As the dandelions bowed their heads in shame, it danced. And while she stood there and watched, it called out her name. But she did not answer. Just watched it explode into the white rain. The wind carried two drops and placed them on the blue window ledge. They landed softly before slipping over the edge, down into the purple hearts of the irises below the window.

She watched her husband walk away from the side of the house towards the barn, the limp in his right foot pronounced. She had noticed it more lately. The extra burden he carried around. The way his shoulders dove into his chest for support. Even her name seemed heavier on his tongue. She had just watched him pleasure himself in the open wind, and yet she could not go to him and tell him that she remembered only parts of him. That behind the emptiness Calum was there. He was inside her. Body and soul. She could feel him move. His laugh. His voice. Sometimes he fooled her by laughing out loud. In his father's voice. Or in Hamish's laugh. Once, she heard him call her by name. She didn't answer, so he called out to her again. She had to answer him to quiet him down. To hear him laugh again. It was the laugh she waited for. Sometimes it would take her from sleep, and she had to stifle it with a pillow to stop it from running through the house. Once contained, it settled into a mellow hush under the quilt, like a butterfly trapped in a jar.

"How do you expect me to make love to you, Joachim?" Her voice was anguished. "With Calum so near, so near I can feel his hand tracing daisies on my ankles. And sweet Hamish brings me wildflowers. My sons have left marks on my skin to comfort me."

On her bad days, she could not remember his laugh at all. She had to go listening for it. Down by the old school. At the sawmill, among the dead curls of wood. In the back fields, where the blueberries flaunted their naked skin in the grass. Beside the sea. Under a fresh snowfall. She listened intently. It sprang from the arms of the pines and curled around the limbs of the evergreens. Side-swiped the white maples. The branches trembled with appreciation, casting off the last of winter's snow in cascades of blue-white confetti. How softly it had echoed when it came through the thick bush this spring. Like a whisper, getting smaller lately.

Ona dressed quickly and walked out the screen door. She could see Hamish and Benny down near the wharf as she walked to the side of the house where her husband had been. How lonely Joachim must feel. How abandoned. She realized that this was not how Calum would want to be remembered, his mother in one room downstairs with her memories, and his father in another upstairs with his.

She had not paid much attention to colour in years. The colour of skies, the rainbows in quilts, Christmas candies, ribbons in girls' hair, vegetables uncut from the cord of mother earth, the colour of shame on the skin, but now she could not help but notice the bold dance of colour where she stood. The red tulips waltzing cheek to cheek with the yellow daffodils. A golden spectacle of dandelions coming between them, as if to cut in. And at their feet, the yellow and purple irises, unable to dance because they had been burdened in the heart.

She returned to Calum's room and lay on the bed. She tried to justify her visit to that side of the house. What had made her get up and go? Did she want Joachim to know she had seen him, had witnessed what he left behind?

A slow fire burned in her throat. She looked in the mirror to check its colour. Orange blossom. A pink blush clung to her face. Almost red. It toasted her dimples. She looked at the green in her eyes. Evergreen. At the darkness of her hair. Night black. The whiteness of her teeth. Pillow white. She coloured herself like a child with a new box of crayons. A splash here, a smear there. She would pull out a red crayon to colour her mouth. Red. Yes. Apple red, that would do.

Joachim stood near the open barn door and looked out towards the house. He watched Ona emerge through the screen door and walk up to her flower bed like someone being escorted by the hand of grief. He had planned another trip to Halifax early the next morning. As he watched his wife reach down to pick up a broken flower, he knew it would be his last trip without her at his side.

Thirty-Four

1947

“Bless me, ather, for I have sinned. I spied on my naked wife through lace curtains.”

Joachim listened as the parish priest in St. Mary’s Basilica in Halifax cleared his throat and shifted uneasily in the confessional.

“Why do you call it spying? She is your wife, is she not?” The priest’s voice was demanding.

“Yes, she’s my wife, but we don’t sleep together any more.”

“Was that your idea?”

“No, she moved into our son’s room when we got the news of his death. He was killed in action in Holland.”

“So, she has been in his room for almost two years.”

“Yes, Father.”

“Has she received any help? She is obviously suffering a deep depression with this loss.”

"The doctor has been to see her a few times. He says it will take time. She is taking the medicine."

"Do you think that spying on her will help her in her depression?" The priest's voice had a sermon edge now.

"No, I don't suppose it will."

"Does she know that you are, so-called, spying on her?"

"I'm not sure, she hasn't mentioned it. You'd have to know my wife."

There was a long pause before the priest spoke again. His voice was critical. "In my profession, I try not to have any interaction with any man's wife, but it is your duty to stand by your wife in sickness and in health. Have you forgotten your marriage vows? They were not written to fill up space. They are a critical part of church doctrine."

"I try. I do what I can." Joachim felt like a child pleading for forgiveness for watching his mother undress.

"When was the last time you did what you refer to as spying through lace curtains?"

"Yesterday."

"What do you get out of this spying business? Many mothers have lost their sons to war. I can't imagine every husband has to succumb to lace curtains to meet his needs."

Joachim squirmed on his knees. He did not like this priest. Or his accusations. He was sorry he had bothered to enter the basilica and stretch out his wounds. He understood now why his wife refused to speak to anyone.

The dark voice spoke again. "I asked you, sir, what you get out of spying on your wife?"

"I'm not really sure, if anything at all," Joachim replied. His anger was loose now, ripping up from his bad foot and lodging between his teeth. He did not tell the priest about the look he saw in Ona's eyes. The dry loneliness. The table she still set for four. How painful it was to look at the empty plate. The times she called the boy "Calum." The times Joachim mentioned Calum's name to her. The times he pulled something from Calum's childhood and presented it to her like a gift. To let her know she was not alone in her grief.

"Remember how he would sing and dance for his brother, Ona? You would always make a candy apple for him after his recitals."

She responded with a blank stare, as if a stranger was speaking to her. He'd thought it would help. Letting her know that he had not forgotten their son. She'd always encouraged him to speak about Calum. Now it was she who went silent when he mentioned Calum's name. The only voice she responded to was the boy's.

"Self-satisfaction is a temporary thrill, sir," the priest continued. "A deadly insult to the flesh. Your body is a temple. A blueprint for the soul. Obstruct the temple and you shall see the ruins."

Silence fell between the two men. Up in the choir loft someone was singing a Latin hymn. The sound thickened as more voices joined the first. They carried a perfect pitch, these songbirds of Christ, on a mission to bring down the rafters. To warn the mischievous cherubs above the altar to be quiet in their helm. To loosen the tongues of the men on their knees. To chant away their mortal wounds. Suddenly, the singing stopped, and the priest, in an aggravated voice, asked, "For what have you come here to seek forgiveness?"

Joachim sighed deeply, and his breath caught in the sleeve of the priest's soutane. He was not sure what pardon he sought. He wanted his wife back, but he had not asked her to leave. How many ways and times had he tried to reach her? To call her back into his life, to tell her that Calum's death had made him realize how much he loved her and the boy. Made him wonder how much longer they would live like this. But he kept this to himself for another time. Another place.

"It's the flowers, Father. I seek forgiveness for breaking the flowers," choked Joachim. He rose from his knees and left the confessional. He heard the priest raise his Latin voice as he walked away. He was a man on the run, with a pardon as close as his heels.

Outside on the street, a white-hazed sun swallowed up what was left of the city breeze. A streetcar rattled by, whipping up dust the colour of toast. When it settled, Joachim noticed the man walking through the cemetery across the street. Two hands behind his back. Moving slowly, his dark shoulders jutting out above the headstones. At last he stood still, bowed his head low like a condemned man waiting for the executioner to land the blow. From behind his back, a gift of yellow and red flowers fell softly on the grave.

Near the harbour, on Water Street, a middle-aged woman in a red housecoat opened the door. "You're late," she said, passing him a key. He nodded politely and walked towards the stairs, his feet heavy and dusty. The room he entered had one window. A young woman stood there, looking at the haze over the harbour. She wore a white satin slip. One strap fell loosely over her shoulder. She turned towards Joachim and smiled, showing a crooked tooth.

Her blond hair was cut short in a saucy bob. In her blue eyes everything collided. The joy, fear, regret, pain, laughter, and dreams of women who live in satin. She looked like the young woman Calum had danced with that night, the last dance before he left.

"Calum." She greeted him by name. "I knew you would show up. That's why I waited for you."

Joachim sat on the edge of the bed and removed his shoes. Infidelity and deceit weighed on his lame foot. She sat beside him on the bed. "I knew you would return," she said, running her hand along his back.

"It was kind of you to pay for all these months, even though…" she paused. "Even though we do nothing but talk."

Joachim looked at the young woman, at her innocent interpretation of kindness.

"Do you think what I do to you is kind?"

She answered by pulling him closer and holding him. Her white slip lay on the floor like a pool of spilt milk. They moved under the sheet like kittens seeking shelter from the light and made sweet love that chased the pain from his foot, put accusations on the run, made choirs silent, and caused temples to crumble in ecstasy.

Later, when he saw in her eyes that wrinkled space that satin cannot smooth, he realized that she had fallen in love with him. He apologized and made his second confession of the day.

"Calum was my son. He was killed in action at the end of the war. My name is Joachim."

The young women listened as she pulled her white slip over her head. "How old was your son when he died?" she asked in a soft voice.

"Twenty-four."

"Does coming here keep him alive for you?"

"You remind me of the young women he probably would have married someday. You look very much alike. For months I have been trying to extend his life. But I must bury him today. He is not coming back. I have a beautiful wife and another son. I have been making excuses to get away for months now, but I know I have not fooled her. Please forgive me."

Joachim turned at the door to say goodbye. To thank her for listening. She was standing at the window, where she had been when he entered. There were white lace curtains on the window. He had not noticed them before.

"I forgive you," she said.

Thirty-Five

1947

Ona knew that her husband had left secrets in the folds of a younger women's skin. No tangible evidence could be found. No trace of fingerprints or scent of sinful cologne. No verbal confession. She knew by the look in his eyes when he returned from his monthly trips to Halifax.

There was always something he needed that only the city could supply. Something for the haymaker, something for the tiller, something for the bull's collar. Something for him. She believed he broke equipment in order to justify his monthly trips by ferry across the Canso Causeway, which linked the island to the mainland. His truck always left with something broken piled in the back and a fresh suit of clothes on the front seat. His overnight stays with an aunt, he said, were always welcomed. Yet she had never stopped loving the man. She had just stopped loving life.

The first time she made love with him after returning to their bed, she wore white socks. A practical, emotional woman, she made a mental note to return to him one limb at a time. She had been more than generous in letting her hair down and wearing a short nightgown. The other garments would fall one by one. Sock by sock.

She was not a jealous person, yet women like her do not drop their armour all at once. The truth was that she loved many things about him. Had always loved him despite her physical absence from the man. Her mind rested somewhere in his parts.

She knew the difference between women who are abandoned and woman who are left alone at their own request. She had chosen the latter and was now tired of living in pieces. She slipped out of Calum's bed one moonless midnight, walked up the stairs, and climbed back into her own bed. Her husband, pulled from sleep, sighed as her stockinged foot slumbered between his thighs. He pulled her to his side of the bed and made love to her with the urgency and clumsiness of a man rescued from infidelity.

After her husband fell asleep, she remembered. Calum had been dead for eight or nine months when Joachim began slipping into the downstairs bedroom at night. A white moon slept on the edge of her sheet the first time he entered the room and stood among the galloping white horses. When she first saw him, she was prepared to speak to a ghost. She was not afraid. Her heart smashed against her chest with joy.

"Is that you, Calum? Don't wake your father or Hamish, my love! I will give them your message," she whispered to herself. But then he moved, and she recognized the limp of her husband's foot as he walked out of the room.

When he came again, he moved quietly through the night up to the edge of the bed. A cough got rid of him. Yet he returned, again and again. Stroking her hair, her wandering curls on her pillow. She eyed him like a cat, waiting for his next move. But it was always the same, the stroking of her hair. Sometimes wrapping the curls like twine around his fingers. He never bent to kiss her. Sometimes he whispered her name. Let it roll from his tongue like a prayer. Her hair was his rescue. The softest strength he could reach in his own house.

In the mornings, they went about the kitchen like strangers.

"Did you have a good rest?" he would ask, over a cup of tea.

"Yes, and you?"

"Fair. I thought I heard something. I had to get up and check it out."

"That's too bad," she said, wishing to add, "Did it have long, dark curls?" But she would not embarrass him. Would not let him know she knew what he was doing. She understood his needs. He was her husband. In a way it was a comfort. She had begun to look forward to his dark visits. This reaching out without words. He had never been a man who could talk out his feelings.

Now she combed out her long hair to feel the warmth of his hands among the curls. How foolish she had been to turn him away. She knew now that passion and despair come from the same heart. With Calum's death, he had suffered as greatly as she, and yet she had turned from him, drove his suffering into a stranger's arms, while she basked in Hamish's love. Nothing would bring Calum back to them. They needed each other. Needed to blend their memories of their dead son. Now, in each other's embrace, it was easier to get through the bad times.

Thirty-Six

1947

Gunner MacDonald strode towards his neighbour's gate with an outstretched hand. It was early morning, and the sun rose between the two men like a small flame. Joachim could hear weariness in Gunner's voice, but the man's stance was firm and his gaze steady.

"I've been meaning to ask you and the missus over," said Gunner. "Hector enjoyed seeing Hamish again."

"I didn't know Hamish had stopped by." Joachim paused. "I hope he was no trouble."

"It was a pleasure, Joachim. Just what Hector needed. That's why I want to invite all three of you for a visit. The only thing I ask is that you not mention the war."

"It was great to see Hamish again," Hector announced when the three MacPhersons arrived the following week.

"Indeed it was," Gunner agreed.

Hector did not meet Ona or Joachim's eyes as he shook their hands. Nor did he mention Calum's name. "Little Rachel waited patiently while Hamish had his tea," he told them, his gaze still aimed at the floor.

They kept the conversation light and upbeat, for Hector's sake as well as their own. Hector, they could plainly see, was still fragile. They did not mention Alex or Benny. Hamish smiled as he forked into a piece of apple pie and patted Hector on the back.

"It will take time," Gunner said, when Hector went off to bed early. "War can make a man believe he is in the presence of a good deed, until it is all over."

The lamp in the hallway, next to Hector's bedroom door, never went out in the MacDonald home, even at night. Gunner heard the screams that night. Rushed in. Saw Hector brace himself against the head of his bed, an imaginary rifle in his hand. Watched him fill the rifle magazine with make-believe bullets. He could hear the panic in Hector's voice.

"Who goeth there?" This was a question only soldiers asked, and only on guard duty.

"It is me, your father," Gunner said in a soft voice, in the soft light.

Hector was calmed by the familiar voice. "Is it really you, Da?"

"It is me, Hector, it's really me."

"I thought it was one of them."

"They are all gone, Hector. It's just you and me."

"Will they come back?"

Gunner MacDonald was a truthful man. "I suppose they will, someday."

Gunner walked downstairs, warmed some milk, and brought it up to his son. Hector was beside the window now, crouched on his knees, his eyes level with the ledge, peering out into the dark night. Watching for any kind of movement. Listening for any kind of sound. Hector held a small object carefully in his hand, his thumb delicately placed at its centre, waiting for the right moment to pull the pin on his grenade. A note from a light breeze crept along the outer ledge of the window. Whispered itself inside with a raspy, lingering voice, then faded when Hector opened the window and threw the grenade. Hector sank to the floor and covered his ears against the sounds in his head. Someday, the gull, watched from the ledge.

Gunner returned to the kitchen after he'd settled Hector back into bed. He flipped over the next card in his game of solitaire. The old king eyed him face to face. In the dim light, Gunner thought he saw a gentleness in the king's eye. No one in Beinn Barra had witnessed such terrors, except Flora and Napoleon Doucet. They had seen it all with Benny. They would understand.

Gunner invited the Doucets for an afternoon. Hector enjoyed their visit, his eyes fixed on a pattern on the floor. Flora's voice floated above his head, sweet and careful, the voice used to speak to a frightened child. The Doucets were happy to see him and to wish him well. They chose their words wisely, and lovingly. Hector believed their good wishes, he knew these people, yet he felt he had injured them in some way, returning to Beinn Barra with full sentences and two hands that got stronger by the week. Hector did not mention any of the boys, and they were not surprised. They knew that Hector felt the pain much more than their Benny ever would.

The next morning, Hector saw three figures standing in the graveyard, the sun on their backs like a splash of yellow paint languidly dripping to the ground. Hector smiled at them through the window, at Hamish and Benny and poor Cassie MacGregor. The red wagon idled beside Hamish. Now and again, Little Rachel stood and ruffled her feathers as if she were caught in a sandstorm. This was Hector's first glimpse of Benny since Europe. Benny was much thinner. His shoulders had surrendered. His walk was weary. Hector watched Benny circle the tombstones, bend down, throw something into the air. A broken white cross from an old grave.

Cassie, meanwhile, had not moved. Her hands remained in the pockets of her old coat. Her head was bare, and the wind crawled through her hair like a snake. Hector could not move from the window. He was remembering Cassie the way she was years ago, the lupin eyes and the delicate round mouth. He and Calum would joke about her beauty when they were young boys, embarrass her son, Alex, to an alarming red, and then stop before he cried. Alex's sister, Joan, looked like their mother, but Joan was strong, like her father. Joan wouldn't cry if you set her on fire. The kids called her Joan of Arc MacGregor. Hector's mother's face came back to him. She was beautiful too, but in a different way from Cassie, who now stands with indifference to the rape of the raw wind on her skin.

Hector noticed something different about the graveyard. The old maple trees were gone. The surrender trees. Cut down, probably, by order of the old priest. "No doubt all this took place under the surrender trees," Hector remembered Father MacDonald saying before absolving him of his sins.

Now Hamish was circling behind Benny and flipping small stones into the air. Hamish picked up the wooden cross, examined it carefully, as if he were reading the name of the owner whose identity had been thrown into the air.

Hector watched them. Watched his past. Hamish and Little Rachel led the parade out of the graveyard, followed by Benny. Cassie did not follow them. She knelt now, as if looking for something she'd lost in the grass. Hamish and Benny walked past the stumps where the maples had once fluttered their leaves, the initials of the sinners who had caused their slaughter carved in their trunks.

Gunner was at the post office when Hector heard the knocking at the door and opened it to see Hamish and Benny standing side by side, Little Rachel behind them in the wagon. Hector's heart raced in his chest, knocking against things he could not name. Benny stared directly at him. He did not avoid the eye of his comrade, his friend. Hamish was telling Hector something about a crow. The hen in the wagon was quiet.

Benny's face was tanned a dusty bronze, and lines scarred his brow, running into his now greying curls. His large eyes were wild. He took deep breaths.

Hector took them into the kitchen and prepared something to eat. It gave his mind and hands something to do.

Benny would not remove his long coat, despite the heat of the kitchen. He would not be stripped of this identity. Hamish was already filling his face with tea biscuits and cookies. Benny sat as straight as a tack, his lean back braced against the back of the chair, military-style, musician-style. There were some things this man's body remembered in rhythm. He ran his stump along the wooden table. Tapped at a knot in the pine. He had not spoken. He ate slowly, studying Hector's every move, listening to Hector's every word.

The sun stroked patterns on the floor. Shot up the wall and down again like a dozen dancing mimes. Benny watched, almost amused. Hamish was still eating. A fierce bolt of sunlight streaked Benny's face. His eyes darted back and forth like shooting flames, looking for little fires of memory to ignite. He heard a voice speak to him through the sunlight.

"Benny, it's me, your friend, Hector."

Benny listened to the voice coming through the dancing speckled light. *The light is dancing on the man's face.*

"How are you, Benny?" Hector whispered.

Benny's face was quiet and hot. *The man's voice is going away. Hiding in his mouth.*

Hamish got up and grabbed a face cloth off the rack, dipped it into a bucket of cold water to wash the sweat from Benny's brow. Benny turned his drowning face towards the stove, like a swimmer turning for a breath of air. *The kettle is singing on the back of the stove. There is music in this house.*

Hector sat at the head of the table, looking at his two visitors. His heart trembled as he held the face cloth Hamish had passed to him. He watched as they ate the last of his offerings, then stared at the empty plates before them. Again, Hector spoke to Benny in a low voice.

"Benny, I'm happy you came to visit me. I'm very happy to see you again."

Benny looked towards the speaking voice, then turned back to the singing kettle. He didn't speak one word to Hector. Words did not suit him.

Hector was remembering a morning in Stalag 7A when a soldier woke him, begged him to look at his best friend. The friend lay dying, his lips sealed together like two wet spoons. "Help him. For Christ's sake, do something, Hector!" Hector could do nothing but tell the soldier that his friend should be in the compound infirmary, that he probably had pneumonia. "No," insisted the soldier. "He said he didn't want to be taken there. He wants to stay with me." The soldier pleaded with his friend to speak to him. To say something, anything. But no words came.

When Gunner returned, he saw two empty plates and two cups on the kitchen table. Hector was upstairs, sitting on the edge of his bed. In his hands, he held a white face cloth rolled into a ball. In his eyes, a quiet panic rose like a bird that had lost its direction over the deep sea. Gunner called his son's name, but got no response. He walked away softly.

Early the next morning, Hector heard footsteps on the stairs. More than one man. They took him gently by the arms, swept him off the bed. In the kitchen, his father put his coat on him, and the two returned men escorted him out to the car waiting to take him to Camp Hill hospital in Halifax. His father embraced him. Over his father's shoulder, Hector could hear the kettle singing.

Thirty-Seven

1947

Ona MacPherson lay crossways on the fresh white sheet.

It had never before occurred to her to do something like this. To let dust settle in the corners of their bedroom, leave unwashed laundry on the floor in a pile, ignore the ironing in the basket near the door, and stretch full-length on her unfinished bed. She felt at peace.

There had been no snow to speak of this fall in Beinn Barra. The mountains were green, and the cattle still grazed on brown grass, now and again raising their heads as if searching for a green patch. She'd watched them through the window, and watched Hamish and Benny down by the sea, before she began to change the bed. A few fishermen were patching and nailing down the hatches for the coming winter.

She grinnedat the thought of the widows looking in at this domestic chaos. The widows could not stand disorder in other people. Sloshed, they would accuse, and with that dear boy and crippled husband of hers to look after. The woman is as full as a stuffed peacock. Scandalous. Can't even make a bed without inviting herself into it. Even with grief's teeth biting into the skin, she should be able to control a broom and a bit of dust. Work will set you free. It's the only way to mend a broken heart.

Men don't last in their prime forever, she'd heard the widows preach often enough at the post office, glancing over their shoulders at the younger women present. You can't varnish them like a pole fence to keep them from decaying. It's his knees that go first, then the hips follow, and the rest of him is as dead as an old sock in no time.

She was smiling in her sleep when Joachim came into the room. Her hair undone, lying like a rope down over her shoulder. He was reluctant to spread a blanket for fear of waking her, so he pulled a light sheet up over her instead. Her hands edged the sheet like ruffled lace. He wanted to bend down and kiss her forehead. But he did not take the chance with his foot acting up. He might have stumbled and broken into her dream.

She had settled for dreams, now that the nightmares were fewer and farther between. It was a relief to watch her limbs respond to something good remembered. Joachim pulled up a chair beside the bed. He could idle awhile. His chores had been completed until evening. Hamish and Benny were still down at the shore, with the fishermen, searching in old lobster traps and broken nets and under the wharf. The fishermen smiled. "Nothing yet?" they called out, as if they, too, were part of the search.

Joachim would have to prepare the runners for the red wagon, get them waxed for the coming snow. The old hen would know the difference, he mused. He had spoken with his neighbour earlier in the morning. Hector had been in hospital for almost two months, but was doing much better and should be back home soon. This was as much as the man would offer. He understood what only time could unravel. There were no knots in Gunner MacDonald's spine.

The Doucets, too, were from strong stock. They'd accepted their loss with quiet dignity. A man hidden from music, or the music hidden from the man, it made no difference. They knew they would never again hear a single note from him.

A dark shadow crept over the western corner of the house. Joachim moved quietly to the window and looked down at Cassie MacGregor. He held up his hand in a friendly gesture, but she did not respond. She bent down, searching for something in the brown grass. Why had she ventured so close to their house? She had not visited their property since the news of Calum's death had arrived. She had stood at the edge of the back field, but would not come any closer. Whom did she want to see? He got up and went down to the back door to speak with her, to invite her in for a cup of hot tea, although he knew she would not enter any door except her own, had not for some time now. When he opened the door, she was gone. Joachim could see Hamish and Benny down at the shore with the fishermen, but there was no sign of Cassie.

In the rustle of a tree branch he thought he saw a hand moving. If Cassie was there in the branches, she was still very close to their house. He watched for a minute, but nothing stirred. Joachim went into the yard and looked towards the graveyard. She was not there. He shook his head. Perhaps he had imagined her. He went back into the house, poured himself a cup of tea, made a fresh pot for Ona when she woke.

Joachim looked around the large kitchen. Grand varnished pine planks stretched across the floor like narrow trails in the woods, hidden here and there by Ona's braided rugs. Oak wainscotting ran along the walls, met up with delicate wallpaper of gold and green. Ona had insisted on making the changes after Calum's death. She had not stopped working. Making new quilts, curtains, braided rugs. Preserving jams and pickles. The root cellar was full, and as colourful as a summer garden. She made woollen socks and mitts for the fishermen, and was rewarded with buckets of mackerel, a crate of dried cod. Yet she could not remember the colour of things. "I believe they were blue," she'd say of the mitts. "No, I'm wrong, they were grey. Do you not remember, Joachim?"

Joachim returned to their bedroom and sat once again beside the bed. He had not seen Ona sleep in the daytime in many years. Not since the birth of their sons. He had heard her singing the other day, not to the boy, but for her own pleasure.

He looked down at his aching foot. Could it have been the reason Calum had gone to war, to let his father know that this family could do as others did? Had he stood with his youthful strength to represent his father? No. No, Calum had his own will, his own strengths. He had made his own decision, Joachim reasoned. He must be reasonable now, with his wife singing again and tossing smiles from her dreams. He felt a gaiety, the elation that comes over a man the first time he tells a women that he loves her. He was about to get up and put more wood on the fire when he felt Ona's hand on his knee.

"Your knees, Joachim, how are your knees?"

For a moment he thought she was dreaming out loud.

"And what about your hips?"

"My knees, my hips, why do you ask, Ona? They are not giving me any trouble."

"Good," she laughed.

Thirty-Eight

1947

Something moved boldly between two blades of October grass. Hamish clapped his hands excitedly as he watched the grass swell and fold, squirm and wiggle. Playing a game with him. A mysterious game that kept him moving. His eyes a merriment of delight and wonder at the secret in the grass that suddenly reared its head. Hamish smiled down at a garter snake. Little Rachel clucked and dipped her beak under the quilt.

"Gonna find the fiddle," Benny said. He stopped and listened to the sounds of the Salmon River, close by. It cooed as it echoed up the brown banks. No one stood fishing from the river today.

"Me can't find it, Enny. Fiddle not here." Hamish scared off two rabbits as he dug up old branches.

The two adventurers were on their own. Straying farther than either had ventured before. They had been in the back woods of the old MacGuspic property. Searching the rusting sawmill. Clearing branches. Uprooting dead twigs. Benny stopped off at Rory's old shack at the edge of the clearing. He entered through the open door and stood on an old piece of floor covering, its pattern worn down into the floorboards, creating a scribbled effect. A slight breeze followed him in and hummed around his head. It sprayed the walls with a dark melody. A light from the open door illuminated a carpenter's hammer leaning against the wall. The hammer felt light in Benny's hand as he picked it up, a dying flower shedding rusty seeds in his hand. He eyed the hammer curiously. The dark melody played up and down the walls. Benny stood still and listened. And then the melody disappeared. *Where did the music go?*

The first strike of the hammer against the wall produced a ringing in Benny's head. Sweet music to him. He pounded the wall for more. Two boards fell to the floor, revealing a dark cedar box. Benny stared at the box, then removed it from the wall. It was covered in dust. He opened the latch. Inside, surrounded by cedar wood chips, lay his beloved Carmen. He removed the fiddle carefully and wrapped it inside his coat. He tucked the bow in the crook of his arm. He paced back and forth in Rory's shack, his arms securely around Carmen. He sat on the floor and rocked in a panic of delight. Then he unwrapped her, brought her out into the light, ran his fingers along her slim body. Her long graceful neck. Her smooth ribs. Carmen's strings vibrated to his touch like long-cold veins.

Hamish did not enter the shack, but kept a close eye on where the garter snake had disappeared. Hamish and Little

Rachel kept moving as Benny reappeared and followed closely behind. Hamish stopped suddenly and did a quick, happy dance above a squirm and wiggle in the grass. He laughed out loud and clapped his hands. They moved on, Benny with his two arms wrapped around himself against the cold.

The smell of fall cleaned the air. Tree branches scratched against the darkening sky. Neither of them noticed that the wind had stopped moving. That the scattered leaves had stopped rustling. That the squirrels and rabbits had scurried under the bushes. That only the river kept its voice. That the silence was growing cooler, much cooler. That day was turning into night.

Hamish noticed the first snowflakes. He looked up from the grass and stuck out his tongue. He danced in circles at this new delight, forgetting for a moment the thrill in the grass. All around him, soft gentle flakes fell on his tongue, into his open hands. They fell on his cap, dotted his shoulders. Little Rachel tucked her head into her breast.

Benny knelt on the ground, withdrew his beloved Carmen. He rocked the fiddle back and forth, as if swaying to a slow air. He held the bow in the air like a champion declaring victory, his face serene, flushed by the ecstasy he held in his arms. Benny positioned his stump around the neck of the fiddle and tucked the fiddle under his chin. His left hand held the bow. Hamish clapped wildly when he heard the sounds coming from Benny's fiddle. He watched the long bow stride savagely across the strings.

Benny began to dance with Carmen to his own fiddle sounds. Two dark figures were unaware of time or place.

Hearing what they had always heard. Believing what they had always believed. Nobody to interrupt them as they danced like dark moths on a spiralling white web. Nobody to warn them that this storm was real, not make-believe. Nobody but Hamish to see Benny dance backwards over the edge of the riverbank. See his flared, dark wings descend, falling between snowflakes, a cascade of dancing feet and ragged sleeves cradling a fiddle and bow.

Only when the music ceased did Hamish stop dancing. A sharp wind trumpeted in the branches. The soft snow rose up from the ground and ran in circles, chasing itself. Hamish pulled his cap down over his ears and tucked Little Rachel under her quilt. She shook the snow out of her feathers. He pulled the wagon a few feet, then stopped near a white tree. Nobody had ever told him which way to go in the dark.

Ona MacPherson took her pie from the oven, put on her boots and coat, and walked quickly towards the barn. Maybe Hamish had stopped there to visit his father. He was always home before dark. Especially when it began to snow. She called out as she neared the barn, but she could tell by the look on her husband's face that Hamish had not come home.

"I'll go to the Doucets'. They're probably keeping him there until the snow lets up."

"Go now, Joachim. The snow is getting heavy!"

"You stay in the house, where it's warm. I won't be long."

Ona watched her husband as he turned down the hill towards Benny's home, moving faster than she had seen him move in a long time. She ran back to the house and set the table. Her kitchen was as warm as a mitten. They would be home shortly. She went to her pantry and took all the ingredients off the shelf. Why hadn't she made the cake earlier in the day? How many times had she made this "war cake" for Hamish? She could not remember from what magazine or paper she had taken the recipe. It was crazy at this moment to be thinking of the war rations they had endured. In the country they were fortunate. They had had plenty to eat. She took down the big mixing bowl.

1 cup brown sugar

2 lbs seedless raisins

½ cup molasses

1 cup hot water

1 tsp cloves

1 tsp cinnamon

1 tsp nutmeg

1 cup butter

1 tsp salt

2 tsp baking soda

Scant 3 cups flour

1 tsp vanilla

2 eggs

Heat the first 7 ingredients on top of the stove at medium heat for about 10 minutes. Remove from heat. Add butter and salt. When cooled, add baking soda, flour, vanilla and eggs. Pour batter into a well-greased 13-×-9-inch pan. Bake in 325°F oven for approximately 1 hour.

She repeated the instructions out loud, as if she were speaking to someone hard of hearing. She had the cake ready and in the oven in no time. The smell of spices filled the kitchen. She wrapped her coat around her shoulders and went out to the creamery to get a jar of cream. Hamish liked it whipped with his cake.

The house was too quiet. They had not returned home a half-hour later. From her kitchen window, Ona watched two lanterns move in single file across the Doucet property, heading in the direction of the shore. Along the way, they were met by more lanterns. Her first impulse was to go down to the water. But the howling wind sent her flying backwards against her storm door, so she kept a watch beside the kitchen window as the lanterns' faint lights dotted the shoreline. She fetched a heavy quilt and held it in her arms to warm Hamish when he came home. The cake sat cooling on the table. Her son would be hungry after braving this storm.

In her own kitchen, Flora Doucet filled the stove with dry hardwood. She could hear nothing but the slow crackling of the burning wood and the tick-tock of the grandfather clock in the hall. She glanced at the time on the old face. She could do nothing now but wait. She made her way slowly up the stairs to Benny's room. She looked into the closet, at the new coats and jackets Benny refused to wear. For reasons Flora could not understand, he insisted on wearing his old army coat, in all seasons.

On his bureau he had lined up pieces of fiddle rosin in a straight row. An array of fiddles stood against the wall, like old men gathered along a fence. He had removed their strings. How forlorn they looked, unable to make a sound. Like him. She could not remember him ever saying where he had left his best fiddle. The one he named Carmen. The one he went about Beinn Barra looking for in a mad frenzy. They all looked the same to her. Many people believed it was part of his madness, that nothing was missing but part of his mind. That he really was searching for his missing hand.

"He knows what he is searching for, Flora," her husband said angrily, loudly. Not directly to her, but for the people who did not believe that what he was searching for had ever gone missing. Benny knew the difference, his music was still in his head. Napoleon had checked the fiddles Benny kept in his room. Carmen was not among them. "I know it exists somewhere. We must not discourage him."

She did not reply. How long did it take a man to reach the end of his beliefs? She could see the way Napoleon looked at Benny. Seeking to take what pain he could from him and rock it to sleep. He held him when medication was needed. Talked to him about boats as if he were still a child.

"The first one I ever built is still afloat, Benny. As sturdy as steel was that juniper. She bent like a petal in my hands when I cast her ribs. When you truly believe in something, it is never too far away."

Gunner MacDonald saw the lanterns from his kitchen window, saw the men leave the Doucet home. Gunner met up with the others as they neared the breakwater. Several others had joined the posse. Someone harnessed a horse and sleigh and met the group of men down at the shore. "I saw them earlier, down by MacGuspic's old mill," Gunner said. "They were walking east. I didn't think anything of it."

Joachim and Napoleon sat up front in the sleigh, their lanterns like fading blooms on their knees, casting a soft light in the white wilderness that surrounded them. A couple of men stood on the back. A trail of searchers followed. They talked about the sudden, unexpected storm. Hadn't the autumn been gentle on the earth, sending only the rain? Joachim and Napoleon listened to the sound of the runners on the soft snow. It had fallen quickly, but it had not packed firmly enough for the runners to get a good glide. They listened to the heaves from the big mare as she stomped along past the trees. Branches swiped at their elbows like children playing tag.

The driver pulled on the reins. The big mare stopped in her tracks. They were in a clearing. "The old sawmill is to the right," said the driver. Two men bolted from the back of the sleigh and made their way to the mill. Napoleon could see the other searchers closing in on them at a distance. He watched as the lanterns moved, some high, some low. They were looking under branches. Calling out to Hamish and Benny in collective voices punctuated by the wind. The two searchers turned and came back.

"No sign of them anywhere in there. We checked Rory's old shack, too," said the younger man. "Nothing but a couple of holes in the wall." The driver pulled on the reins. The horse moved at a slow pace, its large head bobbing up and down, causing the bells on its harness to jingle, a melody from a children's rhyme.

Joachim shifted the lantern on his knee. Rubbed his forehead with a cold hand. Tried to remember the day that had started off with sunshine and a baby's breath of wind. The boy going through the gate, with the hen on wheels. Joachim had thrown a slight salute in response to his son's eager wave. He would have to put the runners on the wagon before long, he remembered thinking.

He remembered something else: he had not thought about Calum on this day. He had taken the wagon runners down and coated them with wax. Amused himself with the idea of Little Rachel gliding over snowbanks like a mad one-eyed monarch taken out in a red chariot for a breath of fresh air.

"Hamish! Hamish!" he called to the dark woods.

Napoleon's calm voice responded. "What we will find, Joachim, is what we will have to accept."

"I should have kept a closer eye on them, Napoleon."

They were interrupted by the driver's heavy voice. "We're getting close to the Salmon River." He pulled on the reins, and the big mare halted again, heaved in her tracks.

"The searchers should go on ahead with the lights," the driver called out over his shoulder.

The two fathers watched as the men marched towards the river, two abreast, their lanterns blinking in the night. There was a sudden shout. Two end lights broke off to the west. The other lights followed.

Joachim jumped from the sleigh, followed by Napoleon. In the instant that escorts a man from life to death, both men stalled. Joachim could see a black huddle a few feet away. He could hear the excited murmur of the men's voices coming through the storm. He could see in the flames' grace a dark figure being pulled erect. Someone swirled a blanket over its shoulders. He heard Hamish stuttering out his explanation.

"Enny fall down. Him fall down in water."

He could hear his own tattered voice as he picked Hamish up in his arms.

"We'd better get him back to the house and warm him up, Joachim. He seems to be all right for wear. He was sitting against a tree when we found him, with that hen in his arms and the quilt wrapped around them."

Joachim moved ahead of the men, awkward with his lame foot. The weight of Hamish was too much for him.

"I'll carry him," said one of the men. "He must be a dead weight."

"Please," he begged. "I want to carry my son. I want to carry Hamish." But Hamish was on his feet now, and his arm bent around his father's shoulder in a protective gesture.

"Take the wagon and Little Rachel with you!" Joachim

called to the man who had offered to help as they moved towards the sleigh.

Joachim watched from the sleigh as a lone lantern light stood vigil on the edge of the riverbank. The river offered up its mixed voices. Chants and chimes. Broken pieces of wind. The wind relaxed and collected in the trees. Men huddled in a circle. A light snow continued to fall.

Napoleon could see nothing but a blanket of white below the riverbank, hear nothing but the fractured lament of the river. He knew there was nothing they could do this night. The river had already issued her warnings. She was too dangerous at this incline to descend. She was too dark a creature to explore without daylight. She was able to draw a man in with her sweet, seductive cries.

In the time it took Hamish to eat his war cake and whipped cream, the river relinquished the body of Benny Doucet at the mouth of Spring Falls. Three men carried his slight body to the bank the following morning and removed the snow from his face.

"If I didn't know better, I'd swear that's a smile on his face," one of them said.

"I don't know what the poor bugger had to smile about. He was always in a hurry to find something," another said to the old doctor, who had arrived along with the priest.

They carried his body to the crest of the bank, put it on the back of the sleigh, and covered it with a wet, frozen quilt.

The big mare heaved and moved slowly through the bright morning. People gathered at the edge of the path. Men removed their caps and bowed their heads as the remains of Benny Doucet passed. Children stood back a few feet. The three widows cried openly in the October chill.

In the Doucets' barn, Napoleon and some carpenters had been working for hours on a maple coffin. In the Doucets' kitchen, women stuffed white satin cases with sheep's wool to line the coffin. Someone covered a pillow in satin.

The bow lay straddled along the riverbank, against the rocks, like a branch that had fallen. A mile downriver, the fiddle found open water. It floated under the rising sun, poised, perfectly balanced, unnoticed, unclaimed. Its bellied top empty of snowflakes. Its stringed face as shiny as brass. Being towed by the wind to the sea for final burial. A glowing Carmen, riding her last ripple of death. She had the birds singing at the crack of dawn.

Thirty-Nine

1947

"Benny Doucet could tune up the wind," observed one of the hundreds of mourners who stood shoulder to shoulder in the old graveyard. They had come to address their own sorrow, the grief they had felt since the hand of the great fiddler had fallen in the Valley of Death, near the Arielli River, far away in Italy.

They looked down at the rough box in the grave where his maple coffin would be placed. Two or three inches of rain had collected. The gravediggers had removed the tarpaulin when the pallbearers, all returned soldiers from Beinn Barra, had appeared on the top of the hill, carrying the coffin.

Hector MacDonald stood firm and tall and recited "For the Fallen" for his friend:

They shall grow not old, as we that are left grow
old:

Age shall not weary them, nor the years contemn.
At the going down of the sun and in the morning
We will remember them.

The pallbearers loosened their grip on the ropes, and the body of Private Benny Doucet was lowered into the grave.

Hamish stood at the edge of the crowd, dressed in a black raincoat and boots, alongside his mother. He was smiling. He had never seen so many people gathered in the rain. He watched as the last of the dirty snow ran down the hill and turned into mud. Little Rachel poked her head out from under a quilt and took in the radius that one eye would allow.

"It's been awhile, Hector MacDonald."

Hector had not seen her walk up behind him, Alex's sister.

Joan MacGregor tightened her grip on his hand. "*Bithidh latha eile ann*," she said softly, as she walked away. "There will be another day."

On the hill's crest, a lone figure bobbed in and out of view, Cassie MacGregor searching for clovers among the living and the dead, strands of wet hair plastered against her face. This was where clovers bloomed best, she believed. She was hostile to other voices now, preferring the jarred dialogue she carried on with the flowers she found and admired.

Gunner MacDonald stood at attention and saluted the Last Post, then turned and saluted his son.

How often Hector had heard this lonely cry of the bugle for the dead. He was grateful that the Doucets could bury their son in home soil. Calum MacPherson and so many other Highlanders rested in foreign soil, in Italy and Holland, ageless, named in full military honour. *How gently does the sun shine on them; how swift is the rain?* Hector wondered.

Under a black umbrella, Flora and Napoleon Doucet walked solemnly to the waiting car, pausing here to wrap their arms around Hector, there to acknowledge neighbours and strangers alike. Many of them had not known Benny personally. They spoke of his music the way they would speak of an old friend. They named their favourite tunes. They remembered the way pain slid from their bones when Strings Doucet played. The widows were mournfully tipsy as they tottered to the front of the line. Flora smiled kindly on them. Napoleon shook their hands.

Flora watched as a slight figure made its way down the hill and stood off in the distance. Flora walked over and held out her hand. "It was kind of you to come, Cassie."

There was nothing but rain and confusion in the eyes of Cassie MacGregor.

"Do you remember, Benny, our son, Cassie?" Flora asked.

Cassie did not respond, but she was carefully watching Flora's face.

"Our son, Benny, died in the storm a few days ago. That's why we are here, Cassie, we are here to bury our Benny. Benny and Alex were friends. You must remember our Benny and his fiddle. I remember your son. Benny is buried not far from Alex."

Cassie mumbled something under her breath. Flora looked down at the woman who stood before her in the rain in a thin brown coat and winter boots. At the exquisite gestures from her bare hands. At the opening and closing of her soft mouth. People passed her by these days with a quick nod. They rarely spoke to her. They didn't say outright that she would be better off out of her misery. But they believed that.

Cassie turned and walked back up the hill. She stood there for a few minutes, watching the mourners leave the graveyard. Blurred figures going off in different directions. Some under umbrellas, others with plastic caps tied under their chins. Men holding down their hats. A few lingering beside a mound of clay. She wanted to make wishes on them with the clovers she had stashed in her pockets. A black car stopped at the crest of the hill. Flora rolled down the window. Cassie put a wish on her and watched three men with shovels toss clay into the muddy hole in the ground.

"What is she doing out in the rain?" a weary Napoleon asked his wife.

"She is focusing on something beautiful, Napoleon," Flora whispered as the car moved slowly away from her son's grave, with its freshly buried wish.

Hector and his father walked home together from the graveyard, Gunner stealing glances at his son's damp face. Hector was composed, despite the fact that he was only recently out of the hospital. Gunner's steps were a dead weight as he walked along the lane. As if he had route-marched for miles. He wondered if silence was his best ally at this time. But Hector turned to him.

"Da, I remembered my POW number when I was in the hospital. What do you think that means?"

Gunner stopped in the middle of the lane. "It could mean that you are on your way to finding freedom. Everything takes time. When I returned home from the last war, I realized that victory and defeat are closer than most people realize."

At the house, Hector retreated to his room. The rain had stopped and the sun was bouncing in and out of the clouds like a ball of fire on the run. From his window, Hector watched the gravediggers. They moved slowly with the weight of the damp earth in their shovels. A few people milled around, leftover mourners dredging up memories. There would be a hundred different versions of how Strings Doucet met his demise. The widows had their own theory. "God needed the best Cape Breton fiddler to play for the troops at Christmas. He had only to look down and gaffle Benny by his long coat."

But Hector knew and Gunner knew that the war had killed Benny Doucet. And sent him home for Beinn Barra to bury him.

There was music in Hector's dreams that night. Hector could hear "The Warlock's Strathspey" in E minor. He could not tell from where in the Stalag the music was coming, but he listened intently. The music awakened several other prisoners, their haggard faces cropped in the light of one match. They had worked until sunset that day in Moosberg. Five of them had shared a loaf of black bread, along with a bowl of watery soup. Someone passed out peppermints sent in a Red Cross care package. Hector set the bag on fire for more light. The soldiers wanted to know where the music was coming from. Who was playing so beautifully to them?

The flame went out, but not before Hector saw one of the older soldiers fall to his knees. He was burning up with fever, and someone broke up a peppermint so he could swallow a piece without choking. The beautiful Joan of Arc MacGregor, dressed in a Red Cross uniform, offered the soldier the broken peppermint from the tip of her tongue.

Hector sat straight up in his bed and looked around through the darkness.

He was not dreaming now, but remembering. He could smell a foul odour from the soldier beside him. The soldier must have died in the night, because his body was stiff and cold and curled in a sphere. He lay on his side, with his hands knuckled into a ball under his chin, as if had kept a close eye on his own demise.

Some of the soldiers consigned letters or small tokens for loved ones to the strongest among them. "Promise me that you will deliver this?" several had begged Hector.

"Sure," Hector had answered. "You can count on me. They don't call me the Stalag Mailman for nothing."

He had tried to maintain whatever it was that must be kept going in a place like this. Watching men rot to death. Beg their mothers, in their delirium, for a glass of water. Call out to their wives. Some of the prisoners complained when the guards marched in with lanterns and pieces of cloth around their mouths and carted off the dead.

The darkness had shapes this night in his father's house. A dull lamp burned in the hallway. He stood. The cold floor sent shivers up his legs as he walked towards the window facing the graveyard. His left leg still hurt from the shrapnel, and it brought him to a stall. He cajoled it, a reluctant child who refused to come in out of the cold.

There was a light in the graveyard, dim and close to the ground. The night was too dark to make out the figure behind the light. Once or twice it stopped and aimed the light on the fresh mound of clay. Who was watching over Benny's grave? Hector could not imagine who could be out at this hour of the night.

Hector noticed a light on in the kitchen. Gunner was sitting by lamplight, playing solitaire.

"Are you still trying to nail the old king, Da?"

"No," said Gunner. "I'm chasing the queen tonight."

"It's not exactly night, Da. It will soon be daybreak."

"I know, Hector. I'm used to these fishing hours—they never let you rest. I didn't hear you get up. Are you feeling sick?"

"No, I must have been dreaming. When I woke up, I saw a light in the graveyard. Someone was visiting poor Benny's grave. I have a feeling Benny found what he was looking for all along."

Gunner looked up at his son, at the quiet in Hector's eyes. "Or it found him, Hector."

Hector watched his father's quick hands shuffle the deck and place a card on the table.

"There. I got her! She's been elusive for a long while, Hector, but I finally flushed her out. I caught up with the queen."

"Good for you. I think I'll go back to bed until the sun hits the roof." Hector walked over to the cupboard and opened a couple of doors.

"What are you looking for, son? Perhaps I can help you."

"I am looking for a peppermint, Da. I would like a peppermint to chew on."

Forty

1947

HECTOR MACDONALD'S NEXT public appearance in Beinn Barra was to the sea. In his rubber boots. Above his head the sky was a cold blue. The morning sun created a dazzling streak across the water. The sea spread in small waves like meringue against the boat as he rowed out to meet the sun.

A lone seagull noticed the intruder and swooped down to investigate. The gull dropped its wings and perched on the bow of the rowboat. Hector smiled at his visitor. The gull's glassy stare was unflinching, a greedy child waiting for a Halloween treat. Hector fumbled in his pocket for a morsel of dry cod and threw it upward. The gull plucked it from the air and flew towards the wharf.

"Don't tell your friends!" Hector called out to the bird, watching it fly off in a southerly direction.

In Beinn Barra kitchens, mothers prepared porridge for sleepy schoolchildren uprooted from warm beds. The school bell waited. Hector had not cared for school, or porridge. He would have been happier if his father had set him adrift every morning on the sea. It was Calum and Benny and Alex who had migrated to the rhythms of foreign languages, to history, to the pure logic of science. And he rode the waves of the second-hand knowledge they'd provided him. Until now. Until war had taught them all the same lessons.

He alone remained. His lungs alone sought a rush of sea air, breathed. Inhaled, exhaled. Caught life in between. He alone tapped the music from the radio between his fingers until his limbs sang for him, danced for him. He alone turned the pages of Percy Bysshe Shelley and felt Shelley's drowning words spill into the night. Out on the sea, alone, Hector realized that they had left it all to him, a gift he had opened slowly over the last couple of months.

The last time he had talked to Calum was on the eve of his own capture. They were at the bottom of Hill 120, taking orders for battle. Calum spoke of the day they had shipped out of Halifax Harbour. He mentioned his father, how he could still see his father standing there at the end of the rope, watching as they walked up the gangplank. It was a lonely image, Calum said, your father standing like a man at the end of a gallows. "I can't get that image out of my mind," he said. "I had no idea he would show up to see us sail."

Hector guided the rowboat slowly towards Dipper's Point, where Alex MacGregor's father had drowned so many years ago. He paused for a moment, looked out over the smooth waters. Not a troubled wave in sight.

He and Calum had sneaked down to the water the day the body washed up on shore. They stood back at a distance. Frightened, yet in awe of the man who had shouted orders from his watery grave to have his son led back to safety. The body's feet were bare. Seaweed wound like thick rope around his body, as if some strange sea creature had bundled him up and spit him out of its watery territory with savage authority.

They moved closer, he and Calum, to see the wrinkled face. Between the wrinkles, Hector thought he saw a look of relief. He was familiar with that look today. The mask that shadows dying men from light. One of the fishermen uncovered the drowned man's face so the priest could anoint him with oil. They removed their caps when the anointing began. Hector and Calum inched closer as the priest came to the dead blue hands.

"May the Lord who frees you from sin save you and raise you up," the priest said in a special voice he used only on the dead. Then he made the sign of the cross on Alexander MacGregor's forehead, nose, ears, mouth, and hands. The fishermen answered, "Amen."

They ran off then, he and Calum, before the priest got to the bare feet. Up to the edge of the cliff, where they looked down.

"Why is the priest blessing so many parts of him?" Hector asked Calum.

"Because the pope said they have to," Calum answered.

With all the oil and prayers being poured over him," said Hector, maybe Alex's father would rise up from the sand and go looking for his boots.

Now, the sun went behind a white cloud, and its rays sketched a mellow pattern on the water. A criss-cross stitch of subdued sunlight. In the distance, Hector could see the outline of the old schoolhouse.

It was always Benny at the front of the school line, telling someone or other about the different types of wood that went into the building of a boat, or a fiddle. "My father knows everything," Benny would inform the kids who listened to his wood stories. "He's the smartest man I know."

"These floors are oak," Benny had told them. "They'll last forever. And the shingles on the roof are made from cedar." Everyone called him the Wood Worm. Nobody knew so much about wood, except St. Joseph the carpenter, but nobody, including the nun, knew of anything he had built, and St. Joseph didn't know how to play the fiddle.

Even onboard the troop ship on their journey to England, Benny had pointed out and named the different woods in the interior of the ship.

Benny was always right. He had always been so precise. He carried information the way he later carried his own fiddles. Carefully. In tune.

Hector remembered the last time he saw Benny. The day Hamish brought him to the house. He ran his stump along the maple table in the kitchen, and the old woodbox on the porch. Carefully, like a doctor checking a pulse.

Hector and Calum never did tell Alex that they had seen his father lying in the sand. Cast from his watery grave only to be lowered into his earthly one. Alex had adored his father. Had sat on his father's knee for hours, his small hands pointing out pictures in the open books they sailed through together. And then came the poetry that his father knew by heart. By the time he climbed off his father's knee, Alex had drifted into words like soft snow into an open well. His father had recited the poems aloud. Sometimes he would recite them in Gaelic so the older clan of fishermen could share his love for the words. Alex held on to his poems like a secret mistress, and had died alone with them.

After his father's death, many of the older people referred to Alex as the lad with no visible existence. "He roams like a blind dog," they said. "Every direction is his path." He walked around with his eyes fixed on things, but didn't remember seeing them. Everything lived outside his soul. Except for the poetry. It was alive inside him. He came to some form of life only when Hector and Calum and Benny sheltered him under their wings. They walked to school together. Shared slingshots made of spruce, and the ice pond. Tin cans and ghost stories. Fudge and comic books. Lemonade and mock wars. Trees and the anticipation of adultery.

When Calum was figuring out arithmetic, and Benny was identifying wood, and Hector longed to drift out on the sea, Alex already knew the answers. He had been introduced to death long before the war lured his friends away from him.

Hector could hear the flapping of wings as he turned the rowboat around, towards the shore. Three seagulls prepared for a landing above his head. Two side by side as the third clung to the rim of the bow and dipped its beak.

"I told you not to tell your friends," said Hector, eyeing the gull that looked familiar.

The other two listened, waiting for instructions. They watched Hector's hands go deep inside his pocket. Hector unwrapped the dry cod from the brown paper, broke it apart in small sections and threw it into the air. The gulls scrambled inside the rowboat and claimed their treat. Again they perched on the rim of the bow. Three abreast this time, lining up for a race. Hector picked up three morsels of cod and flipped them into the air. Again each gull returned to the bow with its beak full.

"You should be catching for the Yankees. You'd make lots of cod there." He took the last bits of cod from his pocket and threw them out over the water. "There's nothing left," he shouted to the gulls.

Hector looked out over the blue vastness that was his on this day. Interrupted only by faint callings of schoolchildren to each other. The wind scattered their voices, drowned their names one by one.

Hector recalled the games he and his friends had shared in the schoolyard. Marbles and Red Rover, baseball and snowball fights. Perhaps he would have children of his own someday. He would tell them about his friends. How brave they were, how the youngest of them made it all the way to the end of the war with a white feather under his helmet. A feather from a hen named Little Rachel.

He would tell them about the great fiddler of Beinn Barra, who died just as his music ran out. And the quiet poet who had buried his father's gift so deep within himself that he forgot how to open it. And his little friend who rode a white horse adorned with a Silver Cross.

He would hold his children on his knees and recall the day he was rescued by the Americans from the Stalag. Tell them how eight or nine prisoners were fitted into an old American fighter bomber that lifted up off the ground like a gull. There were no seats on the plane, so they crouched on the floor as they were flown to Brussels, and then on to London for medical aid. That's when it happened. On the way to Brussels, the old bomber plane crashed and crow-hopped into a field of alders. Nobody died. They all survived to tell the tale by landing on top of each other like wood stacked on a woodpile.

Near the wharf, Hector caught sight of his father, waved to him as the gulls took flight and went scrounging near the old fish sheds, looking for a handout.

Hector could tell by the concerned look on his father's face that he had been watching, waiting for a while. This proud man, his father, who let poetry slip out when he knew someone nearby might be listening. Perhaps he was waiting for a story or two to unfold. A story that Hector longed to tell.

Epilogue

1947

A week after Benny Doucet's funeral, the sky turned a spotless blue, and the sun slipped out like a yellow yolk from a delicate shell and splashed Beinn Barra in gold. Housewives opened up their kitchen windows to let in the colour of the day. It lay on their rag rugs like a striped cat. Cast a shadow on their freshly baked bread. It found the wood, piled in the woodboxes, and set off a fire of its own without a flame. It settled in the steam rising from kettles and sent rainbow streaks up to the ceilings. Fishermen on the sea held up their golden catches. Children on their way to school paraded down the snow-covered hills like fireflies.

Several people caught a glimpse of Hamish and Little Rachel on their morning journey. Hamish was watched very carefully now, as if he were everyone's child.

Hamish walked slowly up and over the hill. Turned into the graveyard and asked Little Rachel to be quiet. He had been here only once before, on the day of Benny's funeral. He manoeuvred the wagon with its winter runners cautiously among the headstones until he found the mound of clay covering Benny's grave. It was frosted with light snow, but today a yellow hue spread over it like a field of unharmed dandelions. Hamish pushed the makeshift marker upright. Stood back to examine his work. The stick stood straight and firm above the clay.

"Benny has gone where Calum and Alex live, to play his music for them," his mother had told him on the day of the funeral.

"Wat colour heaven?" Hamish asked, turning towards Little Rachel. The old white hen pulled her head into her feathers as if she had fallen asleep.

Hamish removed his mitten, plucked a bunch of flowers from a wreath, and smiled peacefully. He walked home carefully, holding the flowers steady in front of him. Like something breakable. Too fragile for pockets. Too dangerous to drop. He could not waste a petal. Little Rachel moved out from under her quilt and looked around. Hamish maintained the smile on his face as he walked towards home. Kept it warm in the golden sun. He could not feel the cold on his bare hand.

People bid him good morning. He smiled and kept walking. He had been told not to wander too far from the house by himself. Perhaps his mother would be finished her chores when he got home, and she would dance with him in the kitchen. Later, he would ask her to follow, and he would lead her to where he believes all the pretty flowers grow.

Author's Note

Hector MacDonald, Benny Doucet, and Calum MacPherson are fictional characters, but the Cape Breton Highlanders are real and enjoy a long and honourable history.

The battalion was first organized on October 13, 1871, from four independent companies, and was designated the Victoria Provisional Battalion of Infantry, with headquarters in Baddeck, on Cape Breton Island, Nova Scotia. On May 8, 1900, it was redesignated the 94th Victoria Regiment Argyll Highlanders. The 94th served in the First World War from 1914 to 1918. Gaelic was the mother tongue of eighty percent of its personnel. Later, the 94th was assigned to the 85th Battalion, Nova Scotia Highlanders. The present motto, *Siol na Fear Fearail*, the Breed of Manly Men, was selected for the 85th Battalion.

On April 1, 1920, the militia was reorganized, and the unit was redesignated the Cape Breton Highlanders. At the outbreak of hostilities in 1939, it was called to active service and tasked in a coastal defence role. The Highlanders trained in St. John, New Brunswick; Ottawa and Camp Borden, Ontario; and Debert, Nova Scotia. They sailed for England in November 1941. They landed in Italy on November 10, 1943.

Battle honours inherited through the services of the Cape Breton Highlanders include the Liri Valley, the Gothic Line, Coriano, Lamone Crossing, Italy 1944–45, Authie, Chambois, Boulogne, Breskens Pocket, and the Rhine.

The last action of the Highlanders was the capture of the port of Delfzijl, Holland, and the liberation of the Dutch people, who had lived under German occupation for five years. Seventeen hundred prisoners of war were taken.

The regiment captured a large wooden eagle from the Dutch headquarters of the German ss troops. This trophy is presently displayed in the Sydney Garrison officers' mess, a proud and lasting memorial to the Breed of Manly Men.

The MacDonald Tartan of Clan Donald—the oldest, most powerful, and largest clan—became the official tartan of the Cape Breton Highlanders in the 1950s. Thus did the prediction of the fictional Hector MacDonald come true.

The Breed of Manly Men: The history of the Cape Breton Highlanders by Alex Morrison and Ted Slaney is an excellent history of the legendary Highlanders.

Request for the Fallen

We lay them down in foreign lands,
Beneath the cold, damp sod.
Their work on earth accomplished,
Their souls we give to God.

Brave lads of our Dominion,
From East unto the West,
Begrudging not their sacrifice,
God grant their last request.

Let's not forget future generations,
As they journey on through life,
Be called upon to settle
Another world of strife.

Give Nations, Lord, the power
Of vision strong, to see
That a world of friendly neighbours
A peaceful world would be.

Let men heed not of color,
Nor criticize of creed;
Abolish, good Lord, from them
Their greatest foe, of greed.

Then we, Thy sons, the fallen,
That freedom might remain,
Will sleep in peace, and knowing
We have not died in vain.

WOII (CSM) Joe Oldford, DCM
Cape Breton Highlanders

Acknowledgements

To my editor and friend Clare McKeon, fellow writers Alistair MacLeod and Dawn and Sheldon Currie, and my brother, Roddy MacDonald, for their clarity of thought and perception. To Ted Slaney, a gifted veteran of the Cape Breton Highlanders, for his superior memory and insight. To veteran Alex MacInnis, who remembered the horrors, for sharing them openly and painfully. To the family of the late F.X. MacNeil, who served with the Cape Breton Highlanders, for sharing their father's personal triumph. To Jerry MacNeil, friend and neighbour, for all his notes and books, delivered to my door. To my friend Tommy Mombourquette for his fishing stories. To my friend Donna D'Amour for her valuable time and research. To Robert McMillin, a lover of history, for providing valuable information to the manuscript. To my friends Father Frank Abbass and Anita MacLeod, who can turn a phrase into Gaelic or

Latin at a moment's notice. A special thank you to my friend and neighbour George Karaphillis for his help with my inept computer skills. To my long-time friends Diane and Penny Ulster for making sure my "white horse" arrived in time for Christmas. And to my brilliant musician friends Michael J. MacDonald and Dwayne Cote, who make music matter in their lives and the lives of others.

Finally, to all the Canadian men and women who have served in the theatre of war, whose courage and daring have made my words possible.

About the Author

Beatrice MacNeil is the author of the bestselling and critically acclaimed novel *Butterflies Dance in the Dark*, for which she received the 2003 Dartmouth Book Award.

Her short story collection, *The Moonlight Skater*, won the 1994 Dartmouth Book Award. Her children's book, *There is a Mouse in the House of Miss Crouse*, won the 1996 Marianna Dempster Canadian Author's Award for Nova Scotia. She received the 1999 Tic Butler Award for outstanding contribution to Cape Breton writing and culture, and is the founder of Cape Breton's Reading Ceilidhs. Her work has been published in the *Globe and Mail*, the *Toronto Star*, and the *Halifax Chronicle-Herald*. She has written ten plays, two of which have been adapted for CBC Radio Halifax.

Of Acadian and Scottish descent, she grew up in Lower L'Ardoise in Cape Breton. She lived in Toronto for an extended period and currently makes her home in Cape Breton, in a big timber house, by a forest, overlooking a lake.